"There ... past you don't want me to know,"

Adam replied, still studying her.

Where her calm originated, Josie didn't know. Out of her desperation, she guessed. She smiled slowly. "Any woman worthy of the name has a few secrets. Life is more interesting that way."

Swallowed up in his jacket, her wide-eyed face pale in the shadows, she didn't look like a threat to his comfortable way of life, yet somehow Adam knew she would be.

"You're free to keep your secrets," he said, "as long as they do no harm to my household. The moment they hurt anyone, the bargain is off."

Josie squared her shoulders, a little flame of indignation lighting her eyes. "I have never deliberately hurt anyone, Mr. Scofield."

"When someone is hurt, Mrs. Cross," he replied, "it hardly matters to the victim if the pain was deliberately or accidentally inflicted...."

Dear Reader,

This month brings us the second historical from popular contemporary series author Muriel Jensen. *A Bride for Adam* is the heartrending story of a mail-order bride who must keep the existence of her own two boys secret from her new family.

Also this month, we are very pleased to have Curtiss Ann Matlock back with her new historical Western, *White Gold,* the unforgettable story of unlikely partners who must face countless dangers and their own growing attraction on the sheep trail west.

Our other titles include *Lion's Heart,* by Suzanne Barclay, the beginning of a new medieval saga featuring the Sutherlands, a clan of Scottish Highlanders, and *For Love Alone,* a tale set in the time of Henry VIII, from Barbara Leigh, the author best known for her medieval, *To Touch the Sun.*

We hope you will keep an eye out for all four titles, wherever Harlequin Historical novels are sold.

Sincerely,

Tracy Farrell
Senior Editor

Please address questions and book requests to:
Harlequin Reader Service
U.S.: 3010 Walden Ave., P.O. Box 1325, Buffalo, NY 14269
Canadian: P.O. Box 609, Fort Erie, Ont. L2A 5X3

MURIEL JENSEN

A Bride for Adam

Harlequin Books

TORONTO • NEW YORK • LONDON
AMSTERDAM • PARIS • SYDNEY • HAMBURG
STOCKHOLM • ATHENS • TOKYO • MILAN
MADRID • WARSAW • BUDAPEST • AUCKLAND

If you purchased this book without a cover you should be aware
that this book is stolen property. It was reported as "unsold and
destroyed" to the publisher, and neither the author nor the
publisher has received any payment for this "stripped book."

ISBN 0-373-28853-0

A BRIDE FOR ADAM

Copyright © 1995 by Muriel Jensen.

All rights reserved. Except for use in any review, the reproduction or
utilization of this work in whole or in part in any form by any electronic,
mechanical or other means, now known or hereafter invented, including
xerography, photocopying and recording, or in any information storage
or retrieval system, is forbidden without the written permission of the
publisher, Harlequin Enterprises Limited, 225 Duncan Mill Road,
Don Mills, Ontario, Canada M3B 3K9.

All characters in this book have no existence outside the imagination of
the author and have no relation whatsoever to anyone bearing the same
name or names. They are not even distantly inspired by any individual
known or unknown to the author, and all incidents are pure invention.

This edition published by arrangement with Harlequin Enterprises B.V.

® and TM are trademarks of the publisher. Trademarks indicated with
® are registered in the United States Patent and Trademark Office, the
Canadian Trade Marks Office and in other countries.

Printed in U.S.A.

MURIEL JENSEN

started writing in the sixth grade...and just never stopped. Marrying a journalist taught Muriel the art of discipline and the playful art of arguing whether it's easier to get the "who, when, where and why" in the first paragraph or to take 100,000 words in which to do it. Muriel lives in Astoria, Oregon, with her husband, two cats and a golden retriever. She also has three grown children.

To Diane Hankins,
my buddy

Prologue

Boston—April 1886

Jonathan Dunlop watched Josephine Cross pace the width of his office and sighed. He loved her like a daughter, but the last ten weeks of her life had been among the worst of his. He'd known her since she was fifteen, when his long-time friend, Benjamin Cross, walked the blue-eyed, dark-haired waif into his office and told him they were to be married.

Her widowed father had worked for Benjamin and earned his friendship. When Will Denehy lay dying, he pleaded with Cross to look after his daughter, and he agreed.

It hadn't been difficult to see how Ben's charity had grown into something else. Josie was pretty, sweet-natured and intelligent. The forty-year disparity in their ages seemed of little consequence to either of them. They had needed each other and made each other happy.

Jonathan allowed himself a private smile as Josie dropped a little black velvet bag in the chair facing his desk and said firmly, "I'm going to California, Jonathan, and I don't want to hear that the journey will be difficult and that I'm unprepared."

Nine years of marriage to a pillar of Boston society had transformed the wide-eyed waif into an elegant young woman of genteel manner. Even in a somber black gown and hat trimmed in the dull black crepe of mourning, she had an air of grace and style. But recent events had taught Jonathan that under that polish was the determination of a hungry grizzly.

"It's not as though I have to bump across the country with the overland mail," she went on, reasoning. "The railroad now stretches all the way to Sacramento. I will travel in comfort and relative safety."

Jonathan made a scoffing noise. "Safety. Snows blocking the tracks, pickpockets, train robbers . . ."

She sighed patiently, picked up her bag and sat in the chair. "It's spring, Jonathan, and train travel has been secure for some time now." She squared her shoulders, the bright blue eyes under a lacy fringe of dark brown curls meeting his without trepidation. "In the two weeks I've been out of prison, I've acceded to your wishes that I be patient and let your Pinkerton man find my children, but now his latest telegram says he's tracked them as far as the Siskiyous but has met with an accident on the trail that will incapacitate him for several months. I won't wait a minute longer." She swallowed with obvious difficulty and blinked away the glaze of tears.

Jonathan tried to harden himself against her vulnerability but failed as she said huskily, "I'm going to find my children myself, Jonathan. Please lend me the fare. With Benjamin's affairs entangled because of the murder, you know I'm temporarily penniless. You have to help me."

He reached across his desk to put his hand over the two delicate gloved ones clutching the edge. "Josie, you know I don't refuse you lightly, but you have no idea what you'd be up against. There are three thousand miles of wilderness between us and the Siskiyou Mountains. And if I gave you the fare, what would you do when you got there? That part of the country is full of miners and lumberjacks and men escaping their pasts." He went on gently. "Have you any idea how long it might take to find your boys? Months, probably. Possibly longer. And how would you sustain yourself?"

"Jon, people are just people everywhere. And I could work. I..."

"Where? In the mines? The camps?"

She slammed a small fist on his desk and stood, anger overcoming tears. "Jonathan, I'm going to California if I have to walk. Will you be able to live with yourself when I head west in my kid slippers?"

He leaned back in his chair and shook his head at her. "You think you're that tough, do you?"

She angled her chin. "My husband was murdered. I've spent two months in prison accused of the deed, and my mother-in-law packed off my children like bags of flour and coffee with a disreputable couple going west." Her eyes darkened with a pain that decimated his defenses. "You would be horrified to know how tough I've become."

Jonathan thought there had to be a special place in hell for Jerusha Cross, Ben's mother, who had hated Ben's young wife for providing the longtime bachelor with two sons of his own. She felt that his love for them diminished her importance in his life. Her hatred for Josie had been so strong she'd told the police she had followed Josie to Ben's office that night and seen her commit the murder.

Jonathan had tried to wire Daniel Cross, Ben's younger brother, who'd always been fond of Josie and the boys, but he'd been travelling through Europe and the messages continually missed him.

The frightened little housemaid Jonathan had finally bullied into coming forward told the court Josie had never left the house that night, that she, the maid, had been ill with the croup and Josie had sat with her until morning.

After Josie's imprisonment, the maid had overheard Jerusha make plans with a couple named Gripper to take the children away. The Grippers were going west to escape im-

pending arrest for their involvement with a ring of dock
side thieves. "She stole my son," Jerusha had said. "Now
I want her to know how it feels."

The only comfort to be taken in the sordid story was that
when the housemaid had finally revealed the truth, Josie
had been freed and Jerusha disappeared. But Benjamin's
murder remained unsolved.

"Well?" Josie prompted. "Do I walk, or will you honor
our friendship and lend me train fare?"

"Neither." Jonathan decided it was time to play his ace.
He pointed to the chair and said, "Sit down. We have been
presented with another solution in my morning mail."

Jonathan took a letter out of his middle drawer and re
moved it from its envelope.

"Jonathan, I won't be delayed further."

"You will be delayed only as long as it takes me to post
your reply, and for him to telegraph the money for your
fare."

A pleat formed between her eyes. "Reply to what? To
whom?"

"A proposal of marriage," Jonathan informed her. He
leaned back in his chair and cleared his throat. Josie's eyes
widened, but before she could open her mouth, he raised a
finger for silence.

"I will read this to you," he said, "because it contains
several passages unsuited to a lady's eyes."

He began to read.

"Dear Jonathan,
I hope this letter finds you well and prosperous. I am
much as I was in our days at Harvard—without sufficient whiskey or women to realize my true potential.
You, however, never lacked for..."

Jonathan scanned the next few lines silently, glanced
guiltily at Josie, cleared his throat and continued.

"I am enclosing this letter from a young man of my acquaintance, also an attorney, who is in the market for a commodity in scarce supply in the California mountains—a single lady. The gentleman in question hopes to find a lady of breeding and good manners with a sweet and patient disposition."

Jonathan looked at Josie over the top of the letter and smiled wryly. "We may have to deceive him a little there." Then he read on.

"I fear delicate Southern ladies would not do well in our rugged mountains, so I've suggested that my client approach a sturdy New England lady with his proposal. I thought you might be aware of a young woman of quality, bored, perhaps, with the strictures of Boston society and willing to start a new life in a beautiful place with a man whose character is above reproach and whose industry has earned him comfortable circumstances and a position of respect in the community. I ask that you give the enclosed letter to a well-bred lady with a sense of adventure."

Josie stared at Jonathan for a moment, allowing the contents of the letter to penetrate her brain. She was shocked—not because she'd received a marriage proposal, however indirectly, but because for the first time in nearly three months she saw a glimmer of light at the end of a very dark tunnel.

"Now, don't turn him down out of hand," Jonathan advised, misinterpreting her stunned expression. "This could be the perfect solution. You need a man to take care of you, and he seeks qualities in a woman that you absolutely define. A positive answer will put you within reach of your children, if they are indeed in the Siskiyous, and in comfortable surroundings while you search. I'm sure if you ex-

plain to this...this—" he scanned the letter for a name
"—Adam Scofield what's happened to you, he'll be more
than happy to help you fi—"

"No." Josie got to her feet, her cheeks pink.

"Josie, think what this could..."

"I don't mean no to the proposal, Jonathan," she said,
her eyes losing their focus as she walked away from him to
the window. Beyond, rain poured down on Boston Common and she drew the draperies back to look out on the
puddled grass.

A man of means, she thought, would probably know
everyone in the area—and the area happened to be where
her children had been taken. This timely letter by no means
eliminated all the obstacles in her path; in truth, it presented several new ones, but it would get her to the Siskiyou Mountains and, at the moment, that was all on which
she chose to focus.

She turned back to Jonathan. "I mean, send an affirmative answer. You may say that I'm a widow, but don't
mention that I have children or that I'm going west to search
for them."

"Josie, that's deceitful," he scolded.

She walked back to his desk with a wry smile. "You're an
attorney, Jon. You have to deal in honesty. I'm a mother
and I'm going to get Charlie and Billy back by whatever
means it takes."

"Josie..."

"Jon, do you suppose for one moment that this man
would marry a woman who's spent two months in jail on the
charge of murdering her husband? Even if I didn't cause
him concern for his own personal safety, I'm sure I wouldn't
meet his strict requirements for a wife."

"You can't begin a marriage on a lie."

"It wouldn't be a marriage, it would be a temporary
means to an end."

"I won't do it."

She sat on the corner of his desk and smiled down at him. "Then you'll lend me the money to go on my own?"

Jonathan fell against the back of his chair with a groan of defeat. "Josephine Cross, if you were my wife, I would—"

"Be guilty of bigamy," she finished for him, settling back in her chair with a rustle of silk and poplin. "You have here an adventurous lady. Finish the letter, Jonathan."

Chapter One

Sacramento—May 1886

Josephine Cross braced her gloved hands on the back of the seat in front of her. Her knees wobbled dangerously, apparently unwilling to support her. They probably didn't remember how, she thought wryly. After five days and six nights on a train without the luxury of a sleeping berth, she would no doubt have to relearn the skills of walking and lying down.

"Thinking about your young man?" Selina McDuffy asked. She'd occupied the seat beside Josie since Denver, and they'd shared confidences. Josie knew Selina had been visiting a sick sister, and Selina knew Josie had come west to be married.

Josie hadn't explained that she and the gentleman in question were complete strangers. She also hadn't mentioned her stint in prison, her missing children or her deceit. She had decided when she left Boston to put those things out of her mind. It wouldn't do for her intended to read them on her face.

Adam Scofield was expecting a respectable, ladylike widow, and she had to look the part or he wouldn't marry her. He'd explained in the telegram that had accompanied the money for her ticket that her taking the trip in no way bound her to him. If she decided, upon meeting him face-to-face, that she disliked him, he would purchase her return fare.

Though he'd worded that paragraph carefully, Josie suspected it provided him as well as her with a way out of the engagement. If he found her unsuitable, she would either have to return to Boston with her problems unresolved or try to find a way to support herself while she searched for her children. The former was not a consideration, and despite her denials to Jonathan, she knew the probability of her finding respectable employment was unlikely. No. She needed Adam Scofield. She had to make this work.

It wasn't until she caught Selina's expectant expression that she realized the woman had asked her a question. She pulled the small photograph that had accompanied the original letter from her portmanteau.

"My!" Selina said softly but emphatically, a hand to her heart in undisguised admiration. "Now there's a face to make a woman travel three thousand miles."

It was a handsome face, Josie admitted to herself. Dark hair over a broad brow, dark eyes, strong, straight nose and a mouth held in a taut line—no mustache and no smile. She had studied the photograph in Jonathan's office, then put it away, a little alarmed by the way it drew her. Now she had to study it so that she could locate its living, breathing counterpart on the crowded platform.

She experienced the same feeling now—a little frisson of alarm coupled with a...something she couldn't quite describe. Longing, perhaps. The face looked so strong, and she hadn't known a secure moment since Benjamin had died three months before.

Selina gave her a quick hug as passengers began to stream past them off the train. "I wish you a wonderful life in Yreka, Josie," she said sincerely, "and lots of beautiful babies."

Josie struggled to maintain her composure. She *had* two beautiful babies—somewhere. She drew a deep breath as the heart-wrenching desperation threatened to overtake her. Adam Scofield was expecting a dignified, cultured woman, not a weeping ninny. If she was ever to find her children, she had to appear to be what he wanted.

She swallowed the lump in her throat, along with the consummate sadness that had dogged her every step since Benjamin's death, and forced a smile.

"Thank you, Selina," she said. "And I hope your family hasn't destroyed your home in your absence—as you suspect."

"There they are!" Selina waved through the grimy window at a portly man in a gray suit with a derby and an elegant mustache. A little girl and two teenage boys standing near him waved back.

Selina hugged her again. "Goodbye, dear. Good luck." She was off the train in an instant and Josie watched enviously through the window as Selina's family encircled her and she was passed from embrace to embrace as they all began to talk and laugh excitedly.

With a sigh, Josie turned her attention from the McDuffys to the sea of bodies on the platform to look for a face that matched her photograph. Suddenly, the scheme that had held such promise in Jonathan's office a brief three weeks ago now seemed foolish and doomed to failure. What if the Pinkerton man's information was incorrect? What if the family the sheriff had seen had not been the Grippers and her children but simply people who had fit their descriptions? What if . . . ?

Josie dragged herself to the few steps that led down to the platform and squared her shoulders. "This plan has to work," she told herself firmly, "because you don't have an alternate one. So get out there, Josephine, find Adam Scofield and render him helpless with your charm."

* * *

"Why am I here?" Miles Carver leaned a shoulder against a depot post and looked over the passengers coming off the train.

"To visit your aunt," Adam Scofield, whose shoulder balanced Miles's weight on the other side of the post, replied without looking at his friend. "Do you see her?"

Miles ignored Adam's question and answered his own. "I'm here because you're a coward and not a very bright one at that. You send three thousand miles away for a wife of culture and breeding, and now that she's about to arrive, you realize what an absurd notion it is—particularly since you possess neither of those qualities."

"Thank you, Miles," Adam said absently, looking over the crowd.

"You bribed me to come along," Miles went on, "reminding me that I could visit my aunt and call on one of our clients at the same time. Actually, you just needed a rear guard."

Adam was silent, searching the crowd for dark hair and a small round face, mentally adding several years to the face on the photograph Josephine Cross had sent him. It had to have been taken earlier. It was the face of a mere girl, yet in her letter she'd explained she was a widow.

"You shouldn't equate marriage with a military skirmish, Miles," Adam said, then glanced around the post to grin at his friend and partner. "On second thought, I suppose there are times when it's appropriate."

"There were times," Miles laughed, "when you and Maggie sounded like field artillery."

Adam smiled thoughtfully, distracted from his search by memories of the beautiful red-haired Margaret Birch, who'd been his bride at seventeen, borne him two daughters as beautiful as she was, who'd loved him, annoyed him, made him laugh, made him shout, made him crazy—then died in a stagecoach accident at twenty-three.

"There!" Miles pointed into the crowd at a young woman in blue looking around uncertainly, as though searching for someone. Tendrils of blond hair escaped her bonnet.

"We're looking for a brunette," Adam reminded him.

"*You're* looking for a brunette," Miles corrected. "I'm open to a variety of…" He stopped when Adam leapt down the depot steps and headed for the rear of the last passenger car.

A small woman, a fringe of dark hair visible under a grim black bonnet, stood on the steps, surveying the crowd on the platform.

Adam wasn't sure how he'd spotted her. She was small and slender in widow's black and clung to the side of the train as though she seriously considered getting back on. In this teeming crowd of humanity, one's eyes slipped right over her—or should have. His hadn't.

As he approached, she looked into his eyes. He saw recognition flash—then a little shock of alarm, as though she found him frightening.

He thought of the poised, controlled woman he'd hoped to place beside him, to put in charge of his household, and felt a moment's disappointment. A scared little rabbit was not what he'd had in mind.

She's a recent widow, he reminded himself. *Of course she's going to be frightened. And look at how young she is. She can't be more than twenty. The photo must have been recent. And this is Sacramento—more boisterous than Boston, to be sure.*

He swept off his hat and reached a hand up to help her down to the platform. Though she was two steps up, his eyes were almost on a level with hers, and when she looked into them, she seemed to pull herself together. She blinked long dark lashes once, and when she looked at him again, he saw no evidence of fear.

"Mr. Scofield," she said in a small, quiet voice. "I'm Josephine Cross."

* * *

A smile made him even more handsome than his photograph, Josie thought, which came as a great relief to her. He was so tall and large that had he been wearing the fierce expression in the photograph, she might have seriously considered wandering the Siskiyous on her own.

"I recognized you right away," he said. "Welcome to Sacramento."

She smiled at him as she brushed at her skirt, hoping she looked calm and capable. "Thank you. I'm afraid the trip has left me wrinkled, short-tempered and considerably aged."

He studied her with a mild frown. "I was thinking how young you seem."

She laughed lightly. "Do I? Well, I was twelve when I left Boston a week ago."

Adam laughed in surprise. Witty and quick. That was good. He'd have to revise his impression of a scared rabbit.

"Your berth was uncomfortable, then?" he asked.

"I booked second-class passage," she said, reaching into a black velvet bag and handing him a small packet of bills. "I thought you could put the rest of the money to better use." She smiled winningly.

"You've been sitting up for six nights?" he asked with a wince.

She continued to smile. "I'm frugal, Mr. Scofield," she replied nobly. If that didn't win him over, she had more virtues to display.

"I imagine you're anxious to have a bath and lie down," he said, still looking astounded but picking up her portmanteau and offering his arm. "I've rented you a room at our hotel."

She slipped an arm in his and lifted her skirts with her other hand. "Our?" She looked up at him inquiringly.

"My friend Miles Carver rode to Sacramento with me. And speak of the devil..." Adam stopped as Miles loped

toward them. He came to a halt several feet away, nar
rowed his gaze on Josie, then shook his head.

"No!" he said. "No, no, no! It isn't fair that you send fo
a wife, sight unseen, and end up with...with an angel, whil
I scour all of northern California and have yet to find a
unattached female who doesn't resemble Ulysses S. Gran
and behave like General Sherman."

Adam expelled a long-suffering sigh. "Mrs. Cross, ma
I present Miles Carver, friend, business partner and bane o
my existence?"

Josie offered her hand. "Mr. Carver, if it's any comfor
to you, I assure you I am far from angelic."

Adam raised an eyebrow and looked down at her. "Oh?"

She nodded candidly. "I'm afraid I'm willful, opinion
ated, stubborn and alarmingly clever when it comes to get
ting my own way." She gave Adam a devastating smile
"Perhaps you'd like to put me back on the train whil
there's still time?"

Adam was to wonder later if that wasn't the moment h
fell in love. She fairly sparkled with wit and style. Most o
the unmarried women he'd met in the last few years eithe
simpered and fawned like brainless little girls or were so bol
and coarse as to completely repulse him.

While Adam studied Josie, amazement and amusemen
alive in his eyes, Miles shook his head and sighed. "Thos
qualities might alarm another man, Mrs. Cross, but no
Adam. He prefers women with a brain and a tongue. Neve
understood it myself, but there you have it." He smiled a
his friend. "I presume you'll want me to join you for din
ner?"

"No," Adam replied without pause.

Miles pretended hurt feelings. "Very well. I'm sure there'
a woman somewhere in Sacramento who'd be happy t
provide me company."

"And let us hope," Josie added, straight-faced, "that sh
bears little resemblance to General Grant."

Miles raised his eyes fervently. "Yes. Let us hope." He bowed formally. "It's been a pleasure meeting you, Mrs. Cross, though I think you far exceed anything Adam deserves." He tipped his hat then turned to his friend. "I'll see you at breakfast."

Adam smiled and clapped Miles's shoulder. "Stay out of trouble."

Miles looked from him to Josie then back to him, a smile twisting his lips. "You appear to be the one in danger, Adam." He turned and disappeared into the crowd.

Adam hired a cab to the Sacramento Palace. Josie listened attentively as he pointed out the gold-domed capitol building, the beautiful stick villa-styled residence of Albert Gallatin, who'd made a fortune supplying the railroad with hardware, the decrepit state of Sutter's Fort, abandoned when Sutter lost his land to newcomers in the gold rush and moved west.

"It's a remarkable city," she exclaimed as they passed a long row of high-shouldered mansions on a wide, tree-lined street. All along their path, new buildings were under construction.

"Yreka, where I live," Adam said, "is much smaller, though we do have an opera house and a school and three churches. It's beautifully set in a small valley with some of the nicest people one could ever hope to find anywhere."

That sounded appealing to Josie. She needed quiet to clear her mind and firm her plan. "It sounds lovely," she said, giving him a smile that she hoped conveyed genuine enthusiasm. "Boston was crowded and busy. I grew up in a much more rural setting and often missed the quiet of country life."

Adam was all for turning the cab in the direction of Reverend Willow's church and taking Josephine Cross to wife immediately. Instead he reminded himself that things and people were not always what they appeared. Surely her beauty was a figment of the long weeks he'd awaited her and

the image he'd built in his mind. Her wit and sweet tempe
were what he *wanted* to see. He must have several days to ge
to know her, to hope to catch a glimpse of the real woma
and not the one on good behavior for their first meeting.

And there was always the possibility she wasn't as take
by him as he was by her. She might have hoped for more c
an aristocratic gentleman than the small-town lawyer h
was. He enjoyed the excitement of the courtroom for wha
it did for justice and the common man. But unlike many c
his acquaintances in the law, he had no political aspira
tions.

Still, she had a way of looking up at him as though h
were precisely what she'd travelled so long to find. She di
it now as the cab pulled up in front of the Sacramento Pa
ace and he had to give his brain a moment to clear.

"What a beautiful place," she said, her bright eye
studying the graceful arches and bay windows of the whit
six-story structure that gave it a sort of bird-cage effec
"Boston has elegance, but it's very austere."

"That's the heart of California," he said, bracketing h
waist with his hands and swinging her out of the carriag
"We never sacrifice beauty or comfort."

He still held her several feet above the boardwalk when I
became physically aware of her. He'd noticed that she w
pretty, and he admired a shapely bosom and waist as mu
as the next man, but since he'd lost Maggie, he'd admire
women without feeling anything. His heart and his phys
cal responses had seemed to be still in her control. He'd ha
several women since Maggie, but they'd been nothing mo
than comfort and distraction. He'd felt nothing deepe
He'd even wondered if that responsive part of him had die

Now he was acutely aware of the tiny waist under h
hands, stiffly restricted by stays and stout fabric. He felt t'
warm swell of the underside of her breasts against h
thumbs. The fragrance of rose water drifted around him a

he found himself staring at pink cheeks and dusky curls as though he'd never seen anything like them before.

"Put me down, Mr. Scofield," she said under her breath, smiling, "Before someone bids on me. It must look as though you're holding me up for auction."

Adam set her on her feet immediately, glancing up to see the hotel's doorman and several bystanders watching them with expectant smiles, obviously hoping to see more. He turned Josie toward the steps and, with a hand at the back of her waist, urged her up. He drew her to a stop in front of the doorman, who was elegantly attired in red-and-gold livery.

"Josie, this is Jack O'Mara, friend to all who stop at the Palace. Jack, this is Mrs. Cross. She'll be staying here for several days."

"We're pleased to have you, Mrs. Cross. Anytime you need anything, ask for old Jack."

"Thank you, Jack."

Adam watched as Josie gave the doorman a small curtsy that completely disarmed him. It wasn't every day a resident of the hotel extended a courtesy to the doorman.

Adam took Josie upstairs in the ornate elevator to the sixth floor, then led her down a red-carpeted hall to a corner room, pushing it open to reveal a wide expanse of Brussels carpet and elegant furnishings.

As Josie wandered in, pulling off her gloves, Adam rang for the maid, then crossed the room to pull open the heavy draperies. Josie followed, stopping beside him to look down on the busy city. People hurried to and fro, a newsboy on the corner shouted a headline, and the clop of horses' hooves and the rattle of wagons and carriages filled the air. In the waning afternoon light, spires and windows were burnished with gold.

Sacramento's population was hurrying home from work and shopping to warm hearths and glowing, gaslit living rooms. For an instant, Josie's mind went back in time to the moments in her life when she'd had that cozy security—those times when her mother had been alive and her father had been well. Or, after she'd married Benjamin, the times when Jerusha had visited friends and she had been alone with her husband.

Forgetting herself, she expelled a long, wistful sigh. "All those people with places to go," she said, staring down at the street.

Adam didn't miss the new note in her voice. He was a well-respected attorney because he seldom lost a case. And he lost so seldom because he missed nothing—not the change of expression in a glance or the subtle suggestion in a tone of voice.

He turned to Josie, wondering what that sad little whisper meant. Need? Loss? Fear?

She looked up at him, and for an instant he saw inside the witty, charming young woman to the pain responsible for that sigh. Then she blinked and smiled, and her expression cleared.

A maid appeared in the doorway.

"A bath for Mrs. Cross, please," Adam said. He turned to Josie. "And a pot of coffee? Tea? Something to eat?"

"A pot of tea would be lovely."

Adam turned to the maid, who nodded and disappeared.

Josie put a hand on Adam's arm, afraid her momentary slip had alarmed him. She needed desperately to win him back.

"I'm delighted with the accommodations, Mr. Scofield," she said cheerfully. "Thank you for your kindness."

He smiled down at her, the same easy smile that had relaxed her at the train station. Maybe he hadn't noticed.

"Not at all. A woman who would travel so far to consider a man's proposal deserves to have her needs second-guessed." He pulled a watch out of his pocket, consulted then replaced it. "Dinner in three hours?"

"Perfect."

"I'll rap on the door at eight o'clock."

"I'll be ready."

He raised a teasing eyebrow. "Really? Boston ladies must be a unique breed indeed."

Josie held the door open for him, smiling. "Of course we are. Isn't that why you sent for one?"

"So it is. Until dinner, Mrs. Cross."

"You may call me Josie...Adam." She was pushing propriety, she knew, but despite his smile she sensed a mild constraint in him and she couldn't have that. He had to want her for his wife.

"Good day, Josie," he said.

"Good day, Adam," she replied.

As Adam let himself into the room next door, he wondered about that glimpse of pain. She was a widow, he reminded himself. The fact that she'd decided to consider remarriage didn't necessarily put a stop to her grief. He still grieved for Maggie after three years. The sharpness of his pain had been alleviated, but the sense of loss sometimes still overwhelmed him.

Yet he would wager that the pain he'd seen in Josie Cross was something more. He couldn't explain why, he just knew. And he saw a secret in her eyes. When he looked at her, it was almost as though she closed off a little part of herself—protecting something she didn't want him to see.

He wondered about that, too, considering her lack of reticence toward him. He liked to think it was because he was devastatingly handsome and charming, but he knew better. Josephine Cross wanted to marry him for reasons of her own.

At the first opportunity he would make it clear that, while he expected loyalty and fidelity and appreciated her politically correct Boston lineage, he did not expect love. He'd had six years of happiness with Maggie, and Josie had apparently been happy in her marriage. If she chose to ally herself with him, he could offer security, comfort and contentment—certainly a fair trade for the little he would ask of her.

He would want to share her bed, of course, but he guessed a widow would not find that a horrifying prospect.

He poured himself a brandy and crossed to the window to look down on Sacramento as sunset approached. This could be a comfortable alliance for both of them, he thought. Yes. Comfortable.

Chapter Two

When it came to telling Josie those things in a corner of the hotel's candlelit dining room, Adam found it difficult. Crystal goblets and polished silver picked up and reflected the tiny licks of flame, casting them around until he began to feel he was trapped in a kaleidoscope. Conversation was soft, violins wept, and across the table from him Josie Cross watched him with rapt attention, her wide blue eyes brilliant and softly but dauntingly candid. The small, firmly rounded tops of her breasts rose and fell under the sheer netting of what was probably supposed to be the modest neckline of a lavender widow's dress.

He had trouble tearing his eyes from the subtle undulation.

"I suppose it sounds callous," he said, offering that qualification after a long, tedious description of their life together as he saw it, "but I've had one marriage in which I had everything a man could want, and you obviously loved and still grieve for your husband, so there's little point in deluding ourselves that we're after anything more than companionship and comfort."

Their marriage as he'd outlined it suited Josie's purpose perfectly, but the pompous detachment with which he spoke of it annoyed her. He was damnably good-looking. In the crisp black and white of evening clothes, Adam Scofield looked like the man Josie used to dream about before Benjamin Cross abruptly became a part of her life and moved her to the big brownstone on Unity Street.

But she'd overheard enough male conversation in her time to know that men could discuss marriage in the most analytical of terms. They sought a woman with the right name, a proper dowry, a face a man would be proud to have at his shoulder—then found love and solace in the arms of a woman required to have nothing but a willing way and access to a bed.

At least he was honest about it, she thought. He wasn't promising undying love, just companionship. And all she needed was financial support while she searched for her children. It sounded very much as though he'd stay out of her way if she stayed out of his.

Then he said something to negate that thought.

"On the subject of..." He hesitated, his long fingers picking up his glass by the bowl then putting it down again several inches away.

Josie watched his downcast eyes, shamelessly enjoying herself. If he was planning to set her up in domestic splendor, then spend his evenings with a fallen dove, she was entitled to at least a little mischief.

He winced as he apparently considered and rejected several words to describe the subject on his mind.

She leaned forward and asked very softly, "Copulation, Mr. Scofield?"

His dark eyes flew to hers, half relieved, half mortified. She stoutly maintained an innocent stare. "Did I misunderstand?" she asked.

Adam looked at Josie's pink-and-ivory face framed by glistening dark curls and knew a moment of serious trepidation. He didn't know what to make of her blue-eyed innocence, but he had a sneaking suspicion he shouldn't trust it. She'd wanted to shock him. As he saw it, his only recourse was to pretend that she hadn't.

"No, you did not," he replied, refilling her wineglass from a crystal carafe. Then he folded his arms on the table and looked her in the eye. "I'm a man of considerable appetite. Conventional," he added, pausing a moment for effect, "but considerable. You understand?"

Josie couldn't help the rise of color in her cheeks. She tried to will it away to no avail. "Oh, quite," she replied, maintaining an even expression. "Will you be incorporating frequency into our contract, then? I presume there will be a contract? This does sound very much like a business transaction."

Adam fought down annoyance. In all honesty, he didn't think he'd ever known a woman more quick-witted than he was. Maggie had been wily, but most of what she'd put over on him he'd allowed. This woman, however, was rapidly becoming worrisome. Trouble was, the more worrisome she became, the more intrigued he became.

"Only the traditional marriage contract," he replied, his voice and his gaze even. "I'll trust your word for the details decided between us."

Josie recognized the words as a compliment and a challenge. "Thank you," she said.

"And what is it you'd like to gain out of this marriage?" he asked.

She smiled. *Speak easily, as though it doesn't really matter.* "A certain freedom of movement," she said with a dry roll of her eyes. "I loved my husband dearly, but life in Boston was very restrictive. I couldn't leave the house without a companion. I ride well," she lied, "and I'd like to investigate the countryside if I choose, go to town and visit neighbors on my own. After governesses, finishing school, a possessive husband and a watchful society, I look forward to finding freedom in your household, Adam."

"I'm afraid I can't promise you that," he replied, a faint hint of apology in his voice. "My home is on the outskirts of town, so the walk or ride would be easy, but you would not be free to roam unaccompanied. Yreka is settled and secure, but the area surrounding it is wilderness and not a safe place for a lady from Boston to explore."

"I would be confined to the house, then?" she asked, her tone polite but deliberately uncertain. She was hoping the suggestion of her refusal of his conditions would make him change his mind. She couldn't find her children if she was confined to his home.

"To the grounds," he corrected, also polite but not conciliatory. "We have forty acres that include a pine woods and a stream. And your confinement, as I said, would be only when you are unaccompanied."

But when you are at your office, she thought, while looking properly amenable, *you will have no way of knowing where I am.*

"I suppose that's reasonable," she said.

Adam tried to read her eyes but couldn't. She appeared convincing, but then she seemed to have a gift for that. He found himself wondering *why* she felt the need for this freedom. Was she truly the victim of a repressive life, or did she have other reasons for wanting free run of the countryside? At this point it was difficult to tell. The problem was, by the time he was able to tell it would probably be too late. They would be married.

He watched her as the waiter brought a frothy cream cake and she fussed prettily over it, denying all ability to eat it then delving into it with enthusiasm. She was an enigma all right, but far and away the most interesting puzzle to pass his way in a long time. And he'd managed Maggie Birch Scofield. He could manage Josie Cross.

When Josie saw him studying her enigmatically, she felt panic. With a great show of compliance, she put a hand on his on the table and said quietly, "I want so to have a home again, Adam. I'll do whatever you ask."

Adam thought he saw sincerity in her eyes, though the tone of her voice was laced with syrup. He knew the statement was calculated to raise his sympathies, but somewhere there was truth in it. He sensed that it was deep down where that private pain lived.

He believed her. She would do what he asked, not out of any concern for him but because securing a husband was so important to her—for whatever private reasons she might have.

He put his free hand over the one she held and he saw the concession register in her wide blue eyes. They became hopeful, almost avaricious, as though she knew success was only a heartbeat away.

This is a dangerous lady, a little voice told him. Don't underestimate her, and don't drop your guard.

But she's exactly what I need, he told himself. *Jane and Lucy will love her.* His eyes dropped to the tantalizing flutter of the netting on her bodice. His body responded uncomfortably.

"Then, how much more time do we need?" he asked. "Will you marry me?"

He'd ignored the voice of reason and followed his own inclinations. Such a stance was completely out of character for him, and that knowledge disturbed him somewhat.

Josie tried not to betray how much this success meant to her. She'd made it clear she was anxious to marry him, but he could have no idea of the real extent of her desperation.

She smiled and topped his hand with hers. "Yes, I will," she said. "I'm pleased and flattered."

This was the closest she'd been in two months to any real possibility of finding her children. The reality of it blotted out the grim probability of her chances, and tears sprang to her eyes.

Because she could now afford to be generous, she said, "You won't regret this, Adam, I promise you."

Adam saw the tears in her eyes and could not determine whether they were genuine. He replied with a smile that was all affability with just an undercurrent of threat. "No, I won't. The other party usually suffers when I have cause to regret. Now, let's talk about what you'll need for the wedding. A new dress, no doubt.''

Did he see through her? Josie wondered. She hadn' missed the subtle threat, and his remark about the dress revealed a suspicion that she was motivated in this curious relationship by the promise of material gain.

That rankled. She'd never asked for a thing in her life And conscience forbade her from taking gifts or bauble from this man, considering the way she was deceiving him

''Thank you, but I have a dress that's suitable,'' she replied.

''Shoes? Hat?''

''No, thank you.''

''Surely there's something you'd like?''

''A clutch of flowers to help me look like a bride,'' she suggested with a smile.

Adam studied her a moment, obviously confused by a woman who refused gifts.

''Very well,'' he said finally. ''Flowers it is. If you're finished, I'll take you out onto the veranda for a little fresh air It'll help you sleep soundly.''

Josie felt the smallest jolt of alarm as he came around behind her to help her out of her chair. It was working. Soon she would become Mrs. Adam Scofield and travel to a town in the Siskiyou Mountains, the last known location of her children. A score of reasons why she might never find them flooded her mind. She pushed them aside with a toss of her head, refusing to consider them. Charlie and Billy were not dead or injured or mistreated. They were simply confused and lonely. Her heart ached at the thought. But she would find them. She *would* find them.

The night was moonless and dark, the soft glow of streetlights blooming like exotic flowers planted in a straight line all the way to infinity. The streets were quiet except for the distant gaiety of saloon music borne on a gust of wind

"Sounds as though someone's having fun," Josie said, resting her forearms on the stone railing and leaning out to draw in a deep gulp of air. She felt herself relax for the first time since she'd stepped off the train. Deceit was much harder for her than she'd anticipated. The constant strain of smiling and pretending a seductive charm that was really foreign to her nature was beginning to tell.

"Does that suggest that you aren't having fun?" Adam asked, his voice right behind her ear.

She rubbed her arms against the wind, keeping her face turned away from him.

"It's been a lovely evening," she corrected cheerfully. "But even you must admit that our circumstances make it difficult to have 'fun' in the true sense of the word."

Josie started as a prickly warmth dropped on her shoulders. Adam adjusted his jacket around her then came to prop his elbows on the railing beside hers, his white shirt bright in the darkness. He, too, looked out on the city.

"You mean uninhibited fun," he said quietly. "Clear conscience fun."

Clear conscience fun. Josie analyzed those words for a moment, wondering if they suggested she might have a guilty conscience. His next words deepened her concern.

"Is there anything you'd like to tell me?" he asked gently.

Josie counted her heartbeats, forcing herself to remain calm. "Confess a sordid past, you mean?" she asked lightly, finally turning to find him looking down at her, the light from the French doors burnishing the strong line of his jaw. His eyes were quiet, questioning.

"A sordid past usually shows in a woman's face." He put a hand to her chin and turned it to the light. His touch was warm and gentle, but she felt steel in his fingers. "That's not what I see."

She swallowed. "What, then?"

"I'm not sure," he replied. He released her chin and folded his arms, still studying her. "It's causing me a little concern because I'm usually very perceptive. There is something about your past you don't want me to know."

Where her calm came from, Josie didn't know. Out of her desperation, she guessed. She smiled slowly. "Any woman worthy of the name has a few secrets. Life is more interesting that way."

Swallowed up in his jacket, her wide-eyed face pale in the shadows, she didn't look like a threat to his comfortable way of life, yet somehow he knew she would be.

"You're free to keep your secrets," he said, "as long as they do no harm to my household. The moment they hurt anyone, the bargain is off."

Josie squared her shoulders, a little flame of indignation lighting her eyes. "I have never deliberately hurt anyone, Mr. Scofield."

"When someone is hurt, Mrs. Cross," he replied, "it hardly matters to the victim if the pain was deliberately or accidentally inflicted. It hurts all the same."

Josie swung his jacket off her shoulders and pushed it at his chest. She'd come as far as Sacramento, she could make it to the Siskiyous on her own. Sparring with this man was becoming more than she could tolerate, and she was getting the uncomfortable feeling that though he had no idea what she was up to, it wouldn't be long before he did. It would be better to leave now than marry him, be discovered and sent away.

"Then let me relieve you of my presence," she said, "before I do you an injury, accidental or otherwise." A gust of wind raised gooseflesh on the skin under the netting of her bodice and the tips of her breasts beaded. "I'm sure there's a woman for you somewhere who is willing to be confined to your home and to open her very soul to your inspection. I am not. Good night."

Josie spun away from him and started for the French
doors.

"Just a moment."

A warm hand clamped on her upper arm, stopping her
before she was two steps away. Adam dropped his jacket
across the railing and turned her to face him. His eyes were
in shadow, but she saw the devilish gleam of his smile.

"It occurs to me," he said, "that both of us have become overly concerned about negatives. There will be many
positives to our association. Perhaps we should explore one
to balance our perspectives."

She tried to ask a very tart "Which one would that be?"
but succeeded only in shaping her lips to form the first
word—a mistake that served Adam's purpose well.

He closed his mouth on hers, cupping her head with one
hand and pulling her against him with the other.

Josie had tried not to think about the physical aspect of
her role as wife to Adam Scofield. Not that she disliked
making love, but she couldn't imagine sharing intimacy with
anyone but Benjamin—and Benjamin was gone. By his own
admission, this man would be a demanding lover. It would
be difficult to pretend enthusiasm, she was sure, so she'd
chosen to put the matter out of her mind until faced with it.

Now she was. Faced with the preliminaries, at least. If she
was to— Her train of thought snapped as she came to sharp
awareness. His mouth, dry and warm, moved on hers with
gentle insistence, teasing, taunting, drawing her cautious
response.

It began as a slow prickle along her shoulders, rose to the
roots of her hair, then broke over her, showering her with
warmth and a strange feeling of excitement.

She wound her arms around his neck as his mouth moved
across her eyes, from cheek to cheek, into her ear, where he
dipped his tongue, making her hunch her shoulder and give
a startled little gasp.

With a jolt, Adam felt her small hands at the nape of his neck. When they went into his hair, he felt the reaction to his toes. She leaned into him, straining for balance, and he felt every small curve of her like a brand against his body. When she opened her mouth to him, he invaded, lost to reason.

Sensation coursed through him, wound around him, threatened to suffocate him. The little witch, he thought in mindless amazement. Charm, secrets and passion, too. A deadly combination if ever he'd experienced it.

They pulled apart, each gasping for air and staring at the other in suspicious surprise. Adam could think of nothing to say. He'd kissed her to prove something, but what that was he couldn't quite recall. He knew only that he hadn't felt this way since Maggie, and since her death he'd been sure he would never want to feel that way again.

Josie put a hand to her waist and asked in a whisper, "I trust, Mr. Scofield, that your perspective is now balanced?"

"No, Mrs. Cross," he said, reaching out to snatch up his coat. He dropped it on her shoulders again and gave her a wry smile. "You have me completely *off* balance."

Josie, upset and disoriented, regretted her earlier decision to refuse his offer. She had to have a base in the Siskiyous from which to operate, she had to have money with which to gain information, she had to have a horse, a weapon, sustenance while she searched.

Deliberately, she put all impressions of that kiss aside. She'd only ever been made love to by a man in his fifties. It was natural that the ardor of a man in his prime would unsettle her. It meant nothing more. And her situation needed no further complications.

She had to marry this man. She resumed her mask of the charming waif.

"If you'll apologize for suggesting I intend to bring you harm," she said, angling her chin, "I'll reconsider your proposal."

You're a fool, Adam told himself, even as he nodded. "Then I apologize."

"Very well," she said. "Then I accept."

They were married in a tiny church in a field of wild daisies with Miles as best man and the minister's wife witnessing for Josie. Mrs. Willow was a small, nervous woman who fixed Josie with a look of such pity that though she began the ceremony as a calm bride, she ended it as a vaguely troubled married woman.

Her groom seemed quieter than usual, Josie noted, handsomely dressed in a suit of blue serge. He'd brought the promised flowers and Josie touched a finger to them as he led her out of the church to a hired carriage.

Miles took them to a light lunch at a restaurant near the capitol building.

"That Mrs. Willow was downright frightening," he said, eating the last bite of a spring chicken. "She kept looking at you, Josie, as though you were being sacrificed for a bountiful crop."

Josie couldn't restrain a small laugh—that was precisely the way the woman had made her feel. Now that the ceremony was over and they sat in this beautiful glass-domed restaurant with sunlight pouring down on them, the mood evaporated.

"You mustn't laugh," Adam teased, buttering a biscuit and handing it to her. "I put in a field of corn just last week. If it looks sickly by mid-July, I might have little recourse."

She smiled smugly at him. "I'm safe. That would never work."

He raised an eyebrow. "Why not?"

"Well..." She glanced at Miles a little uncomfortably, then back at Adam. "I'm not sure I should say."

Adam was tempted to tell her she could say nothing that would shock Miles, then remembered their conversation the previous evening.

"Cover your ears, Miles," Adam ordered.

"Now look..."

"Do you want to embarrass Josie?"

"Of course not, but... Mercy!" With a groan of exasperation Miles put both hands over his ears. "Please be brief, Josie," he said, "I've a bird to finish."

"Now..." Adam leaned toward her, lowering his head so she could speak softly in his ear.

She felt foolish now, but she was sure Miles did, also. She said quietly, "A sacrifice requires a virgin."

He turned his head to look into her eyes, his mere inches away. They showed more amusement than surprise. "A point that escaped me," he said. "I have difficulty remembering you're a widow. You're safe, then, even if the crop fails. Put your hands down, Miles."

When Miles responded to Adam's words with a questioning look, Adam reached across the table and yanked his friend's arm down. "I said you can put your hands down."

Miles looked at Adam then Josie with interest. "Would I have been shocked?"

Adam glanced at Josie with a grin. "Possibly."

Miles sighed gustily, obviously jealous. "I'm the one with all the advantages but you have all the luck. Why is that?"

"I'm smarter," Adam replied.

"And more modest," Josie added. "Will we all be riding to Yreka together?"

Miles shook his head. "I have to spend some time with a client. I'm staying behind while you and Adam take the train to Redding."

"How many days to Yreka?" Josie asked.

"Two nights and a day on the train," Adam replied. "Then two days in our wagon, which I left in Redding. We could take the stage, but I thought it would be more comfortable for you to stop when you want to."

She sighed at the prospect. Since leaving Boston she'd had enough travel to last her a lifetime. Four more days of i seemed like an eternity. But she smiled at Adam. "It'll be lovely to finally get somewhere where I won't be bundled onto something else that moves."

"I know." He smiled and patted her hand. "If it's any comfort, Jane and Lucy will be delighted to meet you at last. They've talked about nothing else since your letter arrived."

Josie nodded. "I'm looking forward to meeting them." It would be important to make friends of his household staff, she knew. He'd said in his letter that he owned a large house and Jane and Lucy had probably kept things going for him since his wife died. She'd need their assistance in order to assume her duties. And their forbearance and discretion when she went in search of her children.

Adam glanced at his watch. "Our train leaves in two hours. Are you packed?"

"For the most part," she replied. "I've just a few details to attend to."

"Then you'd best go back to the hotel with Miles. I have to take care of some things." He stood and pulled Josie's chair back. "Is there anything you'd like for the trip? A novel? Floss for your embroidery? A box of bonbons?"

She looked into his eyes, wondering if he was teasing her, but he seemed genuinely solicitous. "I'm a sad failure at embroidery," she admitted.

He nodded as though he'd expected as much. "And your taste runs to dime novels, no doubt."

Her eyes sparkled. "Do you think you could find one and still run your errands?"

"Trust me." Adam led her out into the bright afternoon, then helped her into the carriage while Miles climbed into the other side. "I'll be back in an hour."

She looked down at him, still holding the hand with which he had helped her up. Her eyes went to his face, lingering for one unsettling moment on his mouth. His heart stopped, like a suddenly stricken bird. She was going to lean down and kiss him. Then her eyes looked into his again and the urgency he'd seen there an instant ago turned to humor. "If you run your errands efficiently and have sufficient time," she said, smiling slowly, "the bonbons would be nice, too."

Disappointed, he made himself return her smile. "Anything to keep you sweet on the journey. Back to the hotel, driver."

Josie stared balefully out the window into the dark night, her novel and the box of bonbons ignored in her lap as the train rumbled north. Nights were the hardest for her. Billy was afraid of the dark, and she usually spent sleepless hours praying that the Grippers were tolerant of that, and that sturdy, capable Charlie remained with him to calm the fears that must plague both of them daily.

She fought back tears with deep breaths. It wouldn't do for Adam to wake up and find her sobbing. He would think she regretted their marriage.

She turned to see him sitting low in his seat, one knee bent against the seat in front of him, his hat pulled forward to shield his eyes. Something about the length and solidity of him relaxed her a little. Her children were still lost to her out there somewhere, but, however unwittingly, Adam had provided her with a way to find them.

She brushed a tear away with a gloved finger and delved into her bag for her hankie.

Josie started as Adam slid upward in his seat, pushed his hat back and flexed his taut shoulders. He focused on her, his gaze narrowing as he noticed the tear.

"What is it?" he asked.

She dabbed at the moisture briskly and replaced her hankie. "Soot, I imagine. Bonbon?"

Adam stayed her hand as she tried to open the box. "You may keep your womanly secrets," he said gently, "but please don't treat me as though I'm deceived by them. Is there something wrong?"

Their fellow travellers were quiet, though the train made considerable noise as it clacked along. The interior of the car was almost as dark as the night, but Josie could see into Adam's eyes. There was genuine concern in them and, thinking of how she was using him, she felt guilt billow inside her, strong and smoky.

"Nighttime," she said softly, "makes me melancholy." Another tear fell to substantiate her statement. "I'm fine, I assure you. Please go back to sleep."

Adam took the book and box from her lap and tucked them under his seat. Then he grinned at her bonnet. "Does that contraption come off, or must you sleep with it?"

She glanced around at their quiet companions. "It does come off, but only in the privacy of..."

"Nothing," he interrupted with a whisper, "is more private than the night. Take it off. Everyone else is asleep."

Reluctantly, Josie removed the pins, then the hat, tucking the pins into the grosgrain band, then propping the hat atop her portmanteau at her feet.

"There." Adam put an arm around her shoulders and drew her against him, turning slightly toward her to make a comfortable pillow for her head. He pulled the coat he had discarded earlier over her shoulders. "Try to sleep," he ordered gently. "I know the conditions aren't the best, but when we get home you'll find our house very comfortable, our household warm and kind and our friends congenial. I can imagine how unhappy you've been since your husband died, and how much you went through to come here, but you're riding into better days, Josie. Sleep now."

Josie wallowed in security. Adam's linen-covered chest was solid yet comfortably pliant. His arms were strong, his grip protective, his cheek against the top of her head a comfortable, comforting weight. The scent of his clean person and a suggestion of bay rum invaded her nostrils.

It was so long since a man had held her. Adam had held her last night on the hotel's veranda, but he'd had a differ-

ent purpose in mind then. This offer of comfort was most
welcome. She felt every muscle in her body relax and the
worries that plagued every waking moment recede to the
back of her mind. She'd lived on her wits for so long. It was
a blessing and relief to know that, for several hours at least,
she was required to do nothing but sleep.

She closed her eyes, let all her weight go against Adam's
chest and fell asleep.

Adam felt her relinquish responsibility for the night to
him. He accepted it easily, though not without appreciation of the confusion and frustration attached to caring for
a woman—physically and emotionally.

Maggie had been gone three years, but he remembered
clearly that she could be pliant in his arms one moment,
then in the next erupt like a pyrotechnics display for no apparent reason—something he'd said or hadn't said, something he'd done or forgotten to do.

This woman promised to be even more of an enigma. She
was both more forthright and more private than Maggie had
been. That confused him further. But she was pretty and
smart, and he felt sure Jane and Lucy would love her. He
would learn to deal with her, and she would learn what he
expected. They would have a comfortable future.

Even as he formed that thought, she became tense in his
arms and said softly, plaintively, "Charlie?" She stirred, her
voice growing more urgent. "Charlie? Darling, where are
you?"

When she tried to pull out of his arms, still asleep, he
tightened his grip, shushing her and rubbing a hand up and
down her spine.

"It's all right, Josie," he said, stroking the side of her
face. "It's just a dream. It's all right."

With a small sigh, she leaned into him again, bringing
both hands up between them, her nose and her mouth bur-

rowing into his neck so that he felt her every breath against his throat. She relaxed again, the brief nightmare over.

As the train streamed on into the night, Adam stared out at the darkness, wondering who in the hell Charlie was.

Chapter Three

"We can spend the afternoon relaxing in a hotel room," Adam said, pointing to the Redding Rest, a one-story building far less elegant than the Sacramento Palace, "and leave in the morning, or we can leave this afternoon and be home that much sooner."

Though he left the choice to her, Josie could hear in his voice that he was anxious to keep moving, to get home as quickly as possible.

Josie would have loved an afternoon's rest, but the two of them alone in a hotel room might have inspired a pursuit there hadn't been the room or the privacy for on the train. She wasn't ready for that. She simply wasn't.

"Let's go ahead, by all means," she said with a forced smile. "I'm anxious to be home."

"Very well." His expression made it obvious he was pleased with her decision. "But we'll have lunch first." He touched a thumb to her cheek. "You're sure you're not too tired? You slept so little on the train."

She shrugged a shoulder, thinking of how often he surprised her with a gentle gesture or some solicitous attention to her comfort. The two nights sitting up in his arms were a memory with which she was loath to part. They'd been un-complicated by sexual tension because, in their circumstances, there had been simply nothing they could do about it.

The change would come now that they would be stopping overnight at a halfway house. She could feel it in the air already. *It's all right,* she told herself calmly. *It's not as though you're a stranger to what goes on in the bedroom.*

"I never sleep very well," she replied. "It's not a cause for concern." Hoping to terminate the conversation, she smiled brightly. "Did you say something about lunch?"

"I did." He told the livery hand they'd return in an hour and led her across the dusty street. "Who is Charlie, Josie?" he asked, startling her out of step.

She looked up at him, her eyes wide with anguish before she could control it. "Charlie?" she asked.

He frowned at her reaction. "Yes. You called to him in your sleep."

Stupid! she berated herself. Careless! She couldn't control what she did in her sleep, but she couldn't afford to arouse his suspicions, deliberately or accidentally. She forced a smile and a tone even she knew wasn't convincing.

"My attorney," she replied, making herself look into his eyes.

He hesitated for only an instant, but it was long enough to unsettle her completely. "I addressed a letter to your attorney, if you'll recall," he said quietly. "I distinctly remember that his name is *Jonathan* Dunlop."

Her mind worked furiously—and came up with a plausible lie. "Jonathan Charles Dunlop. All his friends call him Charlie."

"You called him darling."

Her eyes widened farther, then she smiled. "He is a darling."

Adam studied her a moment, then nodded. "Ah. Of course. Let's eat, then."

Josie chatted as she ate, guilt making her strive to be a scintillating companion. Adam accepted her good cheer with no evidence of suspicion, but she knew she would have to get herself in hand if she were to pull this off. She resolved to spend her first evening home in solitude, perfecting the story of her past.

Adam didn't know what to think. He was fairly certain she was lying about her attorney's name to conceal the mysterious Charlie's real identity. But why? Another man in her life? he wondered. If that were true, why wasn't she with him instead of here, three thousand miles away?

He pushed the concern from his mind. As yet, it wasn't a problem. If it became one, he had the upper hand in this situation, and he could make her tell him. Right now, she seemed determined to be charming, to point out every beautiful vista and rave about how different it was from Boston. He suspected she was feeling guilty. For a woman who'd admitted she had secrets and was apparently determined to keep most of them, she was particularly guileless. For the moment she confused him, but his years in the law had taught him that it was impossible to suppress the truth forever. Eventually, he would learn what she was hiding from him and why.

They made a comfort stop in the middle of the afternoon and took several extra moments to stretch their legs. Josie picked buttercups and collected them in her open bag, twirling a fat one in her fingers and smiling over it.

"That's one of Jane's favorite occupations," Adam said, smiling solicitously at her as she looked up at him.

He caught her hand and led her across a green meadow to the edge of a forest of ponderosa pine. The rich, prickly scent drifted out to them. Josie inhaled deeply. "You must be a very generous employer," she said, closing her eyes as she relished the aroma, "if your housekeeper has time to braid wildflower coronets."

When he was silent a moment, she opened her eyes and looked up into his. They were clearly puzzled. "House-keeper?" he asked.

"Isn't that Jane's position?" she asked, leaning down to the grass as her attention was captured by a bright pink, small-petaled flower she'd never seen before. "Or is that Lucy, and Jane is a secretary of some sort?"

He looked down at her, expelling a surprised laugh. "Lucy and Jane are my daughters."

When her head snapped up, her eyes wide with stunned surprise, he went on encouragingly, as one would to some-one slow. "You remember. I talked about them in my letter to Jonathan Dunlop."

He watched her rise slowly out of her crouch, the sun-light slanting across her face as the expression in her eyes changed unaccountably to one of horror. "You mentioned no children," she insisted.

"I most certainly did," he replied, becoming annoyed. "How could I recruit a wife and not mention that I have two small daughters?"

She made a sound of distress and turned away from him. He grabbed her arm and turned her around. "I've men-tioned them several times since you arrived in Sacramento. We talked about them on the train."

"I thought they were housekeepers!" she shouted.

"Why, in God's name?" he demanded. "I described them in the letter!"

She tried frantically to think back. How could she have missed that detail? She had a mental image of Jonathan reading the letter. "... formidable house, two housekeep-ers..." Then a series of "da-da da-da da-da da-das" as he searched the page to get to the part she'd asked about, just where his home was located. He'd picked up at "Jane and Lucy. We live in a beautiful little valley filled with..." She presumed the da-das had merely passed over details about the two housekeepers, not the illuminating fact that Adam had two daughters. That changed everything.

"Jonathan read me the letter," she said stiffly. "I did not see it myself. Somehow, he skipped over the part about your children."

He frowned at her, arms folded. "Small surprise, considering even his own first name is in doubt. I thought all his friends called him Charlie?"

Josie closed her eyes and turned away from him, trying to gather her scattered wits.

He took hold of her arms and turned her around, leaning down to her, making an obvious effort to be reasonable. "Josie, they're sweet, beautiful little girls. You'll love them. They'll love you."

"No," she said firmly, hardening herself against the shrewish image her refusal must project. She couldn't be concerned about that. She could perpetuate this deceit against a pompous man, but not against two small children. She loved her own too much ever to hurt anyone else's. She looked into his anxious eyes, unflinching. "I'm sorry," she said. "I didn't understand that you had children. This changes everything. You have to take me back to Sacramento."

For a moment he looked at her as though he couldn't believe his ears. Then the expression in his eyes and the muscles in his jaw hardened, and she knew her retreat would not be easy.

"I have to do no such thing," he said. "We are married, and we're going home to Yreka together."

"I refuse."

"Then you may stay here." He turned his broad back on her and strode to the wagon, where he began to pull her things out of the back.

Josie looked at her surroundings, a beautiful view made of great ridges, gorges, bluffs and a road winding into a tangle of trees. She went to the coach and put a hand on Adam's arm as he prepared to embark.

"Please understand," she said quietly. "I have to go back."

"I have to go home," he replied as quietly. "If you're leaving this meadow at all, you're coming with me. We're married, Josie."

"We can have the marriage annulled. Please, Adam." She followed his arm down to the large hand resting on her hat box. "I can't explain."

There were tears in her eyes. He tried to read them, to see beyond the surprise and disappointment he felt to what made a normally charming woman react this way at the mention of children, but she lowered her lashes, and when she looked up at him again, all he saw was stubbornness. Anger began to roll inside him.

"You may come home with me," he said, "or I leave you here. Which is it?"

Josie had no doubt he meant it. The man she'd thought of as kind and caring only hours ago now had a threat in his eye she believed with all her heart. He'd leave her and never look back. Well, she'd find another way to leave *him*—later. There had to be one.

She reached down for the portmanteau he'd dropped to the ground and struggled to lift it up to him. "How old are your children?" she asked, pretending mild interest as he took the bag from her. She climbed into the coach beside him.

"Jane is nine, Lucy four," he replied. He shouted at the horses and they began to move.

Adam measured her with another glance and she couldn't read what he thought, though it was clear the easy camaraderie that had developed between them on the train was dead. If she hadn't been born with Yankee cussedness, and if it weren't for the fact that her children were still out there somewhere—and she wouldn't give Jerusha Cross the satisfaction of having defeated her—she'd wish she were dead, too.

Adam didn't know what to make of her. When he'd conceived the idea of sending for a New England woman to be his wife, it had seemed so simple. Any woman, he'd thought, would be grateful to join his comfortable household, to be under his protection and part of the congenial circle in which he travelled. He'd thought any woman would be proud to raise Jane and Lucy.

It had taken every ounce of fortitude he had not to leave her in the meadow—he'd been that angry with her. He knew that she was keeping something from him, though she could behave like the consummate lady. There was something about her that didn't ring true, and he'd concluded that she'd undertaken this marriage to use him for some purpose.

He'd accepted that because, in effect, he was using her, too. But he'd never expected her to reject his daughters. And, fool that he probably was, he couldn't believe she was motivated by a simple dislike for children.

Hours later they arrived at Kilkenny's, the way station where they would spend the night. He drove through a muddy yard and pulled into a dark stable. Adam climbed down, instructing her to wait a moment as he spoke to a stable hand.

Tired and impatient, Josie leapt down without waiting for his help. A little cry escaped her as she sank to her knees in the straw that covered the stable floor.

"Oh, ma'am!" A young boy with stick-straight blond hair ran to her before Adam could and helped her to her feet. "You shoulda waited for the mister."

"Thank you." She smiled at the boy while darting a glance at Adam that dared him to ridicule her clumsiness. "What's your name?"

The boy glowed under her attention. "Jacob, ma'am."

"Thank you for your assistance, Jacob."

"My pleasure, ma'am."

Adam handed the boy a coin, finding his calflike expression almost painful to watch. He took Josie's arm and guided her toward the inn. "Have mercy," he cautioned quietly. "He's just a boy."

"With good manners," she replied evenly, walking across the yard without looking at him, picking up her skirts against the mud. "Perhaps a day or two spent with him would improve yours."

"Mine are suitable," he said, opening the station house door for her, "to a welcher."

"I . . ." Josie began hotly, her temper rising under the accusation. But she could think of nothing with which to defend herself. If he had mentioned his daughters in the letter, and he probably had, her withdrawal from the bargain at this point was welching. She had no defense. Frustrated, she lifted her chin and sailed past him into a comfortable parlor.

They were greeted by a man who treated Adam like a good friend. Adam introduced him as John Kilkenny. "John," he said, his gaze turning to Josie with a hint of warning, "this is my bride, Josie Cross Scofield."

The man let out a shout, pumping Josie's hand with unconcealed delight, then ran to the kitchen door to shout, "Mother! Come and meet Mrs. Scofield!"

John hurried back to Adam and Josie. "I can't believe it. I can't *believe* it! Do the girls know? Does Bertha?"

Adam put an arm around Josie's shoulders. She didn't resist him, though he felt her stiffness. "Yes. They haven't seen her, of course, but they're all anxious for her to get home."

"Mrs. Scofield?" A very short, very broad woman appeared in the kitchen doorway, wiping her hands on a white apron. Her bright blue eyes assessed Josie as she approached. She looked from her husband to Adam. "You've remarried?" she asked bluntly.

"I haven't acquired a mother," Adam said with a wry glance at John. "Felicity Kilkenny, Josie Scofield."

Josie extended her hand, liking the woman instantly, despite the doubtful look Felicity was giving her. Jerusha Cross had fawned over Josie when Benjamin had first brought her home, and had waited until her back was turned to destroy her life forever. Josie appreciated honesty.

"I'm so happy to meet you, Felicity," she said. "I don't know what that aroma is coming from the kitchen, but it smells like heaven after a week of railroad food."

"Where d'ya come from?"

"Boston."

Felicity, painfully frank but sensitive to praise, took Josie's hand and shook it firmly. "Welcome to Kilkenny's. It's time Adam Scofield had a little light in his life again. John will take your things upstairs, and I'll send up some tea and cake to keep you until dinner. Then I'll set out the finest meal you've ever had—Boston included."

Felicity dispatched John to get their bags and led the way upstairs herself, hips and skirts flouncing.

The room was small but clean—a far cry from their Sacramento hotel rooms but with every comfort one could hope to enjoy in the mountains of northern California.

"It's lovely," Josie said, sitting on the edge of a plump bed covered by a quilt that was obviously made by someone who possessed considerable skill with a needle. Josie appreciated that because she had so little ability in the art.

Leaning against the doorway, Felicity looked from Josie to Adam, who was pulling off his coat. "You're certain you deserve this woman?" she asked with a fond smile.

Adam grinned at Felicity, then let his glance slide to Josie. "I have a feeling she'll turn out to be precisely what I deserve. Thank you, Felicity."

The subtle suggestion that she would provide him more pain than pleasure wasn't lost on Josie. "Oh, I will, darling," she said feelingly.

Felicity closed the door behind her with a silly smile.

Adam hung his coat in the closet and turned to Josie, pulling at his tie. "You'll be on your best behavior at dinner," he said gravely. "John and Felicity are very fond of my girls. When they mention them, you're to say how anxious you are to get to know them."

Josie brushed past him to cross to the window. Green hillsides rippled away to a magnificent white-topped mountain. Cows grazed lazily. In the distance was a small cabin and she wondered longingly if her boys could be in it.

"Did you hear me?" Adam asked, his tone imperious.

She turned away from the window to frown at him. "Have you had reason to question my behavior thus far?"

"Several times," he replied frankly.

She sighed impatiently. "I refer to my behavior in public."

He considered that a moment and again replied frankly. "No, I haven't. You'd be wise not to alter that circumstance."

"You could rest easy, Adam," she said reasonably, "by simply forgetting our arrangement."

He closed his eyes a moment, apparently summoning patience. "I remind you again that we're married, legally and in the eyes of God."

"We could have the marriage annul—"

His reaction was so swift Josie wasn't sure what had happened until she was on her back on the bed, Adam's hands fixing her wrists to the mattress, his knee pinning her skirt between her legs, making it impossible for her to move. Her heart pounded.

"I don't want to hear that again," he said, his voice menacingly quiet, his eyes dark. "Or I'll be forced to change the circumstance that would make that possible."

Josie swallowed. "I'm a widow, Mr. Scofield," she reminded him calmly, though calm was not at all what she felt. "What happens in a bed is no mystery to me. Certainly you don't expect to frighten me with such a threat?"

He had. He was angry that he hadn't succeeded.

"I had expected to lend a certain civility to our relationship," he said, "by waiting until we were both comfortable with the notion. But civility is a quality I sometimes have to work at, and I can put it aside without a second thought."

A firm rap sounded on the door. "Tea," John announced.

"Coming!" Adam called. He leaned closer to Josie's face, his hands tightening on her wrists as she struggled instinctively. "You're coming home with me, Josephine," he said very quietly, "so put any other thought out of your mind. How you behave tonight will determine in large part how I treat you once we get there."

As quickly as he had tossed her on the bed, he straightened to his feet and yanked her up. He crossed to the door and opened it, taking the tray from John. "Thank Filly for us," he said politely.

"Supper at seven," John's cheerful voice boomed into the room. "I'll give you time to have your tea, then I'll bring a bath up for the missus."

Josie, staring out the window at the distant cabin, wondered how Adam intended to occupy the next few hours until dinner. Her heartbeat still threatened to suffocate her. Did he intend to offer further instructions for her behavior this evening? Did he intend to stay around for her bath? Or, worse, carry out his threat?

Adam put her concerns to rest by asking John. "Would you like to buy me a drink while Josie has her tea and rests?"

John hesitated only an instant, but it was long enough to make it clear to Josie that he wondered why Adam didn't want to stay and render assistance.

"Of course. Come along. You can help me carry up the tub."

Adam turned to Josie. "Enjoy your bath, my love," he said, his voice silky and quiet and suggestive enough to allay John's concerns. "I'll be up in time to dress for dinner."

She came to the door to push it closed, now visible to John, who was waiting in the hallway. "Of course, dear," she replied sweetly, leaning up to kiss Adam's cheek, knowing her cooperation would confuse him.

Adam looked for guile in her eyes and could find none. He turned away, grateful to be able to spend the next hour or so in the uncomplicated company of another man.

Josie found dinner interminable—delicious, but interminable. While lolling in her bath, she'd concocted a scheme to slip out to the stable, steal a horse she knew Adam would pay John and Felicity for and head off into the night. She would not let the fact that she'd never saddled a horse herself and had had only two riding lessons in her life deter her. She would hide in the woods until daylight and find her way back to Redding in the morning. If she ran into Jacob, she felt reasonably sure she could count on his assistance and silence.

The plan was loose, she knew, but she'd taken the precaution of helping herself to a little cash from Adam's pocket. She would repay him when she was able. With it she expected to find lodging and begin her search.

For a moment she thought sadly of Jane and Lucy, waiting in Yreka for their new mother to arrive. Then she decided philosophically that it would be easier for them to be disappointed now than to get to know her, and perhaps like her, then have her leave them when she'd done what she'd come west to do.

For a moment bitterness almost swamped her. The knowledge that she could never repay Jerusha Cross for the pain and anguish the woman had caused her, for the liar she'd made of her, was more than she could bear. She envisioned ugly, lengthy retributions. But she'd learned in prison that bitterness was self-defeating. It numbed the brain and the reflexes. It made the body forget to fight back. She'd put those thoughts aside and buoyed herself with thoughts of Charlie and Billy.

"You've grown very quiet, Josie," Adam observed, putting a gentle, husbandly hand to her chin and tipping her face toward him. "Have we bored you to death with reminiscences, or are you tired?"

She gave him a lazy smile, calculated to convey an attitude of sleepy affection. She'd been exemplary tonight, she thought. She'd hung on Adam's every word, she'd met his every glance with a smile, she'd done her best to be vivacious and charming, and when Felicity had mentioned Adam's girls, Josie had been effusive in her impatience to meet them. That was the part that pricked her conscience the most. It hadn't been easy, but she was sure the Kilkennys were now convinced she was a loving bride.

How Adam would explain her defection after all that was up to him.

"I'm afraid," she replied with a delicate yawn, leaning into Adam's shoulder for effect, "the bath and the delicious meal were a soothing combination I seem unable to fight." She smiled at Felicity. "I hope you don't think me rude."

"Of course not." Felicity stood and made a shooing motion toward Adam. "Take her up to bed. We can't keep you up all night just because we're so happy to see you and so happy *for* you."

Adam stood, lending Josie a supporting arm up.

She smiled into his eyes. "I'd like to make a stop first. I'll be right up."

Suspicion rose in his eyes for an instant, but she reached up to give him a quick kiss. The suspicion died and in its place was a little flare of desire—no, not just desire. Something deeper, more complex. She felt victorious, then painfully guilty. She lowered her eyes and pulled away. "I won't be long, I promise." She turned to Felicity. "I've never eaten such wonderful roast, Felicity, even in Boston." She gave the woman a quick embrace, smiled at John, then fled outside.

The night was dark and cool. *A coat,* Josie thought as she ran toward the faint light visible from the stable. *I should have thought about a coat.*

No matter, she told herself, stopping in the open doorway to get her bearings. She'd take the blanket in the back of the wagon.

The sound of voices floated toward her from the back of the stable where the dim light shone. Someone was drinking there, she guessed.

She crept into the dark side of the stable, spotting a tall bay standing quietly.

"Hello, boy," she whispered as the slurred conversation in the back grew louder. "Shh, it's only me. We're going for a ride. Would you like that?"

She hadn't expected the horse's response to be so vocal, or so immediate. He whinnied loudly, nervously, and shied away as Josie reached for him, thumping against one side of his stall, then the other, as she followed him. His cry and the sound of his formidable rump banging the sides of the stall filled the quiet stable. He ignored Josie's efforts to shush him.

"Well, what have we here?" an unsteady voice asked.

Josie turned in alarm from the horse into the blinding light of a lantern held high in a swaying arm. She raised a hand to shield her eyes and squinted into the faces of two men she was sure would not have been allowed in Boston— at least, not where the Crosses had lived.

One was bearded and dark-featured. His gaze wandered over her with an intent difficult to decipher because he was cross-eyed. The other, blond and dirty and several years younger, licked his lips and stared at the low neckline of her dress. His intent was clear.

"Where's . . . where's Jacob?" she asked.

"Goes home at supper," the blond man replied. Then he grinned. "You like 'em that young, do you?"

"It's a lady," the other man said, grinning stupidly. "In our stable. What'll we do with her?"

The blond man handed him the lantern and walked into the stall. "Fix her so's she ain't a lady no more."

Behind Josie, the horse began to dance in fear, preventing her from backing away from her attacker. She searched her panicked brain desperately for an escape. She found it in hauteur, remembering that had always worked for Jerusha.

"Touch me," she said firmly, glaring, "and my husband will kill you."

The darker man caught the other's arm. "She belongs to that big fella came with the wagon. Maybe we better not."

The blond man looked around, still grinning. "I don't see him, do you?" He reached a dirty, long-fingered hand out and caught the sleeve of Josie's dress.

"Then you'd better look this way," a quiet male voice advised, an ominous click following his words, "while you still have eyes without a hole between them."

Adam stood in a pool of light in the doorway, a large revolver in his hand, his white shirt open at the throat, the sleeves rolled up. Beside him, John held a lantern and a lever action rifle. Felicity stood behind John's shoulder.

"We was . . ." The blond man licked his lips, going pale. "We was just . . ."

"I came to retrieve my novel from the wagon," Josie said quickly, relief making her feel light-headed and strangely alert. "I believe these . . . gentlemen mistook me for an intruder."

"That's it," the dark man said, swallowing convulsively. "An intruder."

Adam knew she lied, but John and Felicity believed her. He was grateful for that much. He extended a hand to her, warning her with a glance to take it.

"Take her back to the lodge," John said. "I'll take care of these two."

"It was my fault, John," Josie said. "I..."

"There's no excuse for that kind of behavior," John returned. "Not when a man works for me. I'm sorry you were frightened."

Embarrassed and remorseful, Josie followed Adam without resistance.

At the door to the lodge, Adam stopped her, the angry lines of his face visible in the sudden moonlight. "You frightened the three of us to death," he said in a harsh undertone, the fingers of his right hand biting painfully into her arm.

She lifted her chin. "I was wrong," she said, refusing to cower, though, in retrospect, even she felt she deserved censure for implementing a plan so foolish and so predisposed to fail. "I'm sorry."

"Actually, you were half-right," he said, surprising her into dropping her guard.

"Why?" she asked.

"Because your husband is going to kill somebody." He pulled the door open and pushed her inside.

In the privacy of their room, Adam threw the bolt on the door and turned to her. Josie suspected by the look in his eyes that the worst wasn't over. She stood near the post at the foot of the bed and waited, her mouth dry.

"Your novel is in your portmanteau," he said quietly, taking several steps toward her, "in the closet."

She glanced at him, considered lying again, then dismissed the thought. The man she now confronted was not the same man who'd held her for two nights on the train. This man was at the end of his patience.

She nodded. "Yes, I know."

"Then why did you go to the stable?"

"To find a horse."

"Why?"

She looked up at him, refusing to behave like a coward. "To leave you," she replied.

He reacted as though the answer annoyed him rather than surprised him. "You were going to ride off into the dark, without a coat or a scrap of food, in wild country you don't know?"

"Yes."

"Why?"

She sighed, hating to consider what response her reply would bring. "Because you refuse to annul our marriage."

There was a long, pulsing silence. "You're a very single-minded woman," he said finally, covering the small space between them, and locking his hands over her upper arms. "You leave me no choice but to close that door on you."

Something began to tremble deep inside Josie that wasn't simply fear. She knew it was a dangerous element that could complicate her search and, she felt sure, her very life. A sense of self-preservation made her try to yank away from him. "Don't threaten me, Adam," she warned.

Adam held firm, seeing the flash in the depths of her blue eyes. He, too, saw more than fear. For all her impulsiveness, she seemed to be governed by a dauntless nature. He guessed she experienced something she'd often made him feel—some self-protective instinct, an involuntary need to take a step back from her when every fiber in his being drove him toward her. That made it easier for him to do what he had to do.

"It's not a threat, Josie." Purposefully, he turned her around and began to unfasten the small covered buttons that ran from between her shoulder blades down the length of her spine. "I'm going to make love to you and seal this contract between us."

"If you force me," she said, trying desperately to keep her wits, her heart beginning to pound at the touch of his knuckles through the thin fabric of her chemise, "it will be a crime against me and against your own moral responsibilities as a man."

"My moral responsibilities as a husband," he said evenly, his knuckles now pressing into the small of her back, "require that I keep you safe." The buttons undone, he slipped his fingers into the back of the dress's sleeves and pushed them forward until the bodice fell to her waist. He turned her around.

Her face was pale, her eyes wide with worry and something dark and velvety that strengthened his resolve to see this through. He ran his hands lightly up her bare arms, over the curve of her shoulders to the thin blue ribbon woven into the lace that covered her breasts.

"What...about...the civility you...promised?" Her voice was high and unsteady and a little shudder ran through her as he pulled the little blue bow apart.

"I explained it's an uncertain thing with me," he said, tugging at the crisscrosses until the chemise fell open. Her small breasts spilled free, porcelain white and perfect. He had to wait a moment for breath to go on. He looked into her eyes to distract himself, wanting to remind her that she'd frightened him. "I lost it tonight when that stablehand reached for you. You're mine now, Josie." He drew the chemise off her and tossed it aside.

Josie's heart hammered in her breast, her entire being beginning to tremble as if it were something that existed without her, something over which she had no control. She'd never been undressed by a man in the light before—not even Benjamin. She fought embarrassment and excitement, and something else she couldn't quite define that threatened to rob her of coherent thought.

"You don't know me," she said desperately. "You don't know *about* me."

Adam flattened a hand against her back and pulled her into his chest. "You don't know me, either. That's how most marriages begin. The obvious is very seldom the real."

Josie tried to absorb the words but her brain refused to cooperate, the victim of a body flooded with new sensations. She could smell Adam's cologne, feel his soft linen shirt against her flattened breasts, their tips beading in reaction.

"But we'll be...tied forever..." she protested with the last vestige of sanity she'd clung to.

He put his lips to her shoulder and, contrary to every law of nature, her thighs turned to liquid. "That's why I sent for you," he said, his voice a whisper against her flesh. "That's why you travelled three thousand miles."

No, her mind cried. *That isn't true. It was a trick. You weren't supposed to care. You weren't supposed to have children. It wasn't supposed to matter to me.* She struggled to transfer those thoughts from her brain to her tongue.

But Adam chose that moment to slip his hand into the back of the waist of her dress, following the curve of her hip so that dress, petticoats and drawers slipped with it. He leaned forward until her back touched the bed, then pulled the pile of ruffles and lace off her and tossed them to the chair.

Sensation raced down Josie's body with her clothing, pulsing like something alive at the very heart of her being. Vaguely she remembered her boast about the bedroom holding no mystery for her. It occurred to her that he hadn't even touched her yet—at least not intimately—and she already felt on foreign ground.

"I warn you this isn't wise," she said softly, staring at the ceiling as tears burned her eyes. She should be strong enough not to let this happen. She should tell him the truth. She should...

Shirtless , Adam leaned over her, braced on his hands. "Love has little to do with wisdom, Josie. It has to do with need—the heart's need and the body's need. That's all." He kissed her gently, then straightened to remove the rest of his clothes.

He folded the quilt and blankets back, scooped her up and placed her on the cold sheet. She shivered and he was beside her in an instant, pulling the covers over them and wrapping his long, strong arms around her.

Josie's cluttered mind wondered what could possibly be wrong with wanting the security of a caring man's arms around her for a lifetime—or whatever amount of time she had before he discovered her deceit. She could think of no answer. It was what she'd always needed and never had, until Benjamin, and that had been plagued by his mother and lasted such a short time. Perhaps that was all life would ever allow her, she thought. Short spurts of security. Very little bits of happiness.

With a little sigh of surrender, she leaned against Adam and gave herself over to his care.

Adam held her slender fragility like a gift. He'd tried to remind himself that this wasn't supposed to be so important. They were simply supposed to be compatible, comfortable together. It shouldn't matter so much that he comfort her, calm her, please her. But it did.

He ran his hand from the middle of her back into the indentation at her waist, over the swell of her hip, lingering a moment to caress it. He felt her sigh against his collarbone. He stroked down to the backs of her knees and felt her muscles contract and release under his touch.

He repeated the process several times, finally drawing his hand back up the inside of her thigh, hitching it over his hip to allow him access to her. The pulse there beat frantically.

Josie went still. *Be calm,* she told herself. *You've known this before.* But her body refused to listen. Already it was unlike anything she'd ever known. She didn't recognize herself. She was atremble from head to foot.

The moment his fingers invaded, she tensed, an almost silent cry whispering against Adam's throat.

"Easy," he said softly, his other hand running lightly up and down her ribs. "Be easy. I won't hurt you. You know I won't."

She made a conscious effort to do as he said, though her body seemed to want to do anything but.

His fingers invaded a little farther, farther still, then began to move in subtle little circles. A sensation rose immediately, one she recognized and associated with frustration. She almost felt relief. At last—something familiar!

Again, quickly, the substance of the agonizing little tension that had always promised something and brought nothing changed and intensified. That little movement of his hand seemed suddenly to govern the world, the universe. Her life, her being, seemed to distill into that spiral, and everything she'd ever wanted and never had existed at the heart of it. She began to move with it, in search of it, into it. Everything inside her and around her pulsed with the spiral's life.

Suddenly the spiral flew apart and the tension within her fragmented, her body contracting in pleasure with every heartbeat. She lay still, her little cry of surprise drawing a smile from Adam as she absorbed the awesome wonder of this new discovery. So this, she thought in amazement, was how it could be.

She lifted drunken eyes to tell him that, though she'd been married nine years, she'd never known this pleasure, but she couldn't find the words.

He kissed her gently. "I know," he whispered. "And it's only the beginning."

He kissed her deeply, hungrily, and began the ritual another time. She followed his lead hesitantly, her experience with him so different from what she'd known with her husband that she felt inadequate to the task.

She stroked gently down his chest, feeling a muscle in his abdomen leap under her hand. She wasn't sure for a moment if she'd caused pleasure or distress. "I'm afraid there are more mysteries in a bed than I'd realized," she admitted. "I feel woefully... unprepared."

Adam was touched by her honesty and pleased that its cause was the new pleasure he'd shown her. He pulled her closer and closed his hand over her wandering one, encouraging it farther. "No need for that," he assured her, stroking down her back with new purpose. "You're beautiful, Josie. You need no worldly skill to please me."

Josie reached down to test his theory. He drew in a breath, his body's response immediate and formidable. Gaining confidence, she caressed him, his body's warm power curiously sparking hers. He rose over her and entered her.

Her body accepted his with delicious ease. The world began to spin again, and she held on, refusing to think or reason, wanting only to feel. And so she did. Eddies, ripples, splashes, floods of feeling ran over her then receded, only to cover her again and slip away until she finally lay quietly, Adam a comfortable burden on her body.

Still, she refused to let thought intrude.

With a little groaning laugh, Adam eased down beside her and pulled her into his arms.

"Now," he said, kissing her forehead, "sleep. You've nothing to worry about."

Nothing. Except... She closed her eyes tightly, letting her mind's eye focus on the faces of her children but refusing to let a thought form. Panic tried to surface. "Adam," she said anxiously, winding an arm around his neck.

He smiled in the darkness, thinking her body's betrayal had upset her. "It's all right," he assured her, stroking the hair back from her forehead. "You're mine now. It's all right."

Chapter Four

Adam sat at the Kilkennys' table and sipped his coffee as John and Felicity carried on a fierce but loving argument. The subject of it was lost on him because his mind was adrift on thoughts of his new wife and the remarkable night they'd shared.

Josie had responded to his every touch ardently and enthusiastically. She'd been everything a man could hope for in a woman he'd married for love. But since he hadn't, and since she'd quite obviously married him for reasons of her own, he was now completely confused—a state he couldn't handle with equanimity. It was his nature to be able at every moment to assess his position and plan his next move. That was true in the courtroom and in his personal life. But when he'd looked down on her sleeping form just an hour ago, he'd accepted that that was a luxury he was forced to forfeit, at least until he could deduce Josie's plan. He was certain she had one.

A creaking floorboard brought him back to awareness, a state that became quickly physical as well as mental as Josie appeared in the dining room doorway. She wore a pale blue travelling suit, the fabric molded lovingly to small, high breasts, the feel of which he could remember vividly in the palm of his hand. They'd been silken but firm, and their tips had hardened at his touch.

Tiny pearl buttons cinched the fabric at her waist, reminding him that his hands had closed around her there and lifted her atop him.

He knew that the yards of draped blue fabric concealed straight, slender limbs, and that beneath the ruffles behind her, and the bustle that raised them up like some saucy little entity following her, were small, round buttocks that had filled his hands.

He expelled a sigh, thinking there were other things he'd prefer to do with her today than sit for hours in a wagon. But Jane and Lucy were waiting. He rose and pulled out the chair beside him.

His memories of her physical attributes had been so detailed and thorough that only now, as she came toward him with a polite but decidedly stiff "Good morning, Adam," did he focus attention on her face. It was pinched and pale, its every subtle expression closed to him—almost as though it had somehow been dipped in porcelain overnight.

He refused to concern himself over what this meant, certain it would only confuse him further. Even if she petrified on the seat beside him and he was forced to place her in his garden and fill her lap with birdseed, she was going home with him.

"Good morning, Josie," he said amiably. "Prepare yourself for a treat. Filly makes the best hotcakes in California."

Josie forced herself to smile a thank-you as Felicity placed a mountain of hotcakes before her that would have intimidated a lumberjack. Her pleas against the large slice of ham were ignored.

"You have a long day ahead of you," Felicity insisted, pouring steaming coffee for Josie into a fine china cup. "You'll need your strength."

Felicity refilled the men's cups, then took her place across the table beside her husband and asked Adam eagerly about Jane and Lucy.

Josie pretended interest in her food, deliberately attempting to block out the conversation. She didn't want to know that Jane had memorized the first two stanzas of "The Charge of the Light Brigade" or that Lucy loved to ride Blackie, a gentle mare Adam had purchased for the girls. She wanted nothing to contribute to the guilt she already felt like a burning coal in her breast.

Breast. The very word spread the heat of that guilt up her throat and into her cheeks. Memory flashed an image of herself moaning ecstatically under Adam's hands as he showed her how sensitive her breasts were—something she'd never known before.

Even now, dealing simply with the memory, she had to resist the impulse to arch her back and thrust herself toward him.

"Are you feverish, my dear?" Felicity asked in concern, leaning toward her across the table.

With the knuckle of his first finger under her chin, Adam turned her face toward him and studied her, a frown between his dark brows.

The porcelain remained safely in place, he noted, but her pallor had turned a deep pink. He looked into her eyes and saw a very healthy anger there. He concluded that this was not fever but temper.

Josie closed her fingers around his wrist and tried to pull his hand away. He held firm, wanting her to know he would never be managed that simply. Then he felt it. Her pulse thrummed against his own, fast and erratic. Her eyes warred with him for a moment, and he understood that she was recalling the night as vividly as he had and the red in her cheeks indicated embarrassment.

He allowed her to lower his hand, comforted by that knowledge. He'd had little time to consider the fact last night, but this morning, in light of her blush, he wondered about the sexual prowess of her late husband.

When he, Adam, had made love to her, her body had accommodated his with the ease of a woman experienced in the act. Yet all along the sensual journey she'd behaved with surprise and little cries of unexpected delight, and he began to believe that her first husband had never taken care with her, never seen to her pleasure before his own.

Of course, the answering letter from Josie's attorney had explained that her husband had been forty years older than she. And Josie had charms that had tested his own considerable control. It was understandable that an older man had simply not had time to tend to her before her delights overtook him.

Adam was pleased that his lovemaking had unsettled her. In this nebulous relationship they'd forged—Josie, appearing to change completely from the charming young woman who'd seemed so anxious to marry him, and he, being determined to see that she fulfilled her part of their agreement—he knew he had to gain the upper hand and hold it. He was satisfied that, for the moment at least, he had it.

Josie was sure the gentle strum of his knuckle against her cheek and the indulgent smile were for the Kilkennys' benefit.

"I believe she's anxious to get home at last," he said. Then he glanced in John's direction with a very masculine smile. "She's had little rest in the past few days."

Josie refused to allow him the satisfaction of seeing her blush a second time. She paid special attention to her breakfast, ignoring the three of them as they exchanged knowing grins and laughter.

Felicity sent them on their way with cold chicken pie wrapped in a towel and a winking assurance to Josie that "if the brute becomes too difficult to live with, you're welcome back here anytime."

Josie tucked that promise away in a corner of her heart, just as a glance from Adam as he urged the horses on their way told her to put that notion out of her mind. Her bad luck, she thought, to have settled on the one man in the West who could read a woman's thoughts.

Josie took comfort in the unimaginable beauty of the countryside. Insisting to herself that this "incarceration" was only temporary, she decided that she might have been confined in a far less lovely place.

But they passed a valley where she frowned over a bare area of land scarred by a long snake of pipe and a series of sluices.

"What is that?" she asked Adam.

"Hydraulic mining," he replied. "It's made Siskiyou County a great deal of money. The water they bring in for it makes it possible to grow crops we couldn't sustain before. But it also levels forests and defaces the countryside, so it's a two-headed beast."

Everything was green. The road passed through one natural extravagance after another—deep gorges, high, craggy bluffs dotted with wildflowers, meadows that stretched like emerald blankets under a warm sun.

As they rode on, birds sang, small creatures moved in the fragrant grass, and occasionally, in the distance, there was a primitive roar never heard in Boston.

Josie turned in the direction of one such sound as they sat under a cottonwood on the banks of a melodious brook and finished Felicity's lunch with the jar of lemonade she'd sent along.

"Mountain lion," Adam said, leaning back against the trunk of the tree, one knee raised, his tin cup resting on it. He indicated the mouth of a canyon across the creek. "She lives in there, somewhere."

Josie sat slightly apart from him on the blanket he'd spread for her, her legs tucked to the side, her blue skirt pulled modestly over them. She raised an eyebrow, surprised that the sound had been female. "She?"

"Yes." He smiled lazily. "And, as in most species, the female makes the most noise."

"Frustrated, no doubt," she returned, "by her intractable mate."

He'd been courteous since they'd left Kilkenny's, and solicitous of her needs. She'd begun to wonder if the night they'd shared had given her new status in his eyes. He'd seemed as stunned by it as she had—or did most men engage in lovemaking with such...skillful enthusiasm? She didn't know. She had only Ben with whom to compare him. And making love with Ben had been so different as to make the comparison impossible.

In any case, she couldn't help but feel that he'd been pleased with her, and that, on some primitive level, lent her a power even her earlier amenable behavior hadn't offered.

She propped her hand beside her and leaned on it, smiling carefully at him to test the theory. She must be subtle to allay suspicion.

"No retort?" she asked. "Then you admit to being intractable?"

"Readily." He returned her small smile. "Any man who lets himself be governed by a woman won't survive in this country. Or in this life."

She smiled, staunchly refusing to be stirred from the pretense of her gentle mood. "Are we so inferior, then?"

"That's not the point," he said. "The role of protector and protected becomes reversed. If I became accustomed to taking my direction from you, I would be forced to stand back and let you handle matters if that mountain lion came to the stream for a drink and decided we would make a delicious supper. Could you do it?"

She considered a moment, then pointed to the rifle that lay on the blanket beside him. "Possibly. With a weapon."

"Do you shoot?" he asked with interest.

She considered lying, but except for this complex charade, dishonesty was contrary to her nature.

"No," she admitted, then smiled. "But I would point it with authority."

He laughed. "That might work on a man, who would stop to analyze the situation and decide he had an even chance that you *could* handle the weapon. I don't believe a mountain lion would think of it as anything but something to be spit out to avoid indigestion."

She was forced to laugh. "I have it, then. The perfect arrangement would be that the woman could direct all matters that are nonphysical, and the man would take care of those that require physical strength."

"I believe you'd have difficulty imposing that plan on the men of Siskiyou County."

"But I wager I'd gain the women's support."

He looked doubtful. "I'm not so certain. Women are happiest when their men are happy with them."

She widened her eyes, affecting dismay. "Then I'm doomed to misery?"

"Not if you mend your ways," he said with quiet arrogance.

She very nearly lost her flirtatious pose at that. But she remembered what was at stake. Supremacy. And ultimately escape. She swung her legs to the other side and leaned in Adam's direction. She was within his reach if he chose to extend his arm. But he simply watched her with mild interest.

"And how is it," she asked, her voice low as her eyes looked into the depths of his, trying to snare him into her web, "that you want me to behave?"

He put the cup aside, lowered his knee and swung his legs to the side as she'd done so that they faced each other, thigh to thigh, mere inches apart. The arrogance, she noted, had invaded his eyes.

"I want you to remember that we're married," he said.

That sounded promising to her purposes. She allowed herself to lean forward a little more. "Yes."

Then he touched her arm, and she sensed the difference instantly. This was no caress. She'd experienced that last night and knew the difference. This was threat and warning.

"I want you to credit me with enough intelligence to see through your pretenses so that you're not tempted to use them on me." His eyes were dark, his jaw set. "When we arrive home, I want you to behave in a way that will convince my daughters that you're happy to be with them, and after that, I want your behavior to set them a good example. I want you to be kind and generous to the people who work for me, and to be charming to my friends."

Josie trembled inside to find yet another flimsy plan knocked out from under her. But she pretended control.

"What?" she asked evenly. "You want nothing for yourself?"

His response came so quickly and without warning that his kiss delved right inside her openmouthed gasp. She was swung sideways over his thighs and into his embrace, her hat flying off into the grass. His tongue and his roving hands reminded her keenly of the night before and how very little he'd had to ask of her.

When he rose to his feet and pulled her with him, the trembling inside her had moved outward, fueled partly by anger and partly by a response she seemed incapable of withholding, despite the anger.

"What I want of you," he said, holding her by her forearms, "I'm perfectly capable of taking."

Josie couldn't precisely understand what she was feeling. She'd taken a chance that she'd be able to deceive him and lost. She was growing used to that with him. But despite her time in prison, the absence of her children and the dangerous game she'd begun when she married this man, she maintained an image of herself as a woman that she would allow nothing and no one to stain.

Her blue eyes were determined, despite the glaze of tears in them, and she said emphatically, "Don't think that, Adam. Don't ever think that."

His gaze locked with hers, Adam tried to analyze the sudden, deep emotion in her eyes. He saw pain there, anguish, pride.

"If you're ever tempted to take *that* from me..." she said, passing over the word she'd teased him with on the night they'd met. When it came to a serious discussion of the subject, she had difficulty finding the proper word for it. "Don't think it will be as it was last night. Despite your bullying, you didn't take that from me. I gave it to you."

He knew that to be true, but he was fighting now for that precious upper hand.

"I brought it out of you," he said.

"Because it was new." A tear spilled over and he saw her struggle to hold back the rest. "Because, though I loved Benjamin with all my heart, he never...I never have known anything like that." She squared her shoulders, gave her head a little toss and sniffed. "And now that I have, I won't give it to someone who would take it without respect for the power it holds."

He reached into his breast pocket, withdrew his handkerchief and handed it to her. "You aren't under the misapprehension that I would let you give it elsewhere?"

She looked up at him as she dabbed at her eyes, her lashes spiked with tears. An effort to lighten the moment? she wondered. She felt vaguely surprised. But then, every time she thought she'd second-guessed him, she found herself a thought or two behind instead.

She took the other end of the blanket as he pulled it off the grass and helped him fold it.

"I understand there's a profit to be made in such work," she dared to tease. If he was going to try to frighten her, she would have to convince him that it couldn't be done easily. "I'll have to consider a profession when I do finally take my leave."

He came toward her to take her folded half and join it with his. He was grinning. "I would have to be dead for that to happen, Josie. And since I'm young and healthy, you'll be too advanced an age by then to consider making even a minimal profit."

She pinned her hat back in place as he replaced his, fitting it low on his forehead, shielding his eyes in a way that made it impossible for her to decide whether or not he'd finished with the subject.

He handed her the folded blanket and the cups, then lifted the empty jar, the towel and the rifle and led the way back to the wagon.

"So, let's have no more talk of it," he said.

Now that he'd had the last word, she thought, he most likely did consider the subject closed.

Adam tossed their things into the back of the wagon, then helped Josie up into the seat. He climbed up after her, stepped over her knees and took the reins.

Then he turned to her, a foot propped up, ready to release the brake.

"Remember what I told you about the girls," he said, that edge of steel in his voice once again. "I will not bend where their happiness is concerned."

She had decided hours ago, when it was obvious that escape was out of the question for now, that she had little choice but to cooperate. But she would keep herself aloof from the children. She would care for them, see to their comfort and their safety, but she wouldn't let feelings develop that would eventually end in heartache.

This stubborn man had left her no alternative but to hurt him in the end, but that was his own doing. Had he listened to her when she told him the marriage had to be annulled, had he not made love to her, he'd have saved both of them considerable grief.

In any case, he would probably be more angry than hurt, a circumstance he well deserved.

She smiled. "I will be exemplary," she said, then added before he could, "Or I will be sorry. Yes, I know."

Adam released the brake and slapped the reins against the bays' backs. Good, he thought. She understood. He would feel a great relief if *he* did.

Josie's resolve about the children lasted until the moment she met them. How any woman, particularly one who was a mother herself, could expect to hold herself aloof from two such cherubic faces was beyond her. She accepted immediately that she wouldn't even try.

They'd run out onto the rich green lawn spread before a large, many-gabled white house with red shutters and trim. A young woman, probably in her late teens, accompanied them in a simple calico dress over which she wore a pristine white apron.

The girls' dresses were spotless white, as were the wide ribbons that tied their long curls. The young woman held fast to the smaller one's hand as she tried to dart away to welcome her father home.

Adam braked to a stop on the dusty drive between the lawn and the house, and the little one was upon him the moment he leapt down. He lifted her high in his arms, the delight on his face as vivid as hers as she giggled and screamed. Dark brown curls bounced and dark eyes sparkled. Then he held her to him, growling like a bear into her neck. She continued to giggle uproariously.

The older one came forward at a sedate pace. Josie had little difficulty interpreting her mood as she gave one quick, grim glance in her direction. She was not pleased with the situation, and though she might have to put up with it, no one could make her do it happily.

That one must look like her mother, Josie guessed, with her rich auburn curls and green eyes. She smiled as the child turned her face away, her little nose in the air, and went to her father. Josie understood completely. She found herself in much the same situation as the child.

Adam put the little one on her feet and lifted the older one, who lost all her stiffness the moment his arms closed around her.

"We missed you, Papa," she said. "I'm glad you're home. Even if you did bring..."

"Jane." He stopped her with the gentle reproach in his voice. Still held against his shoulder, she looked down at her hands. He put her down, took each girl by a hand and led them around the wagon to Josie's side. Then he reached up, his eyes rife with warning, and lifted Josie down to the drive. The little girl smiled up at her.

"My name is Lucinda but everybody calls me Lucy, I'm four and I can ride Blackie as well as Amos can only Papa won't let me ride him alone 'cause he thinks I'm too small—" she drew a long, noisy breath that seemed to raise her several inches off the ground before she continued "—Jane's nine and she knows everything!" Dark eyes widened with respect at that announcement, then narrowed with the grave, carefully spoken admission, "She doesn't want another mama."

Completely charmed by Lucy, and sincerely empathetic with Jane, Josie got down on one knee. "I understand how Jane feels," she said as Lucy reached up with a pudgy finger to touch the flowers on Josie's hat. "Your papa tells me your mama was very special. So could I just be your friend and not try to be a new mama?"

Without moving, Josie turned to Jane as she posed the question. The older girl, standing beside her father, her thin arms folded, withheld approval with stubborn green eyes and a firmly set mouth that reminded Josie sharply of her father.

"But I *want* a mama," Lucy said.

Josie hugged Lucy to her, unable to help herself. She searched for a solution that would do the least harm, given the circumstances.

"Well, why don't you let me be your friend first," she suggested, "then, if you like me, I'll be your mama."

The little girl considered that and frowned. "If you're married to Papa, I think you *have* to be our mama. That's what Jane says."

"That's usually the way things are," Josie said, getting to her feet, beginning to feel as though she were already being drawn in deeper than was safe or wise. "But we'll just make our own rules this time."

Lucy didn't care for that solution, either. "Papa says we can't ever do that. We have to follow *his* rules."

Josie fixed Adam with a challenging gaze. "Then maybe Papa will make a special rule for all of us. I'll be the children's friend, then they'll decide if they want me for their mother."

Both girls looked up at him, apparently accustomed to accepting his wisdom. His dark eyes told her that, while he might suspect her motives, he knew the solution to be fair.

"I think that would be a fine rule," he said.

"Then what do I have to call her?" Jane mumbled as she leaned against her father, the dusty toe of a patent leather slipper working in the dirt.

"Why don't you ask her politely?" Adam suggested.

Jane sighed with great forbearance and rephrased the question. "What do you want me to call you?" she asked.

"My name is Josephine," Josie replied. "But like Lucy, no one ever uses my whole name. Josie will be fine."

Lucy took her hand and began to tug her toward the house. "I'm going to call you 'Mama.'" She waved at the young woman waiting at the foot of the porch steps. "Ivy, our new mama is here!"

As Lucy and Josie approached, a tall, sturdy-looking man in his middle years appeared from around the back of the house, and a stout woman in a crisp white apron over a simple gray dress came from inside the house to join Ivy.

Josie suspected immediately that she faced an opposing force. Though Ivy looked less suspicious than the older pair, there was not one welcoming smile among them. But since Josie had been faced with her mother-in-law's hatred at a young age, and since the mysterious circumstances of Benjamin's death had subjected her to the suspicion and disapproval of nearly everyone in Boston, she was not one to shrink under a hostile glare. And since she had no choice but to live here for some time, she intended to make friends. She was going to need them.

Josie returned the collective stare with a warm smile. And it helped enormously, she realized, to feel Adam's arm come around her shoulders.

"Josie," he said. "I'd like you to meet the Donovans, without whom the girls and I could not survive. This is Bertie, who takes care of the house..."

He indicated the older woman, who said stiffly, "Good afternoon, Mrs. Scofield. It's a pleasure to have you home."

"Thank you, Bertie," Josie replied warmly, determined not to notice the woman's adversarial stare. She'd dealt with Jerusha Cross and she knew the type. Housemaid or not, she was queen of her domain, and anyone who didn't comply with her terms was treated with royal disapproval. "I'm delighted to be here."

"This is Amos, Bertie's husband." At Adam's introduction, the tall man doffed his hat and inclined his head.

"Pleased to meet you, Mrs. Scofield." He almost smiled, then apparently thought better of it. But Josie smiled, understanding him. She guessed he and Bertie shared the kind of relationship she'd teasingly suggested to Adam when they'd eaten lunch. Bertie made all the decisions, and Amos supplied the muscle where necessary.

"I'm happy to meet you, Amos."

Adam swept a hand toward the girl. "And this is Ivy, Bertie and Amos's daughter. She helps with chores and keeps an eye on Jane and Lucy."

Ivy's eyes went over Josie's fashionable suit and hat with undisguised interest. Then she caught her mother's disapproving eyes and said quickly, shyly, "Welcome home, Mrs. Scofield."

"Thank you, Ivy."

"And this is Muffin!" Lucy said as a very large black cat wandered out of the house. She picked it up with a stout grip around its middle and brought it to Josie.

Josie reached for it.

"Mind your dress, Mrs. Scofield," Ivy said anxiously. "He's been out in the garden."

Josie lifted him anyway, if only to save him from the little girl's asphyxiating grip. She laughed as a sinister pair of yellow eyes looked up at her.

"He looks as though his name should be Lucifer, or Satan," she said.

Adam lightly pinched one of the huge forelegs dangling lazily from her arms. "When you get to know him, you'll see that he hasn't a hostile bone in his body."

"And our not being familiar with the likes of Satan or Lucifer," Bertie said with a glance that suggested the new lady of the house might be, "it never occurred to us."

Josie nuzzled Muffin's fur, which smelled of sunshine and flowers, and let Bertie's remark slide past her. Muffin purred. She counted that as one very small success. She put him down and watched him walk slowly under a porch chair and lie down with a thud.

"Ivy will see you upstairs," Adam said, pushing Josie gently toward the open door of the house. "Amos, will you take up water for a bath, please?"

"Right away, Mr. Scofield." Amos disappeared and Bertie herded the girls inside.

Ivy led Josie through a wide, cool entryway toward a magnificent mahogany stairway. To her right, Josie glimpsed a beautifully appointed room with gold brocade furnishings, a marble fireplace, comfortable chairs and a bright oriental rug.

"But I wanted to go with Mama," Lucy protested as Bertie tugged her toward a hallway that Josie guessed led to the kitchen.

Adam lifted Lucy into his arms. "Mama has to rest for a little while," he said, "but I'll bet she'll want you to sit next to her at supper." He turned to Josie for confirmation.

"I will," Josie said, all her resolutions about keeping her distance from the children completely forgotten in the face of Lucy's unqualified adoration and Jane's distant, desperate need. "And you can tell me all about Blackie."

Jane, arms folded, frowned up at her father. "I want to sit next to you."

He reached his free hand down to place it atop her head. "Well, that will be a perfect arrangement, because I want to sit next to you. Now, you and Lucy run along and help Bertie so I can check my mail." He put Lucy down and waited a moment until Bertie and the girls had disappeared. Then he looked at Josie. "Jane will adjust," he said, his tone suggesting apology for the girl's behavior.

Josie gave him a pointed look. "It's all right," she said. "I know precisely how she feels, having someone forced upon her like this."

There was a trace of censure in Adam's eyes, though his tone remained quiet and courteous. "Enjoy your bath. I'll see you at dinner. If you need anything, ask Ivy."

Adam watched Josie follow Ivy upstairs, advancing to lean his elbow on the newel post to catch a last glimpse of her as they rounded the landing. Her ruffled bustle disappeared with a seductive sway.

The woman was a puzzle. For all her avid protests against coming home with him once she'd learned he had children, she had reacted to them with a kindness and an instinctive skill that pleased and surprised him. It made him wonder why she'd been so upset at the idea in the first place.

Well. He headed to the library, which he used as an office at home, resigned to being confused. One day he would solve the mystery of Josephine Cross Scofield, but until then he would keep a watchful eye on her—and himself.

Ivy opened a large oak door to a deep bedroom that ran half the length of the house. A subtly striped and flowered wallpaper lent it a cozy atmosphere despite its size, and lacy curtains under claret-colored draperies blew softly in the afternoon breeze.

Josie looked around her, fighting the comfortable pull of the room, then noticed that Adam's things were everywhere. This was not a room she would occupy alone.

She heaved a little sigh of resignation as Ivy walked her around the room, pointing out the closet and the panel that looked as though it opened onto another closet but actually concealed a tub. Josie helped her pull it down and smiled at the clever practicality of it. Even Jerusha had had nothing like this.

Bertie appeared with two large towels, which she placed on the foot of the big brass bed. Then, without ever focusing on Josie or Ivy, she lifted her nose in the air and left.

Ivy touched two long fingers to the beautiful, colorful quilt on the bed.

"Mama and the first Mrs. Scofield and I made this quilt," she said, her gray-eyed glance apologetic. "Mama always said she loved her like another daughter."

Josie nodded, remembering Adam's explanation that he'd had everything he'd wanted in a marriage with Maggie and that she, Josie, could settle for companionship and bedtime privileges.

It was clear that Jane felt sure no one could replace her mother.

Josie found herself filled with both admiration and jealousy at the memory of Maggie Scofield. Of course, she wasn't here to replace her, she reminded herself. She was here with a purpose of her own.

But it was easy to see that everyone was reluctant to let Maggie go—a circumstance she knew to be unhealthy. The temptation to startle Adam, crush Jane in an embrace and stand up to Bertie was almost more than she could deny herself. But that would only divert energy from her goal.

Amos appeared, a steaming bucket of water in each strong hand.

"Bertie knew you'd be needing these," he said with a quick smile as he splashed the contents of one bucket into the tub. "Even before Mr. Scofield asked for them."

This was his way, Josie realized, of softening the stiff impression his wife had made. Just as Ivy had tried to do.

She nodded gratefully as he overturned the second bucket into the tub. "Thank her for me, please."

Ivy looked up from turning down the bed as her father strode away with the empty buckets. "Do you have bath salts with you?"

Josie shook her head. Space in her bags had been at a premium for what could turn out to be a long stay.

"I have some." She left the room.

Josie unpacked while Amos bustled back and forth with buckets and Ivy shook fragrant salts into her bath. When it was ready, Ivy helped her with the buttons at the back of her dress, then left her to her privacy.

Josie stripped down and eased into the hot water, the feeling after the past several days of wagon travel and tension almost indescribable. She determined as she rested her head against the back of the tub that, for the duration of this bath, she would close her eyes and pretend that everyone loved her and that she had complete confidence in her ability to do what she'd come west to accomplish.

Chapter Five

Josie peered into the chandeliered dining room, surprised by its elegant comfort. A table that would seat twenty gleamed with four place settings at the far end. A long buffet, several covered items already in place on it, stood along one wall, and the other was graced by a wide, lace-curtained window that looked out onto the garden.

She walked around the room, absorbing its pleasant atmosphere. Jerusha's dining room had been opulent and ugly, and she, Josie, had always found dinner an ordeal in it. When Jerusha was away, she and Benjamin and the boys ate in the sitting room.

The boys. A fist of pain, sharper and more intense because she'd had so little time to consider it in the past two days, rose up to fight her. She closed her eyes tightly, struggling against despair.

She would find them. She would! And she must work calmly and patiently to allay suspicion. She put her hands to her face and closed her eyes, offering up a prayer for their safety. She shook off images of their faces, finding them unbearable. Her tortured mind imagined them enslaved to a cruel couple, for who else would take two small children from their mother?

Needing another direction for her thoughts, she pushed the swinging door near the buffet, presuming that it led into the kitchen. She learned instantly that she was right.

"I think she's very pretty." Josie recognized Ivy's voice and stopped, the flattery comforting in her anguish. "She has the loveliest dresses!"

Wonderful aromas wafted Josie's way. There was the sound of something being chopped on the block.

"Of course she has lovely dresses." That was Bertie's cold, no-nonsense tone. "*That* kind of woman always does."

"Mama, she's only been here three hours," Ivy said. "You don't know what she's like yet."

"Of course I do. What other kind of woman would travel across the wilderness to marry a man she's never met?"

"That kind of woman doesn't do that," Ivy insisted.

"Unless she's weary of the life," Bertie suggested, "and looking for a man with money and position to make her respectable."

Josie wanted to laugh, and she wanted to die. Since neither recourse would help her position here, she pushed into the kitchen, taking special delight in Ivy's gasp of surprise and Bertie's sudden pallor. She knew it was apparent to both women that she'd heard Bertie's last remark. She saw Bertie square her shoulders and turn away from the chopping board to face her, prepared for a confrontation.

Josie smiled cordially. "Pardon me. I was looking for Mr. Scofield and the children."

Ivy stared. Bertie swallowed but looked her in the eye. "I believe they're all in Mr. Scofield's office. The library, just past the stairs on the left side."

"Thank you," she said, her glance lingering on Bertie as she let the door swing closed. A perverse and vengeful little demon in Josie was willing to let Bertie believe she was hurrying to Adam to tell him what she'd overheard.

She turned to find Adam and the girls walking into the dining room. Jane held her father's hand and glowered at Josie from behind his elbow. Josie suddenly felt herself trapped in dislike and distrust. It occurred to her with grim humor that the latter, at least, was probably justified.

Adam was instantly aware of the distress in her eyes and that her usually rosy cheeks were white as milk.

"What is it?" he asked, holding his free hand out to her. She went to him, needing something solid to hold on to at that moment.

"Hunger, I think," she said with a frail smile. "The aroma from the kitchen has been haunting me since I got out of the tub."

He knew she was lying about what troubled her, but that was no surprise. He was sure she was lying about many things. But he didn't want to press her in the presence of the girls.

He led her to the table and seated her to the right of his place. "You'll enjoy this, I promise you," he said, inhaling the scent of rose water that drifted up at him as he adjusted her chair.

He moved to seat Lucy beside her. "Bertie's pies are always in competition with Felicity's at the county fair."

He seated a quiet Jane on his left, then took his place.

Josie concentrated on Lucy as she told her about Blackie in vivid and minute detail while Bertie and Ivy served supper. This allowed her to avoid Jane's condemning blue eyes and Bertie's vaguely uncomfortable glance. She could feel the woman's tension and guessed she felt certain she was about to be chastised by Adam, or worse.

Adam, ignorant of the affair, talked with Jane, then laughed as Lucy described Miles's fall off Blackie.

"He was telling us about a game the natives play in Afghanistan," he explained for Josie, who was having a little difficulty putting together Lucy's story of something decapitated that was used as a ball. "With...well, you don't have to know the unpleasant details. In any case, as he leaned down to demonstrate their prowess at riding out of the saddle, Blackie made a sudden turn, slammed him against the corral fence and knocked him unconscious."

Josie allowed herself to laugh, comforted by the knowledge that the perfect specimen she'd met in Sacramento had shown no signs of permanent damage.

"Papa had to carry him," Lucy said, now on her knees on her chair in her excitement. "And Amos went to get Dr. Brady."

"Dr. Reed," Jane corrected her sister with a roll of her eyes. "Dr. Brady is an animal doctor."

"Dr. Reed." Lucy accepted the correction without a pause in her story. "And Miles didn't break his head but—" she paused for breath "—but he didn't wake up for an hour!"

About to tell Lucy to sit down and eat her soup, Adam was relieved of the responsibility when Josie took hold of her arm to steady her.

"Sit down, sweetheart," she said, helping the little girl remove her foot from the paddle-back of the chair. "We don't want you to fall into the soup."

Lucy giggled at the notion.

For the most part, Jane maintained her silence except to correct her sister or address her father. She ignored Josie as resolutely as Josie ignored her. Lucy needed little encouragement to assume center stage.

When Bertie cleared away after the meal, Adam praised the pork roast, tomato aspic and sauerkraut relish. She thanked him and hesitated a moment as though expecting him to say more.

"We're finished, Bertie," Adam said. "Thank you."

"Yes, Mr. Scofield." She left with her chin high and a faint flush to her cheeks.

Adam frowned after her then turned to Josie. "Have you two had words?" he asked.

She looked at him innocently over the white linen napkin with which she dabbed at her lips. "Of course not," she said, putting it aside. "I believe we're all expected to adjust."

The girls fell silent, aware of the sudden tension, though they seemed more interested than distressed.

Adam warned Josie with a glance. "Jane plays the piano very well. I'm sure if you ask her, she'll play something special for you."

Josie swallowed back that very little burst of temper and remembered that she was an adult and should be behaving as one. She smiled at Jane.

"I would love to hear you play," she said. "Would you?"

"Because *Papa* wants me to," Jane replied.

Josie nodded with forbearance. "Of course." *Papa gets everything his way.*

Adam led them all into the parlor, where Jane sat at a grand piano and went through a considerable repertoire of simple but perfectly executed pieces. Adam and Josie sat side by side on a settee, Lucy in Adam's lap.

Josie experienced a strange sense of disembodiment—as though she were looking down on the picture they made rather than experiencing it. Four months ago, she might have been sitting like this with Benjamin and the boys, listening to Jerusha play. How had everything changed so completely in that short space of time? Benjamin was dead, her boys were missing, and here she was, in the midst of a plan that had seemed so logical a month ago and now seemed to compound her problems rather than offer a solution.

When Jane had finished, Josie joined in Adam's applause, trying desperately to find her feet in this reality.

"That was lovely, Jane," she praised as they all stood together in the middle of the room.

"Mama taught me," she said, her beautiful little face smug. "Do you play?"

"I'm afraid not."

"Do you embroider?"

"No."

"What *do* you do?"

"Nothing remarkable," Josie admitted with a rueful shake of her head. "Perhaps you could teach me to embroider."

Jane folded her arms and said with the certain authority of little girls, "Why didn't your mama teach you?"

"Because she died when I was very young," Josie replied.

Jane stared at her, apparently finding this news startling and unsettling. Josie wondered if the loss of her own mother allowed Jane to suddenly see her as a kindred spirit.

If it did, Jane was not about to admit it. She simply nodded with that same careful distance and said without inflection, "Maybe. Sometime."

Adam guided all of them toward the stairs. "You girls play upstairs until it's time for bed, then we'll come and say good-night." He turned to Josie. "Rest for an hour. I'll be up shortly."

She smiled her compliance, feeling unutterably weary and anxious for the comfort of the big brass bed in which she'd napped that afternoon.

A small hand slipped into hers.

Lucy tugged her toward the stairs. "You can have one of my dollies to sleep with so you won't be afraid."

Josie prayed a heartfelt thank-you that Lucy Scofield was a part of this household. She clung to her little hand as though it were a lifeline as they made their way upstairs.

An hour later Adam found Jane alone in the girls' bedroom, propped up against her pillows, her embroidery in her lap. He went to sit on the edge of her bed in the glow of light from the lamp.

"Where's Lucy?" he asked.

She gave him a disgusted glance. "With 'Mama,'" she said, adding a disgusted emphasis to the word.

Adam took the embroidery from her and put it aside. Then he tried to find the words to tell her that he understood her resentment of a new mother but wouldn't tolerate bad manners or hostility toward Josie.

In a way that had unsettled him since she'd been old enough to talk, Jane anticipated his intent.

"I know I haven't been very nice," she said in a rush, knotting her fingers on the quilt, "but I don't see why she has to be here. And neither does Bertie. Everything was fine."

"Little girls should have a mother," Adam said patiently. "Families need..."

"We had a mother," she said, her little chin firming in a gesture that reminded him of Maggie. "And I'm not going to forget her. Ever."

"Do you really think I would ask that of you?" he asked gently.

She thought a moment, then her leg kicked in a gesture of annoyance under the coverlet. "No. But you want me to love Josephine."

"I want you to let her be your friend," he corrected. "You agreed to that rule this afternoon, remember? She'll only be your mother if you want her to be."

"I don't."

"Then she'll remain your friend. But I want you to remember how we treat friends. We aren't cruel or sarcastic or inhospitable when they're in our home."

Jane nodded. She knew *that* rule. "We have to pretend to like them. Like when Miles brings Betsy Fulton to supper."

Adam couldn't withhold the smile. Betsy Fulton was a bur in their hospitality that the entire household agreed on to the last Donovan.

"But I'm sure you'll find Josie more pleasant to have around than Betsy. Now..." He lowered the light and pulled the pillows down as she curled up comfortably. "I want you to promise me that you'll be polite. No one wants you to be gooey with love you don't feel, but courtesy is always very important in a lady."

Jane said soberly as he pulled up her blankets, "Bertie doesn't think she's a lady."

He raised an eyebrow. "What do you mean?"

Jane braced herself up on an elbow, pleased to know something he didn't. "She thinks she's just *pretending* to be a fancy lady and that she just married you because she wants all our money and our social . . ." She groped a moment for the term, then announced proudly, "Social position!"

Adam's first inclination was to laugh, then anger welled instinctively at the thought that a member of his household staff, beloved though she might be, was deftly undermining his efforts to help his girls accept his new wife.

"First," Adam said, "we have no social position to speak of. We have friends, but that's not the same thing. And Josie's first husband had much more money than I will ever have."

"But Bertie thinks she's lying about that."

"Jane," he said quietly, "when I sent for her, I wrote to and received letters from her attorney. I know that her husband was very rich. And you've seen her clothes."

Jane nodded, admitting grudgingly, "They're very beautiful."

"And very expensive," he said. "She came all this way to marry me because she was lonely. Because she was sad and probably a little afraid and thought a new family in a new place would be a good way to start all over again."

Jane considered that, then lay back against her pillows, a frown between her eyebrows. "You think Bertie's wrong?"

"I think Bertie loved your mama," he said, "and she's as afraid as you are that letting a new mama into the house will make her forget. But it won't. Love and kindness don't close things or people off, they just make more and more room for more and more love."

"How do you know that?" she asked.

He smiled, remembering the gray, rainy morning she'd been born. "Because when I married your mama, I thought I already felt more love than my body could hold. Then you came, then Lucy, and love just grew and grew, and somehow there was always more to give."

"Do you love Josie?"

Children, he thought, could always back one into a corner from which there seemed no escape.

"We're going to be friends first," he said, aware that while not a complete lie, it was not an entire truth, either. "The same rule you and Lucy have."

"Then what if you don't want her to be your wife, or she doesn't want you to be her husband? Will she go away?"

He shook his head. That did not seem a healthy option for her to consider. Or one he liked to think about. "She has no one to go back to. We'll just remain friends who live in the same house."

Jane's eyelids began to droop. "Will that work, Papa?"

He certainly hoped so. He leaned down to kiss her cheek. "I'm sure it will."

She smiled and snuggled into her pillow, giving him one trusting glance from sleepy eyes before they fluttered closed.

He strode out of the girls' room to his bedroom and was stopped in the doorway by the sight that greeted him. Josie lay fast asleep atop the covers in a long white nightdress, Lucy's rag doll Winifred in her arms. Curled up beside her, sharing the same pillow, was Lucy in her nightgown, holding a china doll he'd brought her from San Francisco.

The scene was so touching, so right, he could do nothing to disturb it for several moments. He remembered Josie's look of distress when he and the girls had found her in the dining room, turning away from the door to the kitchen.

In light of what Jane had told him about Bertie, he wondered if Bertie had been expounding at that moment and been overheard. If she had, he wondered why Josie hadn't told him. Then he realized she wouldn't have. She was a woman who fought her own battles, large and small. He would just have to see that she had more field support.

He went to the bed, gently scooped Lucy into his arms and carried her to her own bed. Satisfied that both girls were asleep, he started back to his room and found Josie in the middle of the hallway, sleepy and disoriented.

"Lucy was with me," she said, putting a hand to his arm in mild resistance as he turned her toward his room. "When I awoke she was gone. Is she . . . ?"

"I put her to bed," he said, continuing to urge her in that direction.

"Oh."

He helped her back into bed and pulled the covers over her. As she curled into the side nearest the door, he gave her shoulder a gentle prod. "Other side," he said.

She moved over several inches, but he suspected she was asleep again before she could complete the maneuver. She'd complained very little on the road, at least in regard to her comfort, and he knew she had to be exhausted.

He shed his clothes and climbed in beside her, moving her over with his body until they lay together in the middle, her back to him, his arm wrapped around her. He felt her lean into him contentedly. He smiled into her hair and let himself drift off.

Josie was vaguely aware of sound in the room. Drawers opening and closing. Footsteps. But she remained trapped in the nebulous area between sleep and wakefulness, still caught in a dream of endless travel along a road that seemed to reach no destination.

Then she heard the whisper, "Mama!" She'd heard it so often in her dreams. Even in her waking moments, it lived in the back of her mind like a constant cry, first Charlie's voice, then Billy's. "Mama! Mama!" But this time it was just at her ear. She tried to pull herself to wakefulness, off that endless road. But the word only seemed to grow clearer and more distinct the more awake she became. And then she opened her eyes, saw the lace curtain blowing, knew she was awake and heard the whisper again, soft but clear. "Mama!"

She'd done it! She'd found them! She sat up with a cry, unseating Lucy, who'd been kneeling over her, and knocking her onto the floor. She landed with a howl of pain and indignation.

As Josie struggled to make sense of what had happened, to push aside the overwhelming depression and accept once again that she had only dreamed of finding her children, Adam burst in from the dressing room, adjusting a cuff link.

"Papa!" Lucy cried from the floor, both plump arms raised to him.

He scooped her up, frowning at Josie. "What happened?"

She shook her head, still blinking in confusion. "I think she must have been trying to wake me, and I sat up with a start and threw her off the bed." She extended her arms to him. "Give her to me. I'm sorry, Lucy."

Adam sat on the edge of the bed and handed Lucy over. She went, eager to be comforted and cuddled.

"I'm sorry," Josie said again, rocking her back and forth. "I didn't know you were there, sweetheart."

"I just wanted to tell you breakfast is ready," she said, a dramatic note of affronted dignity in her tone.

Josie smiled over her head at Adam. "Thank you," she said. "Next time you try to wake me, do it from the foot of the bed," she suggested, easing Lucy away and smiling into her face. "Or hold on tighter."

"Like this?" Lucy demonstrated by circling Josie's neck with her arms and squeezing. Josie saw stars. "That's perfect," she gasped.

Adam lifted Lucy off the bed and put her on her feet. "Tell Bertie we'll be right down," he said.

Josie scrambled out of bed, anxious not to be late to the table and give the housekeeper a legitimate cause for complaint. But Adam caught her wrist as she flew toward the dressing room.

"Did Bertie criticize your behavior yesterday?" he asked.

He looked wonderfully crisp and clean, Josie thought, and she felt so bedraggled. And she didn't want to think about yesterday. She shook her head. "I don't believe she's anxious to speak to me at all."

"I mean," he corrected, "did you overhear her say something disparaging of you when you were in the dining room looking for me?"

"Well..." The last thing she wanted to do was cause trouble between Adam and his staff.

Adam pinched her chin between his thumb and forefinger and fixed her with his dark gaze. "Trust me to handle it sensibly. Now tell me the truth."

She sighed, admitting reluctantly, "Yes."

"Very well. I have several options open to me. I can confront her about this and threaten her with dismissal if she ever suggests anything like it again."

She was already shaking her head before Adam had finished. "You said," she reminded, "that you would handle this sensibly."

"Or," he said, "you could behave in a manner so loving, so attentive toward me that she would be forced to change her opinion of you."

He wasn't sure how he managed to look into her suspicious gaze with sincere innocence, but he did.

"Is it that important," she asked, "that we convince Bertie that she's wrong? You and I know that to be false."

"Do we?"

Now completely awake, she remembered that she had to be careful here. And the best way to do that in this instance, she decided, was to pretend fearlessness.

"Do *you* believe that I'm a former fallen dove who's married you for your wealth and status in the community?"

He considered her a moment, then shook his head and leaned his shoulder against the dressing room doorway. "No. But I believe you've married me for purposes of your own. You've admitted as much."

His watchful gaze reminded her yet again that he may have fallen into her trap, but he'd done it willingly. "You don't make love like a professional," he said. "You've resisted several opportunities to acquire material things from me, and somehow, having been subjected to your outspokenness, I can't imagine that a comfortable social status is your goal."

She swallowed, wondering if he was preparing to demand the truth.

"Then what do you think I have in mind?"

He shook his head. "I can't imagine. But I know when you require me to fulfill my obligation, whatever it is, you'll tell me."

She folded her arms, his calm, easy acceptance aggravating her nerves rather than soothing them. "What if I told you you've already fulfilled it?"

He reached to the back of the chair inside the dressing room for his jacket. "Then I'd say it's time to concentrate on what I require of you. A charming wife, a good mother for my girls." He leaned down to plant a kiss on her forehead, his smile dry. "But I believe I'm intelligent enough to know that nothing involving you would be so simple. Get dressed, and be prepared to give Bertie a stellar performance."

They appeared at the table arm in arm. Bertie looked at them suspiciously and just a little nervously as she placed ham and eggs before them. The girls were already hard at work over their breakfasts. Lucy looked up to smile a good-morning, and Jane offered a polite if cool one.

Josie made light conversation, smiling into Adam's eyes when Ivy or Bertie appeared with butter, more toast, more coffee. Adam studied her indulgently, reaching across the corner of the table that separated them to catch her hand.

By the time he left for town, Josie felt completely addled and noticed that the Donovan ladies were very quiet in the kitchen.

Though impatient to learn more about Yreka and the area that surrounded it in the hope of finding some grain of evidence that would lead her to her children, Josie decided it would be wiser to fortify her position at home.

She wandered the boundaries of Adam's property with Lucy skipping at her side. She saw the stubbly new acres of corn he'd described to her when he'd teased her about sacrificing a virgin to its harvest. There were green pastures where red brown cattle grazed, which Amos had told her were Durhams. Beyond them, a small apple orchard rippled over a little hill.

Amos had also explained that the orchard marked the northern boundary. She stood at the very edge of it, gazing longingly beyond at the white mountain, wondering if Charlie and Billy were somewhere in its foothills or beyond it in a wilderness she couldn't glimpse, much less imagine.

Lucy showed her the stables and Blackie whickered affectionately when she gave him a carrot. The bays that drew the wagon stood quietly in their stalls, apparently enjoying their well-deserved rest.

Muffin dozed in a patch of sunlight atop the flat surface of a stable gate. He opened one eye when she nuzzled him but seemed too involved in his task to extend further recognition.

When Josie and Lucy returned to the kitchen in the middle of the second afternoon, Bertie was obviously in a snit. Feeling righteously innocent because she'd been absent most of the day, Josie asked the nature of the problem.

"It's nothing, Mrs. Scofield," Bertie said with an air that suggested quite the opposite. She peeled potatoes and carrots with quick, impatient strokes while Ivy worked quickly over a tub of dirty dishes and pots and pans.

"The 'queen' is coming for supper," Amos said as he dropped an armload of wood near the cookstove.

"Amos!" Bertie scolded with a quick look at Josie.

Josie had asked Amos many questions about the house and the land in the past two days and she'd found him pleased with her interest. She hoped she wasn't presuming too much when she thought he seemed to be loosening toward her.

"Who is the 'queen'?" Josie asked.

Amos opened his mouth to reply, but Bertie quelled him with a look.

"It's Betsy Fulton," Lucy said, standing on a chair to take a peeled carrot. "She loves Miles."

"Ah."

"Miss Fulton likes things just so," Ivy said. "Her father owns a big logging company and she's used to having only the best of everything. Mama always tries very hard to see that she has nothing to complain about."

"But she usually finds something," Amos said on his way out the door.

Ivy dried her hands and went to put more wood into the stove. "I think she likes Mr. Carver much more than Mr. Carver likes her."

"Ivy!" Bertie shook her head in disapproval. "I don't see how you have time to gossip with a tub full of dishes. I have onions to peel here if you haven't got enough to do."

"Is there anything I can do to help?" Josie asked. "I've been a fair hand in the kitchen."

Bertie shook her head wearily. "Your pretty Boston hands will just get in the way."

Josie's offer to help had been instinctive and sincere. She lifted her chin against the rejection. It was such a small thing in light of all she'd been through in the past several months, but added to everything else, it threatened to overwhelm her.

Then she remembered that she would have to remain here until she found her boys, and that Bertie would have her trussed up like a ham within the week if she succumbed to the petty game.

"Come along, Lucy." She lifted the child off the chair and took her hand. "Let's freshen up so we'll be beautiful when Papa comes home."

Lucy skipped along beside her, munching on her carrot. "You already are beautiful," she said with dark-eyed adoration.

For the third time in as many days, Josie thanked God that this child was part of her situation. She doubted she'd survive it without her.

Chapter Six

Josie disliked Betsy Fulton on sight. She seldom made such snap judgments, but this one was easily reached when the young woman looked over Josie's green-and-white walking dress and grimaced as though something hurt.

Josie knew the dress wasn't appropriate for entertaining guests, but she'd confined herself to a limited wardrobe for her trip west, and gowns had seemed less important than serviceable dresses.

"It's a comfort to know Boston isn't as far ahead of us in fashion as we've been led to believe," she said in tones so charming Josie was certain the men would be hard put to believe it was an insult. Looking into wide blue eyes, an angelic berries-and-cream face and an elegant knot of hair that shone like sunlight, Josie had a little difficulty believing it herself. "Welcome to Yreka, Josie. You'll have to let me take you to my dressmaker. She can duplicate the latest European fashions."

"Thank you," she said, and silently added, *I would rather be nailed to the floor of the wagon that brought me here and be jostled until my bones break.* She smiled and resigned herself to an unpleasant evening.

Over dinner, the men's conversation invariably turned to business. Josie, making every effort to be polite, tried to engage Betsy in conversation as Adam and Miles went on about a case they'd recently won involving a Chinaman working on the railroad and the work-gang foreman he was accused of having murdered.

But Betsy apparently preferred to discuss the grisly details of the crime. She ignored Josie completely and told the men in no uncertain terms that they were foolish to have defended the Chinaman.

"Everyone thinks you're foolish," she told them, delivering the insult with a languid bat of her long, painted eyelashes. Her yellow gown, very décolleté and somewhat overdone for a dinner at home, dipped even lower as she used the exchange of a confidence as an excuse to lean toward them. "Why, Papa told me just yesterday that at the Odd Fellows Hall they said if you hadn't already proven yourselves brilliant attorneys in other cases, you'd be cut *dead* in Yreka business and society."

Miles turned to Adam with just the slightest twitch of his bottom lip. "Horrors," he said flatly.

Adam appeared equally grave. "How *would* we hold our heads up?" Then he frowned at Betsy. "You believe we should have let Mr. Fong hang when it was one of the tracklayers who killed Bristol over a woman?"

Betsy indicated Josie with a gesture of a languid hand. "Well, Adam, you don't want your little bride to be a social pariah when she's just gotten here?"

Josie found it quite amazing that the girl had either missed or *dis*missed the importance of the Chinaman's life.

"Please don't be concerned on my account," she said quickly, lightly. "I'd far prefer to be married to a man who'd defend another man, whatever his nationality or social standing, than one who wouldn't do so because of fear of social ostracism."

Betsy turned to her in horror, but Josie was prevented from saying more by the appearance of Ivy announcing supper.

Miles offered Betsy his arm and preceded Adam and Josie into the dining room.

"She has a flair for the dramatic," Adam said under his breath. "Several of our clients have sought other representation because of the case, but none that matter to us. I don't believe we're complete outcasts."

She smiled up at him. "I trust her father is one who's discharged you."

He grinned and shook his head. "I'm afraid not."

"That is a pity. A far worse threat to me than social ostracism would be social popularity with the likes of her."

Adam hugged her to him and laughed. She enjoyed the gesture and felt comforted by it.

Betsy dominated the dinner conversation with highlights of a recent shopping trip to San Francisco. "I found a bombazine even Madame Elise hadn't seen!" she exclaimed, as though she'd unearthed an archaeological discovery rather than a simple fabric. She turned to Josie, pretending warmth, as Adam watched. "She's the couturier I think you should see. She can help you with *all* your fashion difficulties." Her tone suggested there were many.

As they retired to the parlor once again, Josie actually felt grateful for Betsy's cleverly worded insults. She was certain if it weren't for the ire they raised in her, she would have died of boredom an hour ago.

At one point, as Betsy and Miles argued a detail of the law, Josie caught Adam's eye and crossed hers out of pure devilry. He warned her with a frown that fell short of threatening because of the amusement alight in it.

As Betsy droned on, Josie noticed Jane standing hesitantly in the parlor doorway. The girls had eaten supper early and been put to bed before Miles and Betsy arrived.

Adam noticed Josie's glance and turned. He raised an eyebrow at Jane, who beckoned him toward her.

"Oh, is that little Jane!" Betsy asked in a high voice. "Come out, darling, so I can see you!"

Josie saw Jane blush to the roots of her hair, and she guessed that it was more than simple embarrassment. As Ivy had helped the girls prepare for bed, Josie had overhead their conversation and Jane's clear dislike for the young woman.

Reluctantly, Jane walked over to her father. He pulled her onto the sofa between him and Josie. "What is it, pumpkin?" he asked.

"I forgot to ask you," she said in a barely audible voice, "if Mrs. Brady's class can come to your office one day."

"Your classroom?" he asked.

"Yes." She nodded, a flush that was excitement now, not embarrassment, filling her cheeks. "We went to Dr. Reed's last week and to Madame Elise's before that."

"Of course you can," Adam replied. "But what's the purpose?"

Betsy rolled her eyes. "Mrs. Brady, the suffragist," she said disparagingly. "She's trying to talk women into fighting for the vote and little girls into becoming senators and tradesmen. As though we would want all that responsibility when men already do it all so well."

Josie had learned in the few days she'd spent in Adam's house that Jane revered her teacher, Mrs. Brady. Jane now stiffened, her little chin tilted at a defiant angle.

"I would like to be a lawyer, like Papa."

"And so you should," Betsy replied, "because you're a very smart girl."

Josie's dislike of Betsy became visceral when the young woman added with complete sincerity, "But men don't like smart girls, they like *pretty* girls."

The inference that the child was plain could not have been more clear had she said the words.

Though the child sat between them, Josie felt Adam's temper ignite and sensed his move to rise off the sofa. She stopped him with a hand on his shoulder as she, herself, rose to her feet and pulled Jane with her. She felt coldly, even cruelly angry.

"Well, that's fortunate for you, isn't it, Betsy?" she said with all apparent sweetness. "You'll never be lonely. Jane can recite from memory the first five stanzas of 'Paul Revere's Ride' by Longfellow. Have you heard of Longfellow, Betsy? Or, indeed, of Paul Revere?"

As Betsy, red-faced, tried to stammer an indignant reply, Josie answered her own question. "I don't imagine so. You aren't likely to have encountered either gentleman in a dress shop or a milliner's. Excuse us. Come, Jane. I'll put you back to bed."

Josie was aware of the child running to keep up with her as she stormed upstairs and down the hallway to the children's room. She sat a pale, wide-eyed Jane on the edge of the bed in the soft lamplight and knelt before her to look into her eyes.

"Jane, you listen to me," she began firmly.

"I'm sorry I interrupted," the child said quickly, shrinking away. "I promised Mrs. Brady I'd ask Papa and let her know tomorrow, and I didn't think about it until..."

Josie shook her head. "You have every right to interrupt. This is your house, too. What I want to tell you is that there are many adults who do not have the brains God gave a goose, and Betsy Fulton is one of them."

Jane giggled, then thought better of it and sobered as Josie went on.

"Because she doesn't think that smart women can also be pretty—or that a man will marry a smart woman even if she isn't pretty—doesn't make it so."

Jane sighed, going to the issue that really concerned her in all this. "Do you think I'll ever be pretty?"

"Jane, you already are," Josie said, "and don't you ever let a woman like Betsy make you believe that being beautiful depends on perfect features or perfect clothes. It doesn't. It comes from inside."

"But I want to be pretty outside, too."

"You are pretty outside."

Jane shook her head. "Lucy's going to be the beauty. Everyone says so, not just Betsy."

Josie took the small shoulders in her hands and looked into Jane's green eyes. She was vaguely aware of wading too far into the quicksand she'd been determined to avoid, but she had a point to make—and, first and foremost, she acknowledged with a sense of doom, she was still a mother.

"That's because you're quieter, less animated," she said. "You're very pretty as you are, but I have a feeling you're going to be a late bloomer."

"What's that?"

"It means that when everyone least expects it, you're going to wake up one morning and find that you've grown tall and shapely, that all the intelligence and goodness you have inside now shows in your face, and the men will be lined up all the way to San Francisco to see you!"

Jane's hands were clasped under her chin, her eyes rapt, her smile frail as she listened.

"And I think you would make a wonderful lawyer. One day the sign over your father's office will say Scofield, Carver and Scofield. Now . . ." She threw the blankets back and shooed the child under them, standing up to pull them up to her chin. "Sleep tight. I have to get back to our guests."

Josie turned the wick down until the room was in darkness, then she headed carefully for the frail light of the hallway.

"Josie!" Jane whispered.

Josie stopped and turned. "Yes."

There was a moment's silence, then she whispered loudly, a smile in her voice, "Good night."

"Good night, Jane."

When she turned to leave again, she saw the shadow in the doorway. She squared her shoulders, feeling fairly certain

this was the first time a guest had ever been insulted whil
under the hospitality of the Scofield household. Betsy ha
deserved some kind of dressing-down, certainly, but per
haps if she had let Adam handle it, he might have found
more civilized way to accomplish it.

"Adam, I . . ." she began as he came toward her.

He caught her arms and put her aside. "Wait for me i
our room," he said ominously.

"But our guests . . ."

"Have gone."

Josie left the room as he went to Jane's bedside. She sa
on the edge of the bed and waited for him, praying fer
vently for a way to explain that would make her seem less o
a termagant. But she could think of no reasonable excuse
Betsy had infuriated her and she'd acted upon it. Feeling th
desperate confinement of her clothes, Josie removed he
shoes and her bustle, which made her perch on the edge o
the bed uncomfortable.

Settled once again, she closed her eyes as she heard hi
footsteps on the stairs. *Please God,* she prayed, *don't let m
have destroyed my opportunity to find Charlie and Billy a
ready. Please help me to explain to Adam in a way he'll un
derstand.*

But he didn't seem interested in explanations. He pushe
the bedroom door open then closed it firmly behind him an
came toward her, eyes stormy, jaw set.

"I realize I was rude," Josie said quickly, getting to he
feet, "but I warned you in Sacramento that I have a sorr
tendency to say what's on my mind."

When he continued to approach in silence, she took a ste
to the side. "Why a witty, intelligent man like Miles wishe
to keep company with an empty-headed, bigoted bore lik
her is beyond me," she said, her voice rising just a little.

He followed her side step, and she took another, feelin
about to suffocate.

"I promise you I won't make a habit of mistreating your guests," she said, trying to instill reason into her tone without making it sound as if she were apologizing, "but neither will I allow one of them to make thoughtlessly cruel remarks to the children."

He stopped her sideways progress with a hand to the post at the head of the bed. "You led me to believe you didn't like children," he said, looking down on her with an expression too complex to decipher in her current state of mind.

"I said no such thing," she denied, and tried to take a step in the other direction.

He stopped her this time with a very gentle touch to the side of her face. "When you learned I had children, you insisted on returning to Sacramento."

Aware of the danger she faced here, Josie kept her eyes down, her voice carefully neutral. "Not because I dislike children."

"Why, then?"

She groped for a plausible excuse and found it in what might honestly apply in any relationship such as theirs. She raised cautious blue eyes to him. "I thought it was one thing for you and me to embark on a marriage in the hope that we would suit each other and be... happy together, but quite another to involve children. What if... what if we were mistaken after all and found we completely disliked each other?"

He studied her a long, slow moment, then moved his hand to cradle her chin in the vee between his thumb and forefinger.

"I suppose we can't predict the future," he said softly, his eyes on her trembling lips as his head came down, "but I promise you that at this moment, I believe we will suit very well." And his mouth closed over hers in a soft, tender, sweet kiss that was a complete surprise.

She blinked as he raised his head. "Then, you're not angry about Betsy?"

He shook his head, his eyes roving her features as his hand reached behind her to remove the pins in her hair. He laughed lightly. "In fact, it was probably wise of you to handle it. Had you not held me in my seat, she'd be in the water trough by now."

Her heart began to thump as she read his intention. He hadn't made love to her since they'd arrived home, merely held her comfortingly in his arms at night. She'd found herself dreading and anticipating the night he took her in his arms for another purpose.

She smiled, hating to be distracted from the image of the beautiful Betsy wet and bedraggled, but his hand combing through her now-loosened hair raised gooseflesh on her scalp and along her shoulders, thoroughly addling her.

"I'm... I'm sorry now... that I stopped you," she said on a broken whisper.

With a yank that made her jump, he pulled the covers back, then lifted her and placed her across the cool sheet. Panic threatened. When he'd made love to her at Kilkenny's, she'd felt as though every thought and purpose in her head had fled. She could ill afford to experience that loss of direction again. She had so much to do, so...

The rest of her thought was lost in the softness of the bed and the tumult of her own sensations as he turned her over so that her face was buried in the sweet-smelling pillows as he unfastened the buttons at the back of her dress.

When that task was accomplished, she felt his hand slip beneath her skirt, find the bow that fastened her petticoats at the waist and pull them down.

Then his hands slid under her skirt once more to find the tie at the waist of her drawers. His fingers eased inside the waistband and she felt their touch over her hips and down the backs of her legs as he drew the garment off.

He turned her onto her back. She tried to cling to reason. "Adam, I..."

"Shush," he said gently, and leaned over to kiss her protest into oblivion.

As he tugged the sleeves from her, then let the bodice of her dress lie at her waist while he untied the hooks of her corset, she lost all coherent thought.

He tossed the corset aside as though it offended him. "Why a woman as small as you would wear such a punitive contraption is beyond me."

She'd always thought her waist too thick, but she couldn't pull the words together to make a sensible, cohesive sentence. She could only remember what he'd made her feel the last time, and wondered if that could possibly happen again. Surely not. It had never happened with Ben, as much as she'd loved him. It was possibly something that occurred only at times of high anxiety.

Josie learned that she was wrong about that only a moment later when her dress had been tossed aside and Adam was removing his clothes.

She remembered that it had begun as a vague sense of unease, a tightening little discord at the heart of her femininity.

And here it was again.

Adam saw her fidget and draw a leg up, then turn her head on the pillow to look at him in confusion as he stood to remove his trousers.

She said his name and reached a hand out to him. That gesture intoxicated him as nothing else could have. He saw that her eyes were unfocused, that panting little breaths were making her breasts rise and fall. He hurried to kick his clothing aside and join her on the bed, happy with the thought that his very nearness had aroused her to readiness.

She turned to him, wrapping her arms around him, a little pleat of concern between her eyebrows. "Adam, I don't understand," she whispered. "You haven't touched me."

He turned her onto her back and rose over her. "You want me, Josie," he explained as he eased gently past the instinctive pursing of her body, then thrust home as she wrapped her legs around him in encouragement.

Her body arched in his arms, and she gasped a cry he covered with his hand for fear of inviting investigation by the nosy children across the hall. Then he felt the shudders rack her, felt her tighten around him with the need to share what she felt. He was about to lose himself to the pleasure, as well, when she pulled his hand from her mouth to say on a strained breath, "I do, Adam. I *do* want you." His pleasure doubled by that admission, he erupted inside her.

When he finally moved to lie beside her and take her in his arms, she turned to fold her hands on his chest and rest her chin atop them, her confusion apparent.

Adam brushed the dark, tumbled hair from her eyes and tucked it behind her ear. "What is it?" he asked.

She lowered her eyes, traced her index finger absently over his collarbone, then met his gaze ruefully. "May I ask you a question?"

"By all means."

"It's an improper question," she warned.

He grinned. "I don't believe you're familiar with any proper ones. Ask away."

"I..." She sighed, then the little pleat between her eyebrows deepened. "I shared a marriage bed with Benjamin for nine years, yet I never...experienced what you make me feel. Making love was pleasant enough, but I never even realized that...*that* existed. And yet I loved him very much." She made a small sound of frustration. "How could that be, when you and I...we barely know each other?"

He knew what she meant to ask, though saying it aloud, even though it was the truth, was difficult. "You mean to say, how can that be when we're not in love?"

She made the smallest wince. "Yes," she admitted quietly. "I believe that's what I mean."

He put one hand behind his head and absently stroked her hair with the other, wondering how to explain such a thing to a well-born woman.

"I believe it's because the physical part of making love," he said, "can exist completely apart from the emotional part that makes us want to do it."

"You mean two people could be unwilling, and it would still...happen?"

He smiled. "I would venture to say at least one would have to be willing, or the occasion would not present itself in the first place. And once involved, a man could perform easily whether or not there was love attached to the deed. A woman, on the other hand, I believe, could be coaxed to experience...satisfaction, if the man took care with her."

Satisfaction. She considered the word and found it far too small to describe the feeling it was meant to express.

"But Benjamin loved me," she said. "I'm sure if he was aware that this existed, and that I was not experiencing it, he'd have made an effort to see that I did. Did I fail him in some way?"

"I doubt that seriously," he said without hesitation. "It could be a couple of things." He tugged a strand of her hair playfully. "Many men of Benjamin's generation believed that women did not, and indeed should not, take pleasure in the marriage bed. Even though he loved you, he might not have considered your pleasure in it important because that was what his father taught him. A wife is for producing an heir. Pleasure could be taken with ladies...for whom it was their business."

Josie thought that over. That might have been. While Benjamin had always been kindness itself to her, he'd never spent much time or effort over lovemaking, and once Billy had been born, they'd made love very little. Possibly he thought he'd produced two heirs and anything more would be superfluous, though she doubted he'd ever gone to fallen doves for his pleasure. He'd spent most of his free time at home with her and the boys.

"You said there were a couple of reasons," she prompted.

He drew a deep breath. This one was going to require delicacy.

He stroked her hair. "You're a very beautiful woman, Josie, and Benjamin was an older man. At his age, it's possible that you might have...stimulated him beyond his ability to withhold his pleasure until you had reached yours. He might have considered it afterward, but lovemaking requires a considerable effort of a man's body. Perhaps he fell asleep before he could repair the injustice."

Josie found that a comforting thought. The notion that she'd failed Benjamin in some way had nagged her since that first night with Adam. Now she looked at her new husband in light of her discovery.

Her difficult question would have provided him the perfect opportunity to make light of Benjamin or to compare himself with him and let her make the obvious conclusion that he, Adam, was the superior lover.

Instead, he'd gently explained things she hadn't understood or had failed to consider. He'd absolved her of any guilt in her own deprivation and even provided Benjamin with thoughtful excuses. Adam Scofield, she decided, was in some ways a very remarkable man.

She planted a kiss on his chest and snuggled down beside him. "Thank you, Adam," she said.

"You're welcome, Josie," he replied, and closed his eyes with great relief that she'd finished with her questions.

Chapter Seven

"I wish I could go to school." Lucy leaned against the porch rail as Josie waved Jane on her way. Arms filled with books and lunch basket, she walked down the road with a girl and two boys from a farm just beyond theirs.

As the children disappeared from sight around a bend, Josie felt a prickle of excitement along her spine. At last! An opportunity to begin her search.

"Would you like to come to town with me today?" Josie turned Lucy back toward the house. "I'd like to look in the shops. And perhaps we could find you a candy stick."

Lucy danced along backward beside Josie as she went toward the kitchen to tell Bertie they would be absent for lunch. "Can Winifred come?" she asked, obviously excited at the prospect.

"Of course."

"I'll go get her blanket."

Josie felt a pang of guilt she quickly dismissed. While Lucy skipped along beside her, no one would guess that the trip to town was for the purpose of seeking information about Charlie and Billy. She would look at the faces of children accompanying their mothers. Charlie was old enough to be in school, but even so, she doubted the family had taken her children west to educate them. They were probably being used to do chores on a farm or in whatever

style of life was open to a man and woman running from
Massachusetts law. Her boys had inherited their father's
platinum hair. They would be easy to identify, whatever they
wore.

She would inquire at the newspaper office and at the post
office. If the Grippers were in the area, she might find a lead
there.

Josie pushed her way into the kitchen with a smile of
greeting. Ivy, who'd overheard her words with Betsy several nights before, had warmed considerably toward her.
Bertie was somewhat more civil but continued to regard her
with suspicion. Since Josie knew the woman to be justified,
if for the wrong reasons, she had difficulty finding fault with
her.

Ivy turned away from the tub of dishes while Bertie
looked up from kneading dough, flour on her hands and the
front of her apron.

"Lucy and I are going to town this morning," Josie said.
"I have several errands to see to, so I believe we'll have lunch
there. Is there anything we can do for either of you while
we're there?"

Ivy brightened. "Would you see if my catalog order is in
at the post office?"

Perfect. Josie smiled. "I'd be happy to."

"Amos will take you," Bertie said, concentrating on the
dough she worked over with strong, capable hands.

"That isn't necessary. It's a beautiful morning."

"Amos will take you," Bertie repeated. "He has to go to
the lumber mill to pick up posts. Then he'll stop to visit with
his sister, who lives near there. He'll pick you up on the way
back."

Josie wouldn't have minded walking, but on the chance
that this was a gesture of kindness on Bertie's part—though
she seemed to be doing her utmost to suggest otherwise—she
didn't want to turn it away.

"Thank you, Bertie," she said. "That would be very convenient."

"Yes, ma'am," Bertie replied as Josie left the room. Josie thought the title held a little less scorn than usual.

Yreka was a lively, bustling place by midmorning. Amos leapt down from the wagon to lift Lucy down, then Josie. He pointed out several places from which he thought they should keep their distance, then indicated a brick building in the next block.

"Mr. Scofield's office is right down there if you need him, or if I'm running late and you need a place to wait."

Josie smiled at him. "Thank you, Amos."

Amos tipped his hat, then started toward the wagon. But apparently having a second thought, he turned back to her again.

"I believe I'm speaking out of turn," he said, looking vaguely uncomfortable, but also as though he were holding back a smile with difficulty. "Ivy told me what happened with Miss Fulton."

Josie grimaced. "Seems you're not the only one who speaks out of turn, doesn't it?"

He shook his head. "If ever a set down was deserved," he said, "that young lady had it coming." He tipped his hat again. "Good day, Mrs. Scofield."

"Good day, Amos."

Lucy knew precisely where to find the candy shop. "Sometimes Papa brings me and Jane here. He likes the butter candies, but I always have a cinnamon stick."

Josie bought a bag of cinnamon sticks, making Lucy promise to eat only one and to remember that half of them were for Jane, then, on an impulse, bought a bag of butter candies.

To force herself to behave in a calm and reasonable manner that would not arouse suspicion in even the most casual observer, she went to the telegraph office to wire Jonathan that she'd arrived safely and was married. Then she made herself go to the fabric store next, take time to pretend interest in all it had to offer and save the newspaper and the post office for later.

She wandered slowly from one bolt of fabric to the next, from the practical calicoes to the sumptuous silks, then studied the lace and the buttons. But all the time her heart was racing, and her hands fairly trembled with the urgency to be on her way and be about the business for which she'd come to town.

The newspaper office was quiet and smelled strongly of ink and whatever other compounds were used to apply it. A man in spectacles with a green shade over his eyes came to a low counter on which several issues of the *Journal* were spread.

Josie glanced over her shoulder to assure herself that Lucy remained in the chair where she'd placed her and saw little feet kicking back and forth as the girl sucked on her cinnamon stick. Josie returned the man's cordial good-morning.

She had been fully prepared to tell this man she was searching for a man and woman who'd escaped the law in Massachusetts and were purported to have settled somewhere in the vicinity. If he questioned her, she would say they'd stolen several heirlooms belonging to her sister in Boston and that she'd written to ask her to look into their whereabouts.

It hadn't occurred to her that the man behind the counter would know who she was.

"You must be the new Mrs. Scofield," he said. He leaned sideways to smile at Lucy, who gave him a red-mouthed grin.

Josie struggled not to appear abjectly stupid. What was wrong with her? This was a very small town. Of course everyone would know everyone else and be quick to identify a new face with the gossip Ivy told her was circulating about Adam Scofield's new bride. Particularly since she had

Adam's child with her. For a moment she could only stare at him.

"I'm Peter Elliott," he said. "Associate editor of the *Journal*. Your husband has represented me several times."

Josie gave him her most charming smile as she quickly changed her story.

"Josie Scofield," she said. "This is a lovely town. Lucy is taking me on a tour to help me get acquainted."

He laughed. "I see she's introduced you to the candy store."

Josie nodded gravely. "She insisted that should be our first stop."

"Hope you bought butter candies. Adam eats me out of them when he comes to help me with the legal news."

Josie held up the little white paper-wrapped package and said with a smile, "Oh dear. Perhaps I should replenish your supply before I leave town today."

He laughed good-naturedly and shook his head. "I'm happy to share with him. He's given me better legal counsel than I've ever paid for, I assure you. But is there something *I* can do for *you*?"

She nodded as she reassembled the important elements of her story into a new fiction. She could imagine Adam's reaction if the next time he came to see Mr. Elliott he mentioned that his wife had inquired about two fugitives from the law who'd made off with her sister's heirlooms.

She'd kept the fabricated story of her past as true to the reality of it as possible to avoid confusion or a misstep on her part. She had not mentioned a sister because she had none.

And he would certainly wonder what interest she could possibly have in a pair of criminals.

"My friend and attorney in Boston, Jonathan Dunlop, has asked me to look into the whereabouts of friends of his who've recently relocated in the Siskiyou Mountains—a Mr. and Mrs. Gripper." She waited, her heart pounding.

He frowned. "Gripper," he said, slowly shaking his head. "The name isn't familiar to me. But there could be new people somewhere in the county. I travel around once a week for news. I'll be sure to let Adam know if I hear the name."

That was safe enough. She thanked him and reached back for Lucy's hand.

"It was a pleasure to meet you, Mr. Elliott." She held up her candy-store package once again and smiled. "Guard your butter candies. Adam now has his own supply."

The man saw her to the door and waved her off with a loud guffaw.

The postmistress was also unfamiliar with the name Gripper, but she did have Ivy's package. As it was large and cumbersome to carry, the next logical stop was Adam's office.

As Lucy skipped along beside her, excited about "visiting Papa," Josie tried to swallow her crushing disappointment. *It was your very first step,* she told herself. *Certainly you didn't expect Mr. Elliott to say, "Gripper! Yes, of course. He sets type for me. Gripper, come out here and meet Mrs. Scofield!"*

Still, her throat ached and she blinked back the threat of tears. Her brain knew this could be a long, slow search, but all her heart knew was the gaping hole in its center.

"Josie!" Miles was walking out the office door as Josie and Lucy approached. He lifted the child into his arms, uncaring of her sticky fingers and face, and swept his hat off to Josie. "What a nice surprise. Come to visit Adam?"

Josie indicated the package in her arms. "We've been shopping and picked up a package for Ivy. I was wondering if we could leave it in a corner of the office until Amos comes to take us home."

"Of course." He put Lucy down, pushed open the office door and took the package from Josie. "Come inside. Adam's with a client, but he shouldn't be much longer."

She drew a deep breath as Miles ushered her and Lucy inside. She tried to put her personal concerns aside in the overriding need to don her wifely role and maintain her position.

The office was sedately appointed, all large desks and tables, certificates on a panelled wall, the other two covered with books. From an office at the rear she could hear the sounds of quiet conversation. She picked out Adam's voice and was surprised by the little frisson of feeling that drifted over her at the sound. She had a sudden, vivid image of hearing it in the night, its strength blotting out her fears.

Miles placed Ivy's package behind a cabinet, then seated Josie and Lucy in chairs around a wide oak desk. Josie noticed a photograph on it of Jane at about four and Lucy as a baby in the arms of a beautiful young woman with a face filled with laughter. Maggie.

"I have an appointment at noon," Miles said. "Adam should be out very soon."

Josie shooed him toward the front door. "Go on. We'll be fine."

"Before I go..." Miles perched on the edge of the desk, his back to Lucy, who crooned to Winifred in the chair. "I want to apologize for Betsy's behavior the other night."

Josie shook her head. "You're not responsible for her behavior, Miles."

"I'm responsible for keeping company with her because her father's an important client and because she's a young lady with... an adventurous nature."

She smiled. There were such interesting euphemisms for a woman who was free with her charms. It occurred to her that she was hardly one to criticize. She'd done something very similar herself.

"Jane took it very philosophically, and she's the only one I was concerned about. It's forgotten. But my advice would be to find a young woman who is less... adventurous and more kind."

"You're absolutely right. If such a young woman would have me. I'm quite the reprobate, you know."

Josie laughed. "That might be the way you like to think of yourself, but I don't believe it for a moment. You'd be a wonderful husband and father. I think it's time you gave the matter some thought."

He pretended to shudder. "Thank you, but my father struggled under my mother's yoke, unable to move an inch without her consent. I vowed that would never happen to me. However..." He bowed gallantly. "I'd best be on my way. If *you* ever decide that life with Adam is unbearable, we could run off together to the Sandwich Islands."

"That sounds delightful," she replied with a laugh as he backed toward the door. "I'll be certain to let you know."

Several moments later, the door to the back room opened, and Adam stopped in the act of walking a tall, portly gentleman out.

He reached down to scoop Lucy up as she ran to him. Josie, standing with a smile and donning her role as wife, noted that he looked wonderful. He'd shed his jacket and stood in crisp white shirt and suspenders and the pants of his brown serge suit.

She hadn't seen this professional side of him before, and it seemed to lend a polish to the dark danger of which she knew him to be capable.

He held an arm out to her and she went into it, thinking that even now, in this civilized setting, what she felt for him was an unsettling combination of comfort and trepidation.

"Josie, I'd like you to meet the man responsible for your journey west. This is my friend and attorney, George Burton. George, this is Josie, the young woman who, fortunately for me, was bored with 'the strictures of Boston society.'"

Josie laughed as Adam quoted George's own letter to Jonathan.

Josie offered her hand, and the big, cheerful man took it in his two.

"Thank you, Mr. Burton," she said, glancing with an affectionate smile in Adam's direction as her role required. "You made Adam sound so nearly divine. I can't imagine that any woman in her right mind could have remained in Boston."

"And you have to be the most beautiful bride, accidental or otherwise, to ever grace the streets of Yreka." Burton kissed her hand. "And please call me George. My wife, Julia, is anxious to meet you. I believe she'll be calling on you regarding a ladies' group she belongs to that claims to get together once a week to do charitable works, though it's my belief they exchange gossip and scandal over needlework."

"Mmm," Josie said with a saucy roll of her eyes. "Sounds like something I'd enjoy a great deal."

Adam shook his head at George. "Incorrigible, even the beautiful ones. Meanwhile, I was thinking Josie and I would host the after-church social this Sunday to introduce her."

"Excellent."

Josie continued to smile as she and Adam, still carrying Lucy, walked Burton to the door. Meeting new people would be helpful to her cause, though it seemed unlikely Gripper and his wife would make an appearance at church. There could be someone who would recognize the name, though, or who would remember two towheaded little boys.

On the other hand, hosting a party meant she would have to play her role to perfection. Other wives would be watching her and would recognize a fraud, she felt sure. She would have to be careful. And there was the possibility that Gripper was using another name.

She came back to awareness in time to bid George Burton a charming goodbye.

Adam wasn't sure what unsettled him. Josie looked beautiful in a soft yellow suit, her straw hat cocked at a sassy angle over her sweep of rich, dark curls. She could not have been more charming to old George, and Lucy bubbled as though they'd had a delightful morning together. But something subtle in her communicated itself to him, some edge of tension he couldn't isolate.

Though he knew very little about her, and knew she kept a part of herself distant from him, he was beginning to think that he knew the woman in her very well. Since that night at Kilkenny's a week ago, he'd learned everything that pleased her and felt as though he could chart her body in the dark— as, indeed, he had done over and over.

The night he'd first met her in Sacramento and decided to marry her despite his awareness that she hid secrets, he'd thought it would be an easy matter to ignore them as long as they didn't affect their life together. Now he was not so sure. He found himself feeling very possessive toward her, and jealous of those things he didn't know.

He also knew that pushing her would yield nothing but innocent denial or stubborn resistance. He decided to trust that one day soon she would decide to share her secrets.

"Mama and I are going to the hotel for lunch!" Lucy announced as Adam carried her back to his desk.

Adam frowned at her red mouth and fingers as he put her in his chair. "You already look as though you've eaten something large and wild raw."

Josie came behind him with her handkerchief and tipped water from a pitcher onto it.

"It was a cinnamon stick," Lucy said as Adam shrugged into his jacket. "And Mama bought you some butter candies."

Adam raised an eyebrow at Josie as she leaned over Lucy and scrubbed. "You did?"

"I was forced to. According to Mr. Elliott you're in debt to him for roughly four pounds of butter candies. If we're to repay the debt, you'd best have some at home."

He laughed in surprise as he smoothed his collar. "You have been getting acquainted. What were you doing at the newspaper office?"

"Looking for friends of Jonathan's with whom he's lost touch. Last he'd heard from them, they were supposed to be somewhere in the Siskiyou Mountains. I promised Jonathan I'd carry his greetings if I could find them."

"The Siskiyous stretch up into Oregon," he said.

Her quick glance surprised him with its deep distress. She quickly looked away, pretending to fuss with the ruffle of Lucy's skirt. "Yes, well, I didn't promise anything," she said. "Simply told him I'd look into it for him. Would you like to join us for lunch?"

She straightened and smiled at him and he began to wonder if he'd imagined that anguish in her eyes. No. He'd surprised it in her glance too often to be mistaken. But what in the hell did it mean? What did a well-bred widow from Boston who'd just resettled in comfortable circumstances have to be troubled about? Until he knew the answer to that question, he decided it would be futile to speculate.

"I would love to," he said as Lucy twirled in his chair. "That is, if you really want my company and aren't using me as a means of holding on to your shopping funds."

Josie shook her head. "We've finished our shopping and even have enough to treat *you* to lunch. Lucy, stop!" she ordered, raising her voice slightly. Lucy complied. "Thank you," she said quietly. "Your father might want to use that chair again."

Adam followed his women to the door of his office, thinking that his wife was certainly an enigma. Though she'd come all this way on her own, he sometimes got the distinct impression she did not want to be here. But if she didn't, she seemed to have embraced at least her duties as mother with wholehearted dedication.

His feelings about her duties as wife were less clear. On the one hand, she seemed to perform her part before the household staff and friends. On the other hand, in bed, he felt sure her behavior was completely genuine and not a performance at all.

Of course, he'd explained that to her himself the night she'd pounced on Betsy for the slight against Jane. The *act* of love could be executed to perfection without the involvement of the *emotion* of love. Well, possibly not to perfection, but certainly to pleasure.

Adam closed and locked the office door, leaving his thoughts behind, as well. They were simply too much to consider on an empty stomach.

Jane talked nonstop at supper. "Mrs. Brady is very pleased that you're going to let us come to your office, Papa. She thinks I would make a fine lawyer, too, just like Josie does. And she thinks it's a silly notion that smart girls can't be pretty or that men won't marry them, just like Josie does. Because she's very smart and very pretty and married a very nice man." She turned to Josie without taking a breath and added, "That's Dr. Brady, the animal doctor. Just like you."

Josie lost the thread of the conversation at that point. "The animal doctor is just like me?"

Both girls laughed. Adam pushed his plate away and leaned back, apparently enjoying the conversation.

"No. She married a nice man, just like you married Papa. And you're smart and pretty, too, so Betsy was all wrong."

"I'm going to marry a prince," Lucy said, spearing a tender bite of carrot with her fork. "Then I'll be a queen."

"No, you'll be a princess," Jane corrected. "You have to marry a king to be a queen."

Lucy concentrated on the important details. "Will I have a crown and a black horse?"

"You'll have a crown," Jane assured her, then turned to her father with a questioning look. "I don't know about the horse."

"She'll have a carriage," he said gravely, "drawn by four very beautiful horses."

"Black ones?" Lucy asked, her eyes alight, the carrot still untouched on her fork.

"I imagine a princess can ask for any color horses she wants."

"Could you and Mama and Jane and Muffin come and live with me?"

He nodded. "Palaces usually have lots of room for everyone. Please eat that carrot before it dies of old age."

She grimaced, closed her eyes and chewed with her small thumb and forefinger pinching her nose shut. Josie turned to Adam in alarm.

He shook his head in a calming gesture. "She doesn't like carrots and goes through all manner of theatrical measures to avoid eating them. Protracted conversations about incredible things, then dramatic chewing and swallowing when she's finally forced to get them down."

Josie laughed softly. "I was rather enjoying the prospect of her moving us into a palace."

He shook his head with feigned regret. "I'm afraid there isn't a drop of royal blood anywhere in the Scofield line. What about your side?"

She laughed again to forestall any feeling of panic. She'd created a story; all she had to do was remember it.

"The Denehys? I'm afraid not. They're Beacon Hill blue bloods all right, but the royalty exists only in their attitudes, not their lineage."

"I like living here," Jane said, laying her fork daintily on the edge of her empty plate. "When I grow up I'm going to stay in this house, work with Papa and march in suffragist parades with Mrs. Brady."

Adam laughed aloud. "A truly noble future, Janie."

Josie could see that Adam was delighted with Jane. She would have never guessed how animated Jane could be, judging by their first few days' acquaintance. Now that the ice had thawed between them, she was as charming and gregarious as Lucy.

"May I be excused?" Jane asked. "If I wait until Lucy finishes her carrots, I'll be too old to hold my pencil to do my homework."

Adam sent her on her way, then excused himself. "I have a few things to prepare for court tomorrow. Time to take your plate into the kitchen, Lucy."

"But if my carrots aren't finished, I can't have my apple dumpling," she complained, her big eyes disappointed.

"You've had ample time, Lucy..."

"I'll sit with her for another five minutes," Josie bargained. "If she finishes her carrots in that time, I'll get her dumpling. If she doesn't, I'll put her plate away."

He studied her a moment and she was afraid she might have made a mistake in interfering with his discipline. He didn't seem particularly severe, but she guessed he must be firm because both girls obeyed him instantly and without question.

"Five minutes," he said finally, then added with a grin. "And watch her. She tries to give what she hasn't eaten to Muffin."

As he walked away, Josie smiled at the child beside her, feeling for the first time just a little comfortable in her role here—at least the maternal part of it. And she refused to pursue that thought too far because it would be bound to bring on thoughts of her boys and that sick, hollow feeling that made it difficult to function. She tried instead to concentrate on the child at hand.

"Did you know that carrots give a lady sparkling eyes and beautiful hair?" she asked.

Lucy, her eyes screwed shut as she chewed another bite of carrot, opened one to look at her in surprise.

She nodded. "And a princess must have sparkling eyes and beautiful hair."

"Carrots all gone?" Adam asked several hours later when he found Josie propped against their pillows, reading a book by lamplight.

She glanced up at him over the rim of the book. "Every last one."

"How did you manage that?"

"I told her carrots would give her beautiful hair and eyes and that a princess had to have them."

He went to sit on the edge of the bed beside her, placing an arm across her body to rest his hand on the mattress. His eyes dark and a little tired, he looked over her features one by one with slow deliberation.

"And is that your secret?"

"To what?" she asked, her voice suddenly low and breathy. It was always like this. All he had to do was draw near and her mind launched into vivid imaginings of what he could do to her and how he could make her feel. And she grew greedy and wanton.

He took the book from her, closed it and placed it on the bedside table.

"You look like a princess."

"In my old nightdress, with my hair bundled up from my bath?"

He nodded, the way he looked at her indicating that the affirmative referred to more than her question. "With your cheeks pink and your eyes closing sleepily." He asked with sudden concern, "Are you tired?"

"No," she denied quickly, afraid he meant not to make love to her after all.

As his grin acknowledged her hasty denial and the desire for him that had prompted it, she fluttered her eyelashes playfully.

"I was lost in the tale of warm desert sands in my novel. It made me feel languorous."

"Languorous." He repeated the word while leaning over her to take her lips. "Let's see if I can't make real life more exciting than fiction."

Chapter Eight

Bertie produced more fried chicken, sweet corn, roasted potatoes, biscuits, apple dumplings and lemonade than Josie had ever seen in one place at one time in the whole of her life.

She had slipped into the kitchen before she and Adam and the girls left for church to see if there was anything she could do to help prepare for the social after services. She could only stare openmouthed at the fare that covered every surface.

"We'll be ready for you," Bertie said briskly, though she did add a very small smile.

The woman was close, Josie suspected, to offering friendship. She was careful to do nothing that would make her retreat.

"There's enough here to feed all of California," Josie said in wonder.

Bertie shook her head as she whipped a bright yellow mixture in a bowl. Josie noted that the platter beside her held four or five dozen halved eggs, yolks missing. "My cooking never goes begging."

"I'm well aware of that. Is there nothing I can do before we leave?"

"Nothing," Bertie insisted, then added belatedly, "thank you."

The girls, excited about the party, were a handful in church. Adam finally pulled Lucy firmly into his lap to prevent her crawling under the pew in front of them after Winifred, whom she'd dropped for the fourth time.

Josie retrieved the doll and placed it beside her atop her pocketbook. Jane kicked absently at the pew support as the minister preached about the dangers of women abandoning their homes in search of a place in trade or government. Josie put a hand to her knee to stop her. With a sigh of boredom, Jane pulled at her hat.

Josie readjusted it, then gave her a supportive smile to assure her that the ordeal of stillness would soon be over and she could spend the rest of the day in wild play. She imagined that Paleolithic mothers had probably done the same thing around their tribal fires. The task of keeping fidgety children happy while confined was as old as time.

Josie looked up to find Adam watching her, his eyes warm and mysterious, questioning while still filled with a ready acceptance that went straight to the heart of her. Finally quiet, Lucy had ripped off her hat and rested her dark head against his shoulder. Josie found that easy to understand. There was something very solid and comforting about that particular spot.

She turned her attention to the minister, sure if she indulged that thought it would lead her onto a path of thoughts unsuitable for the inside of a church.

"Mrs. Scofield," the minister said warmly as he shook her hand after the service. "I'm so happy to meet you and to know that you've brought a woman's warmth and gentility back to Adam's life."

Josie smiled acceptance of his praise, knowing it was fraudulent to do so but knowing also that her role required it. If she'd brought anything to Adam's life it was heat, not warmth, and a certain challenge to his domestic situation that could never be mistaken for decorum.

Lucy wrapped her arms around her hips. "She's our mama now."

The minister looked pleased with the child's approval. Josie blessed it for its confirmation of all the minister believed to be true.

Jane beamed. Adam smiled on all of them with gentle indulgence.

"Prudence and I and the children will be along as soon as I get the flock on their way—" the minister raised his arms to indicate the formal robe he wore "—and as soon as I can get changed into something more suitable for playing baseball."

Adam made several quick introductions as they wended their way through the throng of families and carriages in the churchyard. Josie was embraced by women, bowed to by men and generally made to feel welcome.

She let herself enjoy the sensation without giving any thought to guilt, because this acceptance was something she'd never experienced in Jerusha's home. Though she'd had Benjamin's unquestioned love and his brother Daniel's offhanded acceptance, she'd never known that all-enveloping love many of her friends had enjoyed, that sense that whatever happened, loved ones would gather around you to support you and keep you safe.

"You ate worms before we came to church, didn't you?" Adam asked as he lifted Lucy into the carriage for the impatiently awaited return home.

"No," she replied seriously, apparently not considering that an unusual question.

He put Jane up beside her. "Then why were you so wiggly?"

She held up her rag doll. "Winifred was kicking me."

"Well, if Winifred is going to one day live in a palace with you," he said, absently reaching for Josie and swinging her up into the carriage, too, "then she's going to have to learn that ladies are very quiet and sit very still in church and at court.''

''At court?'' Lucy repeated with obvious confusion. ''You mean where the judge is?''

Adam, his elbow leaning on the edge of the carriage seat, looked into Lucy's eyes with a barely concealed smile. ''No. I mean when the queen and the princess have all their friends to visit them in the palace, that's called court, too. You'll have to behave like a lady then.''

Lucy puzzled over that, then shrugged and smiled. ''Then I won't marry a prince. I'll marry a lawyer, like you. Because Mama doesn't have to act like a lady.''

Adam swung his gaze to Josie, who looked up at the sky, pretending interest in the flight of a wood duck.

''Mama doesn't act like a lady?''

Josie turned to warn her with a glance, and Jane elbowed her in the ribs. But subtlety was lost on Lucy.

''No,'' she said, eyes wide as she leaned across the front seat to reveal what she knew. ''She can throw beans in the air and catch them in her mouth. She got in trouble yesterday because she was wrestling under the kitchen table with Muffin. And the day before, she mucked out the stalls when Amos got hurt.''

Adam frowned at Josie. ''Amos was hurt?''

''He cut his hand open trying to fix the broken window in the carriage house,'' she said, trying to honor Amos's insistence that Mr. Scofield had enough on his mind without worrying about the smooth running of his household. ''I didn't think he should do such a dirty job with a fresh injury, and I've done it before.''

It wasn't until the words were out of her mouth that she realized her mistake.

Adam raised an eyebrow and inquired in disbelief, ''On Beacon Hill in Boston?''

She laughed softly, groping for an excuse. ''It was a kind of...'' She laughed when nothing came to mind. ''A kind of... entertainment," she said finally, knowing she would now have to explain. "You know. A welcome relief from cotillions and bicycling and croquet."

She was relieved that he seemed to be accepting the lie. He was confused by it, but she knew he was confused by many things about her. But she felt sure he wouldn't question her further. He was probably waiting for the day she would confide in him about all her well-kept secrets.

That thought stabbed her with guilt and sadness, but she dismissed it. It was far too beautiful a morning, and he was climbing onto the seat beside her, his strong thigh and shoulder touching hers, his eyes going over her with that possessive gleam she now found herself looking for.

"Can you truly toss a bean in the air and catch it in your mouth?" he asked.

"Every time," she boasted.

"You won't do that this afternoon, will you?"

She pretended to consider, then conceded finally, "I might be persuaded not to flaunt my skill for the right price."

He glanced down at her as he adjusted the brim of his hat. In the shadow his eyes were turbulent with humor and danger.

"Would a kiss guarantee your decorous behavior?"

There were moments, she thought, when she would do almost anything to have him take her in his arms.

"Only one?" she asked in a tone that suggested the guarantee he wanted was in jeopardy.

"One now," he bargained, "one when the last guest is gone."

She needed only a moment to think about it. "Agreed."

He swept off his hat to avoid conflict with the brim of hers and gave her one long and simple kiss. Except she had learned that nothing was simple with him. Probably because the girls were only inches away from them, and because the churchyard was still filled with people, he did nothing to deepen the kiss and kept his hands on the reins.

But passion stirred and rose in Josie. She was becoming concerned that even the smallest contact with him made her lustful and greedy for more. Already she found herself hoping that when it was time to collect her second kiss, they would be alone.

Either Josie was a consummate actress, Adam thought as he stood in a group that included Miles, George Burton and Pastor Knox and watched Josie talk and laugh with several women, or she was beginning to feel like his wife and the mother of his children.

He could not fault her behavior this afternoon. She was warm and charming and seemed genuinely anxious to become acquainted with everyone present. She saw to their comfort and entertainment with a graciousness worthy of her Boston heritage and California hospitality.

She played with the children, drew the shy ones into games with Jane, who'd apparently been told to keep a watchful eye on them, and still managed to keep a rein on Lucy. He was impressed.

She'd even greeted Betsy Fulton with courtesy when she'd arrived just after lunch. He'd been surprised that Betsy made an appearance after the other night, but it soon became clear why she'd come. At her side was a handsome, elegantly dressed young man whom she introduced as Clayton Brown, a family friend from Red Bluff who was visiting with his father. Adam noted, though, that Brown seemed more interested in the buffet table than in Betsy.

She searched the crowd with avid eyes, then spotted Miles. She left her beau to join Miles where he stood with George Burton's three daughters.

Adam saw her loop her arm into Miles's and try to draw him away. He resisted with a smile and a gesture that indicated his absorption in his conversation with the Burton girls. She tugged on him again, and he shook his head again. Then she walked away, her chin high. She stopped near the buffet table and looked around, probably for her escort, whom Adam had seen walk off into the trees behind the barn. When she didn't find him, she picked up a plate and began to fill it.

Bertie and Ivy brought out more lemonade and punch and another platter of fried chicken and more biscuits. But the amount of food being consumed didn't seem to lessen the sounds of cheerful conversation.

Adam was distracted from his perusal of his guests by Reverend Knox. "She's a lovely addition to Yreka society," he said, pointing to Josie as she cradled someone's newborn baby. "Oh-oh, Adam. Look at that. You might be facing sleepless nights again soon."

Adam watched her hold the baby to her, rocking gently from side to side, the smile on her face turning slowly to a frown that seemed to indicate pain. No one else noticed, he felt sure. But he knew every nuance in her expression. He didn't understand what had prompted it, but he knew what it meant. A sudden pall had slipped over her cheerful party demeanor.

Then a familiar, shrill scream split the air, and he turned with everyone else within earshot, knowing the cry was Jane's. She'd apparently sailed off the swing in the oak tree and fallen.

Josie was there before he could reach her, investigating the long tear in Jane's stocking that revealed an angry scrape.

"I... think I'm all right." Jane sniffed back tears. She wiggled her foot experimentally. Adam noted with relief that it moved well and that she had color in her cheeks.

He lifted her to her feet and she took a careful step. "Want me to carry you inside?" he asked.

She gave him a look of mortification. "No, Papa. I just have to change my stockings."

"I'll help her inside," Josie said, that same pinched expression of a moment ago on her pale face. It was obvious she, too, needed momentary escape. "I'll put some witch hazel on it and a bandage and she'll be fine. Come on, Jane. Lean on me."

Arm in arm, Josie leaning to accommodate Jane's lesser height, they headed for the back door to the kitchen. Adam watched them go, grateful for the resilience of children, wishing that whatever was upsetting Josie could be daubed away with witch hazel.

Josie told herself she should have known better than to hold the baby. Had she expected that the infant smiling at her with pink gums *wouldn't* bring to mind her own children and revive the desperation to find them that lived in the shadows of her awareness every single day?

"Josie, you're going too fast," Jane complained as they reached the back porch.

"I'm sorry, Jane." Josie guided her slowly up the few steps, then held the door open for her.

She heard the harsh whisper of protest immediately. "Mr. Brown, please! Stop!" There was the sound of a piece of crockery breaking.

She propped Jane against Bertie's chair-ladder and rounded the corner to investigate. She found Ivy cornered by the young man who'd arrived with Betsy. He had one arm around her and, with the other, had pulled down her hair. His large hand was clenching in it and he was leaning over her in an attempt to kiss lips that were desperately dodging him.

"Stop that at once!" Josie ordered as she stormed toward him.

He glanced at her over his shoulder. He was very blond and very handsome and completely unimpressed with her intervention.

Josie reached out to pull on his arm. He swept her off with a shove into the cupboard.

"This young lady has no respect," he said, turning his attention back to Ivy. "And she has to learn that I won't be dismissed by a little housemaid."

There was scorn in the slightly slurred words. Josie assessed the situation as the result of whiskey hidden somewhere on his person, coupled with an unhealthy dose of self-importance.

She turned to Bertie's rack of pots and pans and found that all of them had been pressed into service for the social. Her eyes roved the worktable for a weapon and rested on a two-pronged serving fork with a long handle. She took it and poked him in the back with it. He turned, his bleary eyes taking on a new gleam of interest.

He came toward Josie, who backed away. She stopped when she felt the cupboard behind her, wondering if she would be able to use this ugly weapon if she had to.

She held him at bay with it, levelling it at his broad, flat stomach as he tried to close the last few inches between them.

"You will get out of this kitchen now," she said, consciously trying to use the tone Adam used when forcing his will on someone.

He made a grab for the fork, but Josie jabbed at him and he withdrew, interest turning to anger. Josie now understood this confrontation was turning dangerous. She squared her shoulders and tried to will the tremor out of her voice.

"You will leave now," she said again, "or you will be on display at the next county fair as the only man with three navels." She waved the two-pronged fork at his middle as proof that she had every intention of turning him into an oddity.

"I don't believe you would do that," he said, his arms away from his body, his hands flexed for action. "A genteel lady like yourself. Betsy's told me all about you."

He seemed to surface from the cloud of drunkenness sufficiently to focus his attention on her with a sudden clarity in his eyes she knew meant trouble.

"Trust me," she warned, keeping her eyes on his hands, "when I tell you it's simply a veneer."

He swung the hand opposite the fork at her, and when she moved the weapon across to strike at him, his free hand caught hers and squeezed.

For an instant, pain blinded her as he seemed perfectly willing to crush her hand.

She kicked at him, then an arm shot past her cheek from behind her and a fist slammed into the young man's face. For a moment he simply stood there looking stunned, his hands falling from Josie's wrists. Then his eyes rolled back and slowly closed, and he crumpled to the floor with a groaning expulsion of air.

"He was trying to kiss Ivy!" Jane said for the third time since she'd found her father playing horseshoes and dragged him to the house. "She didn't want him to. Mama told him to stop, but he wouldn't listen. She told him she was gonna give him three navels!" She looked up at her father with a wrinkled brow. "What are navels?"

Adam ignored her and turned Josie to him. "Are you all right?"

She nodded, unable, for the moment, to find her voice.

Miles, who'd followed him into the house, went to Ivy. She still stood in the corner, her torn dress held modestly to her shoulder. He pulled her out of the corner and sat her on a bench, then put his coat around her.

The room was suddenly filled with people, Bertie and Amos going to their daughter, Betsy kneeling over her escort with a gasp of dismay, Reverend Knox looking in to see if he was needed.

"What happened?" Adam demanded of Josie.

"Precisely what Jane said." Her voice trembled and she swallowed in an effort to steady it. "He had cornered Ivy, who was trying to fight off his attentions. When I tried to pull him away and he ignored me, I threatened him with the fork."

"You!" Betsy said, rising to her feet in a cloud of blue-and-white gingham fury. "You think you can dictate everyone's behavior. Well, let me tell you—"

"Betsy..." Adam spoke calmly as he held her way away from Josie with one hand on her arm. "Your friend is drunk and tried to force himself on Ivy. I think you'd better take him home."

Betsy digested that information in obvious embarrassment, then turned on Ivy. "That's what happens when you flaunt yourself in front of all the eligible and wealthy young men, trying to marry your way out—"

"Don't say anymore, Betsy," Adam warned, his glance at Bertie stopping her when she would have advanced on the young woman. "I'll get someone to drive you home. Miles, will you help me put Mr. Brown in Betsy's carriage?"

"I'll drive them home," Reverend Knox said as Adam took the inert head and shoulders and Miles the legs. His glance took in the young man being carried out and Betsy following. "Seems I have work to do here."

The party, and the excited relating of details by those who'd seen the altercation to those who hadn't, went on late into the afternoon. Guests began leaving with flattering reluctance close to the dinner hour.

Reverend Knox, who'd returned from his task, shook Adam's hand as Miles helped his wife and children into their wagon.

"Seems you have yourself a handful," Knox said, indicating Josie, who leaned up on tiptoe to hear the reverend's wife describing something with great animation. "You think she would have stabbed him with the fork?"

Adam smiled ruefully. "I've little doubt. Do you think her soul is doomed?"

Knox shook his head. "The Lord is pleased with those who take up their weapons in defense of the defenseless." He clapped Adam on the shoulder. "You might remind her, though, that you're a little better equipped to handle someone of Mr. Brown's size and attitude."

"I'll do that." He'd had every intention of making that clear even before Knox suggested it.

When he'd seen the last guest off, Miles walked him back to the house. "You realize that between us we've probably lost Robert Fulton as a client—I rebuffed his daughter and you broke her beau's nose."

"They both deserve worse."

"I agree. Well, thank you for a most exciting afternoon."

Adam frowned at him as they reached the kitchen door. "Aren't you staying for supper?"

"Well..." Miles shook his head with uncharacteristic uncertainty. "I was able to hang around and enjoy your family when you were a single man like myself. Now that you have a wife I..."

"Don't be absurd. You can keep the children occupied while I educate my wife on the fine points of calling for assistance when in trouble."

"Oh, now don't go shout at the girl for having the courage to..."

Adam stopped, a hand on the doorknob, taking exception to his criticism. "I have no intention of shouting at her. I simply intend to make the point that—"

"You make all your points loudly," Miles interrupted. "In court and at home. I remember you with Maggie. Whenever she frightened you, you shouted. Josie looked a little fragile today, I thought."

Adam had noticed that, as well. He pushed Miles into the kitchen, where the Donovans and his girls were gathered, putting the remnants of the party away and tidying up.

Ivy had changed the torn dress, he noted, and looked quite composed—until she caught a glimpse of Miles, blushed and turned away.

Josie was absent.

"Where's Mama?" he asked Lucy.

"In your room," she replied. "She said she wanted to rest for a little while."

Miles went to help Ivy replace a stack of dishes on a high shelf. Adam saw her give him a smiling glance that spoke volumes. So that was how it was.

"Please set an extra place at dinner for the reprobate Mr. Carver," Adam said to Bertie, "and I think all of you deserve to take tomorrow off. It was a wonderful party."

"Mr. Scofield!" Bertie stopped him at the swinging door and handed him a cup of steaming brown liquid. "Tea for Mrs. Scofield," she said. Her eyes brimmed and she sniffed. "Thank her again for coming to Ivy's defense. And thank *you*. I know Mr. Fulton will likely take his legal business elsewhere after this."

"And he's welcome to do just that."

Adam found Josie lying on her back atop the quilt, an arm across her eyes. She looked so delicate, her breasts so small in the snug bodice of her dress, her flat stomach and thighs all but disappearing in the folds, her stockinged feet almost as small as a child's.

He went to sit beside her, wondering if she was asleep.

"Hello, Adam," she said quietly, her arm still in place over her eyes.

All in all, she thought grimly, it had been a less than fruitful day. She had not seen one child who even remotely resembled her boys, and no one had ever heard of anyone named Gripper. Added to that was a step backward in another direction—that of dutiful wife and social success. She would have liked to die if it wouldn't leave so many details unattended.

"Hello. Bertie sent you a cup of tea."

"Tea?" She lowered her arm and turned her head toward him in interest.

He placed it on the bedside table, then sat her up and held her against him while he propped up her pillows. Then he leaned her back and handed her the cup and saucer.

She took a sip and made a small sound of ecstasy. "This is just what I needed."

"Headache?" he asked.

She smiled at him in self-deprecation. "I'm certain you must have one of your own."

He shook his head in denial. "I feel exceptionally well."

She lowered the saucer to her lap, then carefully placed the cup in it. "I know precisely what you're going to say," she said with a level gaze into his eyes. "So go ahead, by all means. I'm quite prepared."

"Are you?" He braced an arm across her legs and leaned on it. "Then perhaps you should simply tell yourself what I want to say and I'll simply listen to make certain you leave nothing out."

"Very well." She took another sip of tea, then put the cup aside. She folded her hands in her lap and gave him an underbrowed look he could only presume was an imitation of one of his expressions. "Josie, not only have you succeeded in completely disrupting a very pleasant party, but now you've revealed to my daughters—whom you were brought here to teach by your example—and everyone who managed to crowd into the kitchen that you're prepared to fight like a common back-street doxy. You've embarrassed me in front of my friends and my neighbors. I'm appalled."

Josie sighed, retrieved her tea, took another sip, then asked with a pale glance at him, "Wouldn't you say that I've come to know you rather well?"

"I would say," he replied with a steady gaze from which she had to finally look away, "that if that's an indication of how well you've come to know me in nearly two weeks, either I'm too complex for even an intelligent woman to understand, or you're not as bright as you appear."

She returned her gaze to his, half mutinous, half interested.

"Although you're right about my being appalled," he said, setting her off balance once again. His eyes darkened and his jaw firmed. "I'm appalled that you set yourself against a very large man in a drunken and unpredictable state, with the protection of a simple kitchen fork, when I was just a shout away."

"I was occupied," she said defensively. "Ivy was crying, and he had torn her dress..."

"You should have shouted for me before you intervened."

"You arrived in time," she pointed out.

"Because Jane came for me. Thank God she's not paralyzed by a crisis. Brown might have broken your hand."

She subsided, unable to explain that a childhood on the Boston docks had taught her to stand up for herself, that nine years as Jerusha Cross's daughter-in-law had been like attending a class in defending oneself against the strong-willed and selfish, and that two months in jail had taken whatever gentility life with Benjamin had lent her and squashed it like an insect. Curiously, pitted against Clayton Brown, she'd felt on fairly familiar ground.

"It's difficult for me to understand," Adam said, pushing to his feet and pulling off his jacket, "how a gently bred woman from Boston—" he tossed his jacket at a chair and gave her a wry smile "—even one with your quick temper and your dangerous tendency to obey even the most ridiculous impulse—" he yanked off his cravat and came to the bed with the top buttons of his shirt open, leaning a hand against the bedpost and frowning down at her "—can be so ready to travel across a wilderness into the arms of a stranger, be willing to run off in the middle of the night in dangerous and unfamiliar country and not give a second thought to picking up a weapon and taking on a man twice her size. Something about that doesn't fit, Josie.''

She felt the panic bubble up inside her like a sickness that rendered her momentarily helpless.

Adam saw the fear in her eyes, the sudden clutching of her fingers on the quilt, the dangerous tottering of the cup in her lap.

He took it from atop her skirt and put it on the night table. Then he looked into her eyes, trying to determine what might have brought such fear. ''What is it?'' he asked gently. ''What has made a woman who should have been protected all her life so ready to do her own fighting?''

He would understand the desperation that drove her to search for her boys because he loved his daughters so much. It wouldn't be difficult to explain the fear for their safety that tortured her daily, the probably vain hope that whoever had them was tolerant of their childish weaknesses, and the simple misery of missing them that would never allow her to feel whole again until they were found.

But that would involve admitting that she'd lied to him, explaining that she'd done so because she'd been in prison and he would never have accepted her with that knowledge, telling him plainly that she'd married him to use him and his family as a way to retrieve her own.

Adam watched emotion roil in her eyes. He sat beside her and took hold of her arms in an earnest bid to reach past whatever it was that kept them always too far apart to connect completely.

He shook her gently. ''Tell me,'' he demanded.

The only explanation for her behavior that would present itself was the only truth she'd shared with him when she'd answered his letter.

"I fight for myself," she said, with a shrug that suggested it should be obvious to him, "because my husband is gone."

She saw the lines of his jaw harden, saw the tenderness go out of his eyes and a dark purpose replace it. Then she realized what she'd said.

His grip on her became painful. "I am not gone," he said, shaking her. "Boston is thirty-three hundred miles away, and *Benjamin* is gone. But your name is Scofield now and *I* am your husband. I'm very much alive, I assure you."

"Adam..." She wanted to explain that she hadn't meant to suggest she'd in any way forgotten her new marriage in memories of her previous one. But his hands were already under her skirt, yanking slips and bloomers down.

He forestalled her explanation with a shake of his head.

"Please don't offer excuses," he said, sending the foaming ruffles over the side of the bed. He pulled off his shirt and his boots. "I'm to blame. In an effort not to bruise the secrets you hold so closely, I haven't taken possession of you as I should have."

"Haven't taken...?" she gasped, trying to brace herself on her hands and sit up.

He aborted the action neatly with one hand trapping both her ankles and yanking her down again.

My God, she thought as he kicked his trousers aside, he'd already diluted her concentration so that feelings for him and his children lived right beside her desperation to find *her* children. She could not afford to be possessed any more completely; her task was impossible as it was.

Now naked and aroused, he drew her ankles apart and made a place for himself between her legs. He lowered himself down to her, placing himself at the gate of her femininity, that dark velvet place that suddenly represented to him the haven for all her secrets.

"You're my woman, Josie Scofield," he said, his lips against her ear as he cupped his arms under her and fitted her to him. "My wife. You won't forget again, I promise you."

Josie felt him against her, hot and hard and as immodest as the man himself. Her body tightened instinctively against him as did her spirit, as though to shout, "No, no! I can't admit you any farther! You confound me and distract me and make me feel things too difficult to contend with at this moment."

But he stroked her back and her bottom with that insidious skill that was at once both fiercely possessive and unspeakably tender—and made her forget the danger he presented and remember only the physical and spiritual wonder of making love with him.

Her knees bent up of their own accord to ease his entry, and she stopped trying to push against him and instead pulled him closer.

He entered with a swift and graceful thrust and she felt him fill her body, her being, her thoughts—so that, for the moment at least, there was room inside her for nothing but Adam.

Chapter Nine

"Athena Prescott is with child again," Milly Forsythe said, glancing up from her embroidery, dark brown eyes roving the room with an eyebrow raised. The dozen women gathered in a circle in Julia Burton's living room on Monday nodded knowledgeably as though that raised eyebrow indicated something each of them understood.

"Joshua Prescott is a drunkard," Julia explained quietly to Josie, who was seated beside her on the oak and silk brocade settee. "She has six little ones already under seven years old. Scrubs floors and takes in laundry to feed them. Joshua works at the mill but spends it all at Duenkel's Saloon."

"Is her family nearby?" Josie asked.

Julia nodded. "But her mother's in the same state as Attie."

Josie pretended to study the pathetic little blue flower that was all she'd accomplished in more than an hour of trying to imitate Julia's stitches. But her failure was due to more than lack of skill. She listened eagerly to all the women's boasts and tales of their children, hoping to hear something that would give her a clue about her own. With half her concentration on the conversation, the other half was insufficient to support her paltry efforts at needlework.

"Not much of a needlewoman, are you?" Julia finally asked bluntly but without malice. She was a plainspoken woman, Josie had learned, but as kind as the day was long.

Josie laughed and tucked her needle into the edge of the fabric outside the hoop.

"I'm afraid I spent my spare time reading novels."

Julia's eyes brightened and she leaned toward her conspiratorially. "Have you read *Captives of the Wild Frontier?*"

Josie shook her head.

"I'll lend it to you. And I have a few *Lippincott's* magazines."

"Oh. I love the short stories!" Josie whispered. "I used to read the housekeeper's copies at home in Boston."

"What are you two whispering about?" Milly asked. "If Josie's telling tales on her handsome husband, then we all wish to hear."

"We do." Susan Elliott, whose husband Josie had met at the Yreka *Journal,* looked up from the most beautiful black-and-white work being applied to the hem of a dress. "Perhaps we can set him up as an example to spur our husbands to be as considerate of us as he is of you...." She looked around the room knowingly. "To be as fearless as he is about being affectionate in public."

The women laughed and *aahed* their approval, probably remembering that kiss in the carriage in the churchyard. Josie was surprised to find herself blushing.

"Now tell us the truth," Milly challenged. "What brought you over three thousand miles into the household of a man you'd never seen before?"

The oldest woman among them, a short, round woman Josie guessed to be in her late fifties, passed a scolding glance around the room.

"That's none of our business, ladies."

While some agreed with her, Milly and several other women leaned forward eagerly, their needlework put aside.

"We aren't requiring intimate secrets, Nan," Milly spoke for them. "I suppose we're just a little envious of her courage and would like to know what prompted it."

As that sounded reasonable enough, all the women turned to Josie, awaiting an answer.

She forced a smile and made herself remember that she would skirt trouble if she shared only the single fact she'd shared with Adam.

"I presume you all know this is my second marriage," she said. The ladies nodded.

"My first husband, Benjamin Cross, was considerably older than I and...and passed away last winter. I was alone and...aimless." That sentence held great conviction. The ladies nodded again, sympathetically this time. "When George Burton's letter on Adam's behalf arrived at my attorney's—" she smiled in Julia's direction, and Julia took a little bow as though her husband's part in bringing Josie west entitled her to some small fame, as well "—it seemed like an answer to prayer." That also sounded sincere, because it was. "Enclosed was Adam's photograph."

She hesitated a moment, recalling that at the time she'd thought his good looks just a little dangerous. She experienced a blush at the knowledge of just how intuitive she'd been. Her body still ached, though pleasantly, from his reminder last night that she was his.

The women read her blush and put the proper if not detailed construction on it.

Nan laughed wickedly. "So he is as wonderful as he looks."

There was laughter again, and Josie, thinking she'd committed enough lies of omission in front of these kind-hearted women, answered with complete sincerity, "Oh, yes he is."

Shrieks and laughter followed, then Julia served coffee and nut cakes with frosting. While they ate, Josie overheard Milly and Nan discussing other newcomers to Yreka.

"Unfortunately," Nan said with a shake of her head as she speared the last bit of nut cake with her fork, "we're getting our share of undesirables as well as good citizens. I saw a man at King's store the other day that I'd have liked to take a horsewhip to. All he did was shout at his wife and children, two beautiful boys apparently so worn down by his verbal abuse that they kept their heads down. All I could see of them were their red flannel yacht caps, probably acquired from some charity barrel somewhere." She shook her head pityingly, then sipped her coffee. "Poor tykes. Those hats were the only things about them that weren't thread-bare."

Josie's heart lurched. She sloshed tea over her skirt, then smiled an embarrassed apology at Julia, who ran to the kitchen for a towel. Josie listened with what she hoped appeared to be simple casual interest.

"I know just who you mean," Milly said. "They're rude and dirty. Not from around here as far as anyone seems to know."

Josie thanked Julia for the towel and mopped at her skirt, looking up to ask casually, "Where do they live?"

Nan pointed vaguely in a westerly direction. "A few miles out of town—in the canyon, according to Mr. King. I believe their name is Jones. They don't seem to have much."

Josie's brain turned in hectic circles, examining all the details that seemed to be fitting into place. As the women discussed the interesting matter of the Joneses, Josie concluded that the name could very likely be one taken by a couple on the run. They were new to the area, no one local knew of them, and they had two small boys. Add to that the fact that she and Benjamin had given Charles and Billy red yachting caps for Christmas, caps they loved and wore all the time—and they were missing from the boys' wardrobes—and Josie felt sure she had her first serious clue to the whereabouts of her children. She wanted to scream with excitement and run out of the house in the direction Nan had pointed until she found them.

Prudence Knox suggested they gather food and blankets to be taken to the Joneses. "Even if the man is ungodly, we must think of the woman and the children."

"I think that's a splendid idea," Josie said, pleased that her voice sounded far less frantic than she felt. "I'd like to volunteer to take the things to them."

"Oh, no." Julia shook her head in horror and all the ladies supported her with grim expressions. "Our husbands will see to the delivery of our food and blankets. The canyon is not a safe place."

Josie forced herself to nod and smile at Julia's well-meaning decree. The rest of the afternoon was interminable. She pretended to work on her embroidery but succeeded in adding only one pathetic leaf to the very sad flower.

Josie mentioned the meeting to Adam that evening. They sat together in the parlor, the girls in bed, the Donovans retired to their wing of the house.

"We're gathering food and blankets to take to the poor family," she said. She tugged on a length of white thread as she replaced a button Lucy had torn from an old dress she wore to play outside.

"Good Christian charity," Adam said with a grinning glance at her as he studied a folder of papers in his lap. "It's time you learned how that was done."

"Aren't we amusing this evening," she teased, trying desperately to keep any suggestion of urgency out of her tone and manner. "To show you how eager I am to learn to be charitable, I suggested that I take the things out to the family."

He looked up with an expression she'd grown used to in the past several weeks. It said "no" as clearly as though he'd spoken the word.

"There are diggings between here and the other side of the canyon."

"Then you could accompany me."

He shook his head. "Reverend Knox always takes care of those things. Sometimes Peter Elliott accompanies him to report it in the *Journal*." He smiled. "It's diligent of you, Josie, but quite unnecessary."

She dropped the subject rather than risk his suspicions by insisting. She concentrated on the button with an intensity that drove the tip of her needle so far into her finger that it stuck.

She gasped and quickly moved the dress away as blood puddled and dropped off her finger. She pinched the needle to remove it and gasped as it stuck fast.

Adam leaned over her, held the pierced hand in one of his, then removed the needle with a firm pull. As blood spurted from it, he pulled her to her feet and took her into the kitchen. He pumped water into the deep sink and washed her finger until the bleeding stopped.

He dried it with a towel, then brought witch hazel from a cupboard at the back of the room and dabbed it on.

"I suggest you abandon needlework in favor of your novels," he said with an indulgent smile. "You left the work you did at Julia's this afternoon on the bed and frankly, Josie, I think we can safely conclude it isn't one of your inherent skills."

The pain of the needle had served as a sort of safety valve, and she was able to tear her mind from the possibility that her children were only several miles away and behave in a somewhat normal manner. Except that she felt the hum of excitement under her skin.

"I was simply trying to round out my accomplishments. Jane is determined to teach me. She gave me a lesson before she went to bed last night so I wouldn't completely humiliate myself this afternoon."

Adam felt her frantic pulse when he placed a hand to the side of her face, concerned with the flush of color there. Her words and her movements were urgent and quick, like Muffin on the attack.

"Are you feeling ill?" he asked.

"Not at all," she denied quickly, wishing he were less discerning and more like George Burton, who, Julia had confided, would not notice if she came home a foot taller and with her bustle in the front. "I've been going strong since early this morning, what with helping Amos retrieve Lucy from the barn roof and all that needlework and gossip this afternoon. I'm just ... restless, I suppose."

"Amos told me about that when I arrived home." He took her hand and led the way through the dining room and the parlor, snatching a crocheted blanket from the back of the davenport before taking her out to the veranda.

"The child takes after her mother. Maggie could climb trees like a boy."

Josie sighed as she went to the railing that in daytime looked onto the lawn that rolled down to a stream, then to the pasture that stretched to the orchard. Though she couldn't see it in the darkness, the sweet fragrance of the apple trees wafted toward her. She found her tension easing into the simple restlessness she'd fibbed about only a moment ago.

"I'm afraid my physical accomplishments are no more impressive than my embroidery."

His arms wrapped around her, warm and strong in the chilly darkness. "Oh, I can think of one physical skill in which you excel."

She leaned back against him, needing his solidity for balance on this moody evening. But that was all she could take from him right now. Her boys were out there somewhere. She could feel it. And they were all she could think about.

Adam thought it curious that he was able to sense her withdrawal while still feeling her lean her weight against him of her own accord for the first time in their acquaintance. It was as though she unconsciously summoned him closer for support, while telling him without words to intrude no further.

He would play the game for a while. He had no idea as to the nature of the contest—only that they seemed usually to be on opposite sides. Except for the moment, when they'd somehow met in the middle like friendly adversaries shaking hands.

He put the blanket over her shoulders and pulled her back to the wooden settee against the front window, sitting in a corner of it and pulling her into his lap.

"Try to relax," he said, resting an arm comfortably over her hip and tugging her closer. "You won't be able to sleep tonight if you don't settle down."

Josie didn't even attempt to struggle. His arms enclosed her in a comforting embrace that unknotted her tight muscles and eased the tension that had gripped her since the moment Nan had mentioned the boys.

She lifted one arm from under the blanket and wrapped it around his neck. "Oh, Adam," she said on a sighing little whisper.

To Adam's ear, the sound was filled with the mystery of this woman. Though the two simple words seemed to express some deep feeling on her part, they required no comment on his. As was becoming his habit with her, it was a communication he didn't understand but stored way, confident the day would come when he would put them all together and finally understand her secrets.

Until then, he simply held her closer, leaning his cheek against hers as she sighed sleepily and burrowed her nose in his neck. For now, at least, he was willing to wait.

Josie's opportunity to go in search of the Joneses came the following day while Jane was at school and Ivy took Lucy with her to town on an errand for Bertie.

"Where are you planning to take him, Mrs. Scofield?" Amos asked with a mild frown as he saddled the gentle black for Josie.

"Just for a little exercise," she replied with a bright smile that she hoped concealed the heartbeat that was about to choke her. She added with wide, guileless eyes, "Mr. Scofield told me I could ride Blackie whenever I chose."

"He told *me*," Amos corrected courteously, "that I was to accompany you if you wanted to leave the property."

"Amos." The horse was saddled and Josie took the reins in her left hand as they'd taught her at the Bayside Riding Academy, reached for the pommel, then waited expectantly for Amos to lend her a hand up. "What danger could I possibly encounter on a ride around the orchard?"

He studied her one more moment, during which she continued to smile while certain she would blurt out everything if he didn't comply, then he cupped his hands around her foot and boosted her up into the saddle.

"No farther than the creek, Mrs. Scofield," he warned.

She smiled winningly at him and kicked lightly at Blackie's flanks. "Thank you, Amos," she called as she and the horse galloped off across the yard. She was certain theological scholars might not agree with her, but as far as she was concerned, a lie of omission was not a lie. And she'd worded everything carefully. She *would* be riding around the orchard—and beyond it. And her reply to Amos's caution about crossing the creek had been a noncommittal thank-you.

The first few minutes of Josie's ride were spent trying desperately to remember everything she'd learned about riding astride a confoundedly uncomfortable animal. Hands loose, knees tight, back straight, eyes ahead.

She gained confidence as they went down into the stream and rose up the other side with her backside still firmly in the saddle. Excitement gradually began to replace trepidation and she found herself urging Blackie a little faster.

She passed the cornfields and the pasture dotted with cattle. Then she spotted the apple orchard rippling over a hillside, white blossoms catching the sun and looking as though some clever alchemist had learned to grow silver.

She remembered Adam's insistence that she not leave the property and heard Amos's voice still ringing in her ears. "No farther than the creek, Mrs. Scofield."

She put both men's warnings aside without a qualm. In her exhilaration at being finally on a trail she felt sure would lead her to Charlie and Billy, she was certain her husband would not learn what she'd done until he could no longer do anything about it.

If she found the boys, she would make her way straight back to Kilkenny's and then home to Boston. If she didn't find the Joneses' cabin in a reasonable amount of time, she would return home to be there smiling and changed for dinner when Adam walked in the door. Either way, she wouldn't lose.

Her conscience throbbed for a moment as she considered how the girls would feel if she did find her boys and failed to come home. Tears pricked her eyes at the thought as she cleared the orchard and reined Blackie in on the banks of the creek.

She sat taller in the saddle as she forced that thought aside, too. Adam would simply have to deal with it. God knew she'd tried often enough during those first few days to make him understand that she couldn't stay. But he'd insisted on having things his way.

She would wire him from Sacramento and explain. Yes.

She waited for that decision to expiate her guilt. When it didn't, and her mind created, instead, an image of Lucy wondering where "Mama" was, she kicked Blackie's flanks and urged him across the creek.

Josie thought it might be her imagination, given Adam's and Amos's warnings, but the other side of the creek did seem to be a sudden change in environment. After a mile or so the grass thinned and the ground became rocky and steep. Vegetation was sparse. Then she saw the mouth of the canyon yawning wide with sharp, granite teeth. She reined in again and stroked Blackie's neck.

She remembered when she and Adam had stopped to picnic and she'd heard the primitive screech of a mountain lion. A little ripple of fear ran up her spine now at the realization that it was in there, somewhere.

But she was sure Charlie and Billy were on the other side, and she hadn't the time to go around, if, indeed, that could be done.

"Well, Blackie," she said, leaning over him to stroke his head. "I'm counting on you to get us through this. You won't take fright at the cry of what's nothing more than a distant cousin of Muffin's, will you?"

Blackie proved instantly that he was not at all worthy of her confidence. A covey of quail burst out of a dry thicket as she urged the horse forward. They filled the air around them with the rapid flutter of wings in startled flight.

Blackie reared in alarm, tossing Josie through the air like one of the birds.

Josie landed on her back with a vicious thud. Even before she became aware that the wind had been knocked out of her and she couldn't breathe, she was aware that her trusted steed had bolted for home. As she gasped for air, her mind screamed, "No! No! No! Only two or three more miles. No!"

As breath eased back into her lungs, she sat up gingerly, every muscle in her body feeling as though it had been kicked. She rose to her feet with a groan, straightened, rotated her arms and shoulders and was relieved to find that everything seemed to be intact.

Then the realization dawned on her that she would never make it home on foot before Adam arrived home for dinner.

For a moment she considered walking through the canyon in search of the Joneses but knew that was too foolish even for her. The cabin could be anywhere in either direction, and without a horse she simply couldn't follow all the possibilities. And she didn't want to blunder around in the dark and perhaps end up like her Pinkerton man.

She turned in the direction of home, trying to shake off the crushing disappointment. She would simply try again at the earliest opportunity. It had taken this long to come this far. She could be patient one or two more days. Well, she couldn't but she had no other choice.

She was crossing the grassy meadow on the far side of the creek when Miles rounded the bend on the dusty road that led to town.

He reigned his frisky bay to a stop and stared at her in mute surprise for a moment.

"Good afternoon," she said cheerfully, brushing at her skirts. "You're a welcome sight."

"Josie," he said finally, leaning out of the saddle to offer her a hand up. "What in the name of Hades are you doing out here?"

"Learning my way around the property," she said, settling her bruised body behind his with a groan. "Blackie was frightened by quail and threw me."

"You're off Adam's property when you leave the orchard," he said over his shoulder as his horse danced sideways, eager to be off. "I thought you knew that. This isn't a safe place for a woman to explore on her own. Adam would not be pleased to learn you had been out here."

"Then if you hurry," she suggested, "we might arrive home before he does. There's no reason to upset him over what was simply a mistake."

Josie knew by his over-the-shoulder glance that he didn't believe her for a moment. Even the children knew that the orchard marked the end of their property—it was highly unlikely that after two weeks in residence in the Scofield

household she didn't know. And he probably knew that
Amos would not have saddled a horse for her without being certain she knew the boundaries.

She could only hope that he put her wanderings down to
nothing more suspect than simple curiosity.

As Josie's fortune was running that day, Adam was in the
yard, still astride the large bay he rode to town and back
every day, when Miles rode up with Josie behind him.
Gathered around Adam were the girls and every one of the
Donovans, and they all seemed to be in a state of agitation.

Then Lucy pointed in her direction. "There's Mama! She
isn't lost!"

Miles reined in right beside Adam, who leapt down and
reached up to swing Josie to her feet, his expression dark
with concern.

"What happened? Amos said Blackie just came back
without you."

"I was learning my way around and a covey of quail
frightened him and he threw me."

"Where were you?"

In a purely feminine tactic, she cuddled both children as
they danced around her and said with a suggestion of hurt
feelings, "I'm fine and seem not to have broken anything,
thank you very much for asking." She smiled up at Miles
with a silent plea not to reveal where he'd found her. "I was
walking home and Miles happened upon me and brought me
back."

Adam looked from Miles to Josie, then back to Miles. "I
thought you went to Hawkinsville today. How did you encounter Josie?"

Josie felt sudden panic. The road to Hawkinsville ran a
considerable distance beyond the orchard.

She prayed that Miles would give Adam a plausible reply, but he remained silent. She understood with a grim
smile at Adam's friend that while he honored her unspoken

plea not to reveal where he'd found her, he wouldn't deliberately lie to Adam.

Horrified to find herself falling back on another feminine wile, she put a hand to her forehead and made a small sound of pain. It helped, she was certain, that her hand trembled of its own accord.

Ivy gasped, Adam swept her up into his arms and carried her inside as Bertie cleared the way.

"Poor thing's probably faint from hunger," Bertie clucked as she followed Adam to the settee in the parlor where he put her down. She knelt beside her and fanned her with her hand. "Ivy, get some water and a cold cloth. Are you sure you aren't hurt, Mrs. Scofield?"

Josie smiled weakly. "I don't think so, Bertie. I jus landed awfully hard when I fell. Everything hurts, but don't believe I've broken anything."

The girls clustered around her and Adam drew them back insisting that Josie felt faint and needed room to breathe.

She smiled at the girls as Bertie propped a pillow behind her head, then placed the cold cloth Ivy brought on her brow. Though abysmally disappointed that she hadn't succeeded in finding the Joneses, she was given a measure of comfort that she was here to assure the girls she was safe an sound. That made no sense, she realized, since she was preparing to leave them again at the first opportunity, but for the moment she chose not to consider that.

"Would you like to rest upstairs?" Bertie asked solicitously. Since the afternoon of the social and Josie's defens of Ivy, Bertie had become Josie's self-proclaimed champion. "I'll bring your supper up."

"Goodness no," Josie said with another smile. Miles who had followed them into the house, would doubtless be invited to dinner, and she didn't want Adam and him talking over the events of the afternoon. "I think I'm fine now and ravenous for your roast. The aroma was already taunting me when I left to ride around the property this afte noon.'' That wasn't a complete lie, she thought. She simply hadn't been specific about *whose* property she'd ridden around.

She sat up with a carefully executed wobble that made Adam reach for her hand. She gave the cloth to Bertie and, with a sigh and smile at everyone gathered around her, tried to prove that she was fit once again.

Bertie and Ivy headed off to the kitchen, and Amos left to tend to Adam's horse.

Miles tossed his hat in his hands. "Well, since you won't be needing someone to ride for the doctor, I'll be on my way."

"No," Adam said, an arm around Josie's shoulders. "Since you've accomplished a gallant rescue, the least we can do is see that you're properly fed."

Miles glanced at Josie, as though expecting her to protest. Instead, she gave him a bright smile. "Please stay, Miles. No one brightens the dinner table like you do."

Miles glanced at Adam, who responded with the questioning arch of an eyebrow. Something passed between them that Josie couldn't read and left her with the uncomfortable feeling that her little theatrics hadn't deceived anyone.

Chapter Ten

"How did everything go in Hawkinsville?" Adam asked Miles. He stood in the doorway of his partner's office, right next to his, and sipped coffee from a tall china cup.

Miles, apparently completely absorbed in the book he consulted, answered absently as he turned a page. "Routine."

"You located Mrs. McGovern?"

"Yes." Miles ran his finger down the page, then turned it and frowned over the next one. "She'll be ready to vouch for our client's sterling character when we go to trial."

"Good. That's good."

"Yes."

Adam waited for Miles to look up at him, but Miles seemed just as determined not to meet his eyes. Adam had to smile. After almost twenty years of friendship—through school, a year in the gold camps and the last twelve years of beginning and maintaining their law practice—he felt he knew Miles almost as well as he knew himself. Miles was hiding something, and Adam suspected it had to do with precisely where he'd encountered Josie the day before.

Adam sat in the client chair facing Miles's desk and stretched his legs out, determined not to be ignored.

"I suppose," he said, "that you made her some chivalrous promise not to tell me where you found her."

Miles shook his head as he turned back a page. "No. She knows you know she lives in Hawkinsville."

Adam rolled his eyes, though Miles did not look up to see the gesture. "I'm speaking of Josie, not Mrs. McGovern."

Miles finally looked up from the book with an air of impatience. "Adam, perhaps you have time to fritter away this afternoon, but I happen to be busy. Has it escaped your notice that I have work to do?"

"Where did you find her?" Adam asked.

"Adam? You-hoo! Miles?" Both men rose as Julia Burton walked through the outer room. They met her at the door to Miles's office.

"Oh dear," she said, looking from one preoccupied expression to the other. "Am I interrupting an important consultation or something?"

Adam leaned down to accept her maternal kiss on the cheek. "Julia, we would suspend jury deliberation to make time for you. What is it?"

Julia moved to Miles, who also received her motherly attentions. "I just need a few moments of your time, Adam," she said, waving a sheaf of papers. "George asked me to bring these to you regarding that parcel of land we're purchasing. I believe he needs you to file them or something." She smiled. "And I want to talk to you about your wife. May I distract him for a few moments, Miles?"

Miles pushed Adam bodily toward her. "Please. He's been a hindrance to me most of the morning. It must be love. I find him very difficult to deal with. Perhaps you will have better luck."

Adam seated Julia on a small settee in his office. He put his cup and the papers aside, then pulled his client chair closer to her and waited for her to begin. Julia was always direct.

"I am *so* happy that you brought Josie Cross west and married her," she said, obviously certain he'd been awaiting her approval on the matter. "Every one of the ladies in our needlework club thinks she's wonderful. And it doesn't hurt your reputation that she blushes when she talks about you."

He tried not to betray surprise—or satisfaction. "She does?"

"Well, Milly Forsythe asked her what made her decide to come west when she'd never seen you before and had no real idea what you'd be like."

He'd wondered that himself more than once and waited for Julia to go on.

"She explained about being widowed, which we all understood. And then..." She hesitated, building dramatic tension. He found the ploy very effective. He wanted to shake the words out of her. "She said she had seen the photograph George enclosed with the letter. And then she blushed so prettily. It was easy to see that she'd fallen in love with the photograph—and that the reality had been anything but a disappointment."

"She said that?"

"Not in so many words. But she made every one of us who loves her husband dearly but wishes he'd remember her existence once in a while besides a Saturday night when he's feeling like a stallion..."

Adam kept a straight face with difficulty. Poor George.

"Well...she made us wish our marriages were new again and our men as in love with us as you are with her." She sighed and stared glassily over that thought for a moment, then went on to add in tones of high praise, "She talked about the girls—about Jane's class visiting the office and about how clever she thinks the child is. Don't be surprised if you find yourself faced with the prospect of sending her away to college one day. And she adores Lucy. You can just see it in her face when she talks about her."

She leaned toward him, her smile slipping just a little. "Your Maggie was such a wonderful young woman. We all adored her. But I wonder if you have any idea how lucky you are to have found a treasure twice in one lifetime? And by mail to boot?"

She stood without waiting for an answer. Adam stood, too, and followed her to the door.

"I know you're not one to live your life according to public opinion," she said. "I just thought you might like to know that your lady is a complete success in Yreka. Maggie left such an empty place, but Josie is filling it beautifully."

He hugged her. "Thank you, Julia. I appreciate all of you making her feel so welcome. She told me how much she enjoyed getting to know all of you."

He opened the door. Julia stepped out onto the boardwalk, then stepped back toward him, her eyes grave.

"One thing," she said.

"What?" he asked warily.

"Her embroidery is a sad thing indeed."

He laughed and nodded. "Jane is helping her with it."

Julia shook her head, apparently convinced that would prove hopeless. "She should stick to her books. In fact, I sent several home with her."

He frowned teasingly at Julia. "Yes. I saw the *Police Gazette* on her bedside table last night. You hoyden. Does George know you read such things?"

She patted his cheek. "I borrow them from him. Good day, Adam."

"Thank you, Julia. Tell George I'll see that the papers are filed first thing in the morning."

Adam closed the door and walked back to his office, feeling a vague relief that Josie had found a comfortable place among the other women of Yreka. Personally, it wouldn't have mattered to him who approved or disapproved of her, but there were times when she seemed so lonely, times when he couldn't seem to touch that sadness in her eyes no matter how near she allowed him physically. He was pleased to know that she was making friends, that there were women she could turn to if she needed understanding he couldn't provide.

He peered into Miles's office and found it empty. He was not surprised. Miles had been singularly determined not to talk about yesterday afternoon.

Adam decided suddenly that where she'd been yesterday didn't matter. She was apparently doing her best to fulfill her part of their marriage. She'd spoiled Lucy, had managed to win over Jane, and then Bertie, and was apparently making him look like a hero among the wives of his friends. He couldn't help the burst of pride that made him feel. He would do something to show her his appreciation.

Adam snatched his jacket off the peg, shrugged into it and went in search of a wise old Chinese gentleman he knew who imported elegant jade jewelry.

Josie accepted the hot water bottle Ivy had wrapped in a towel and placed it on Lucy's stomach. Lucy lay back against her pillow, pale and wan.

"I tried to tell her what would happen!" Jane said with big-sister superiority. "I told her that green apples made *me* retch for a whole afternoon, but *she* said peaches wouldn't do the same thing. Children are so... *childish.*"

"We learn best by our own mistakes," Josie said, fighting the frustration Lucy's sudden attack of indigestion had caused. She'd planned to go off again that afternoon while both girls attended a birthday party at the neighboring farm. She'd felt sure she could travel more quickly on Blackie this time and still be home for dinner if she was unable to find the Joneses.

But Lucy had found a bowl of dried peaches Bertie had put aside to use in making a pie and eaten all of them while she was supposed to be napping.

Josie didn't realize it was dinnertime until Adam walked into the room to lean over her and touch Lucy's face.

She looked up at him, guilt reflected in her eyes.

He shook his head. "Overindulgence, Bertie tells me."

She nodded. "I'm sorry."

He frowned at her. "Why? You didn't force her to eat them, did you?"

"No, but I should have looked in on her." Instead, she added silently, I was planning my search for my own children and ignoring yours.

"She was supposed to be napping. Bertie told me."

"But I..."

For a woman who was usually very calm around the children, she seemed unusually upset. He placed his hands on her shoulders and rubbed gently.

"What child hasn't made him or herself ill with too much of one thing or another? Jane did last summer with green apples. Lucy will be all right. Come on. You need some supper. Ivy said she'll sit with her while you eat."

"But, Adam, I don't want..."

"And I'm telling you you have no choice in the matter. Now, come with me."

Instead of taking her directly downstairs, he pulled her into their bedroom and removed a small white box from his breast pocket. He smiled with an almost shy indulgence as he handed it to her.

Josie stared at it, praying that it wasn't what it appeared to be. Then she looked up at him, trying to withhold any outward sign of the misery she felt. "Adam, what...?"

"A small gift," he said, taking her reluctant hand and placing the box in it. "Just because I wanted to give you something."

"But why?"

"Must I have a reason other than I'm your husband?"

"No. Of course not." Josie looked away from the tenderness in his eyes and opened the box. In it was a gold ring with a pale jade stone set in delicate filigree.

"Oh, Adam." She couldn't help the little sigh of pleasure at something so beautiful.

He took the ring from the box and placed it on her finger atop the simple gold wedding band. Then he placed a kiss there.

"I thought you should have something pretty on your wedding finger as well as something functional—to remind you that we've found a little happiness in each other, even though that isn't why we came together."

Guilt flooded Josie's being, and she leaned her forehead against Adam's shoulder in the hope that he wouldn't read it in her eyes. His arms closed around her like a warm protective shelter. Guilt swelled and she leaned closer, hiding her face and an unsteady bottom lip against him.

"Thank you," she whispered. "It's beautiful."

She felt his lips in her hair and the comforting stroke of his hand up and down her spine.

"I'm glad you like it." He held her for another moment, then straightened away from her at the sound of footsteps in the hall. Ivy passed their open door on her way to sit with Lucy.

Josie pulled herself together and smiled at Adam, hoping she had indeed acquired sufficient skill at this deception that nothing showed in her face but surprise and pleasure at the gift.

He put an arm around her shoulders and led her down to the dining room, thinking that he probably understood her no more clearly than he ever did, but he'd definitely shaken her with the jade ring and he considered that a step forward. It meant the secure little distance she kept between herself and him now remained unguarded. And he was never one to ignore an advantage.

Supper was quiet without Lucy. Jane held forth, enjoying having the stage to herself for once, telling them about school, about the new puppies on the neighboring farm and Mrs. Brady's new bicycle.

After supper, Jane settled down to do schoolwork in the parlor, while Adam excused himself to do an hour's work

in his office. Josie sat in a corner of the settee with one of
the novels Julia had lent her, hoping to put her frustration
at being kept home this afternoon and her growing guilt over
Adam's gift out of her mind.

Jane looked up at the restless fidgeting, gave her a warm
smile and went back to her schoolbooks.

Josie took comfort from the small gesture.

"Mr. Scofield?" Adam looked up from Miles's notes
taken from the McGovern woman in Hawkinsville to find
Amos standing uncertainly in the doorway.

"Yes, Amos?"

"May I speak to you a moment?" Amos asked, looking
distinctly uncomfortable.

Adam pushed the notes aside, accepting that he was ac-
complishing nothing with them anyway. Not only did they
reveal nothing significant, he couldn't concentrate on what
they did tell him. His mind was full of images of his beautiful wife and her wide, tear-filled blue eyes when he'd given
her the ring. He was already planning the gift they would
give each other when they went to bed.

"Of course, Amos." He waved him into the office. "Sit
down."

He noticed in mild surprise that Amos closed the door
behind him. Then with a frown, the man came to occupy the
leather chair beside Adam's desk.

"I'm sorry to interrupt your work."

Adam shook his head. "You're not interrupting. What's
the problem?"

"Well..." Amos, who was usually the epitome of calm
confidence, began several times, then shook his head and
tried yet again. "Sir, I don't want to cause a problem for
Mrs. Scofield, but I want to get your instructions clear. You
told me she was free to ride around the property."

"That's right."

"But if she left the property, I was to go along."

"Yes."

"Well . . ."

Adam leaned back in his chair and felt his nerves tighten. He could see the nature of the problem Amos was so reluctant to divulge.

"You suspect she left the property the day she took Blackie?"

"I'm sure she did, Mr. Scofield. I combed cottonwood leaves out of Blackie's tail. She had to have gone as far as the creek near the canyon to pick up cottonwood. I'm sure she just made a mistake, wasn't sure where she was going. I warned her not to leave the orchard when I saddled up for her, but she might have gotten confused. She's such a kind, accommodating lady, I don't think she'd have deliberately disobeyed you."

Adam managed not to react to that suggestion. For all Bertie's control over the details of the Donovans' lives, Adam knew that when big decisions were made, Amos Donovan considered his word law and Bertie complied. The man was probably certain his employer controlled his own marriage in the same way.

"I'm just concerned about her safety, Mr. Scofield," Adam went on urgently. "If she crossed the creek into the canyon, anything could have happened to her. I thought you might want to know she must be confused about your instructions."

Confused, Adam wondered, anger settling over him, or deliberately defiant? Or simply following through on earlier threats to leave him at the first opportunity? In view of the way she'd behaved earlier this evening when he'd given her the ring, he could only conclude she was trying to ensnare him with her charms so that he'd be oblivious to all signs of her deception. The signs he'd chosen to ignore like some lovesick youth because Julia told him Josie had praised him in front of the ladies.

Disgusted with himself for being so easily swayed, he stood with purpose.

"Thank you, Amos," he said, shaking the man's hand to assure him he understood his motive in bringing the matter up. "I appreciate your concern for Mrs. Scofield. You're absolutely right. As far as you're concerned, my instructions stand. And I'll clarify them to her."

Amos nodded with relief. "Thank you, Mr. Scofield. Good night."

"Good night, Amos."

Josie knew she was in trouble the moment she heard Adam's step in the doorway. She'd spent the past hour certain he would want to make love to her and wondering if she could in all conscience accommodate him after deceiving him and accepting his gift. And, if he insisted, if she would have the character to resist his artful seduction.

But when she looked up with a smile and saw him leaning a shoulder against the doorframe, she could see that making love to her was the furthest thought from his mind. His eyes were angry, his jaw set and his body tense, despite its casual pose.

He beckoned to her. "I'd like to see you in the office for a moment."

He knew! The suspicion rammed into her stomach like a fist. No. He couldn't know. Another quick perusal of his features seemed to confirm the notion that he did. But she'd played the role of well-bred lady so long she could do nothing but follow it through.

She stood with a smile, pretending not to notice the thundercloud on his brow. "Of course. Jane's just gone to bed, and I checked on Lucy and she's sleeping soundly."

He would know that, of course. Ivy also checked them every evening, and had there been the smallest problem she would have reported it instantly. But Josie sailed past his dark presence in the doorway, hoping that little bit of cozy family information would placate him.

When she stood in the middle of his office and turned to face him as he closed the door behind him, she could see that it had not.

He pointed her to the chair and went to take his place behind the desk. With the few feet of his desk all that stood between her and the turbulent anger in his eyes, she maintained a bright innocent expression with difficulty.

"Yes?" she asked. "What is it, Adam?"

He remembered this look from the night he'd found her in John and Felicity's stable, trying to make her escape. Her eyes were wide with that ingenuousness she was so adept at pretending but dark with the secrets she kept. He maintained his own equanimity with care.

"Why did you lie to me?" he asked quietly.

Josie felt the fist slam into her again. She reminded herself to remain calm, to get a true picture of her position before she admitted anything.

"About what?" she asked with a subtle blend of confusion and indignation.

He studied her a moment, his eyes roving the innocent set of features, then settling on her own gaze with an expression that told her he wasn't deceived for a moment. "About where you rode Blackie yesterday."

"You said I could explore the..."

"I said you could explore the property," he interrupted. "Then I told you you could not go beyond it on your own. Amos reminded you of that fact when he saddled Blackie for you."

So that was how he knew. Amos had told him. But how had Amos been sure? She doubted Miles had betrayed her or he'd have done so at the time.

"I...became confused," she said defensively, her cheeks growing pink with temper at the situation in which she found herself, as well as at his autocratic attitude. A situation of her own making, she reminded herself as she demanded, "Is that so unforgivable?"

"Then why didn't you admit at the time that you'd strayed off Scofield land? Why did you involve Miles in your deception? Where did he pick you up?"

She shook her head. "I don't know. I'm not sure where it was. And he didn't lie to you, he simply said nothing."

"Out of a misguided sense of chivalry, no doubt."

"No doubt," she agreed. "I imagine he knew you'd react in this way and tried to spare me this interrogation."

"Josie." He leaned toward her across his desk just as she strained toward him in frustration and indignation. "I told you what your boundaries were and I have no reason to believe you didn't understand me."

Josie folded her arms and glared at him, determined to fight the constriction he seemed just as determined to place around her. "I'm your wife, Adam, not your child. I don't have to memorize your edicts as though they were handed down from God, Himself."

It was all he could do to maintain a reasonable frame of mind. Violence flowed through him as he considered what might have happened to her in the canyon, and how her attitude might still leave her vulnerable to the possibilities if he didn't take a clear stand.

"This is not Boston, Josie," he said in a firm and quiet voice. "This is the Siskiyou Mountains. Yreka is warm and hospitable, but outside of town, particularly beyond the creek, are dangers you would not begin to be able to deal with. I told you to stay this side of the orchard, yet Amos found cottonwood leaves in Blackie's tail. That means you went at least as far as the creek."

So that was how Amos knew. It seemed everyone with whom she came into contact had all the investigative qualities of a Pinkerton man. Except *her* Pinkerton man, who had all the qualities of an invalid.

Faced with irrefutable evidence of her misdeed, Josie used the only defense left to her. "You did not say I couldn't go beyond the orchard."

"I most certainly..."

"You said you *preferred* that I don't go beyond the orchard," she corrected. "That's not the same thing at all."

When she saw his eyes react to her words, she acknowledged what she already suspected. It had been a paltry defense—and one that only served to intensify his anger.

She remained absolutely still as he came around the desk. The tension emanating from him suggested his temper was being controlled by a thread and the wrong word or move would snap it. Her heart was pounding, her mouth dry, but she looked him in the eye, knowing he watched her for one betraying glimpse of fear.

He sat on the edge of his desk, propping his foot up on the seat of the chair she occupied.

"That's a point well taken," he said mildly.

But Josie was already alerted to the danger of her situation. She wasn't fooled.

"So there will be no question in the future—" he leaned his forearm on his thigh and fixed her with a dark and even gaze "—I forbid you to go beyond the orchard. I believe it is therefore understood that I forbid you to go anywhere near the creek or the canyon. This is not an arbitrary rule on my part, as I know I've explained before. You might encounter a bear or a mountain lion. Now listen to me carefully." He added the last in an even quieter tone so that everything around them seemed to still. For the duration of his brief pause, the silence was very, very loud.

"Do not defy me," he warned, the words still quiet and distinctly spoken, the threat of retribution implied. "It isn't wise."

Josie wanted to bolt out of the chair and tell him she wasn't afraid of him. But that would have been a lie.

She remained still and let her eyes tell him what she thought of his threats. "Do your friends and your clients know about this tendency to...what?...violence?"

It didn't work. He replied evenly. "They know I'm a man of my word—and that I always attend to my responsibilities, the pleasant and the unpleasant."

He lowered his foot to the floor and the tension between them eased but did not disappear.

"I have several hours' work to finish," he said. "I won't be up for a while."

"Considering your attitude," she said, rising regally to her feet, "I won't be waiting for you. Good night."

Adam watched her sail through the door, shoulders square, head at a defiant angle, and got the distinct impression the issue was not resolved.

Josie was just drifting off to sleep when the bedroom door opened. Since she had turned her back to Adam's side of the bed, she could only hear the thud of his shoes to the floor, the clink of his watch chain against the bedside table, the soft rustle of clothing as he undressed.

She felt the mattress take his weight, then the firm curve of his arm around her as he pulled her back against him into the curve of his body.

Warmth and comfort surrounded her, despite their altercation in his office. She knew his attitude about the canyon was not the result of meanness but of genuine concern for her. Unfortunately, it placed him squarely in the path of her search for her boys. And that made it necessary to defy him.

Adam was not entirely surprised the next day to arrive home and find his household in an uproar. Amos was saddling one of the wagon team and Bertie stood in the yard, an arm around Jane, Ivy holding a weeping Lucy.

"Mama's lost again!" Lucy wept.

Amos climbed into the saddle and shook his head at Adam in apology. "I'm sorry, Mr. Scofield. I went to the mill for more boards, and when I got back she'd taken Blackie." His look held mild censure for a man who couldn't control his wife. "I never thought she'd defy you again."

Adam had thought she might, but he'd felt fairly certain she'd have had the good sense to give him time to recover from yesterday's anger. Could escape be that important to her?

"Blackie came back again without her," Bertie said, her features tight with anxiety. "It'll be dark in an hour."

Jane said stoutly, "Papa will find her. And he'll have to teach her to be a better rider."

Yes, he thought. That would be lesson number two.

"You girls have your supper," he said, "and I'll be back with Mama in time to tuck you into bed."

"What if you can't find her?" Lucy wept.

He reached out to pinch her flushed and tearstained cheek. "I'll find her. I promise."

He didn't have to think twice about which direction she'd taken. Adam set off at a gallop for the creek. Amos right behind him.

By the time they reached the canyon it was dusk. And dark shadows reached out from every cranny and crevice. Adam slowed his horse to a walk, thinking that if she'd fallen it would be almost impossible to see her in the encroaching darkness. Fear for her safety and anger that she'd chosen to put all of them through this filled his being, equally potent and merging into one determined purpose.

"Josie!" he shouted. "Josie!"

The only response was night sounds. The rustle of brush, the scurrying sounds of small creatures, the unsettling, indistinguishable sounds overhead in the rock.

Amos had lit a lantern and now led the way, casting at least a small amount of light on the road. If escape was her intention, Adam reasoned, he didn't think she'd have left the road to explore the canyon's interesting but dangerous side trails.

He shouted her name again and again to no avail—until they'd almost reached the other side of the rocky corridor.

He heard her scream so clearly that it stopped him in surprise. "Adam? Adam!" The first cry had held disbelief, the second desperation. And then he heard the cat.

"Oh Lord!" Amos exclaimed, holding up the lantern.

Blinded by its glare, Adam rode up beside him, his heart giving an uncomfortable lurch even as he pulled his rifle from its scabbard.

All he could see of Josie was a flurry of skirts and feet flailing the air as she tried to pull herself up into a scruffy pine tree growing out of a rocky crevice. Under her, a broad, clawed paw swiping within a foot of her as she screamed and tucked up her feet, was the mountain lion.

Amos held the light steady as Adam drew a bead on the beautiful, snarling head. He waited as it fell back, fighting to maintain his control and his gentle touch on the trigger as Josie screamed in fear. He watched the cat bunch its muscles and leap at Josie's dangling feet—and fired.

The cat froze in flight for one heart-stopping moment, then crumpled to the ground. He shot it one more time to be sure, then slid the rifle into its scabbard and leapt from the saddle. His hand shook just a little, and he took an instant to draw a deep, steadying breath. Then he turned to Amos.

"Start back," he told him. "We'll be right behind you."

Amos complied, his features grim.

Josie's arms ached abominably. Terror had gotten her up here, but now, as she looked over her shoulder, the drop seemed too far to simply let go. And Adam was coming.

She could not remember a moment, except perhaps once or twice in prison, when she'd felt more desperate, more close to despair. She'd almost made it through the canyon! She was probably within a mile of Jones, who was probably really Gripper, who had her children. And she'd been foiled again! Blackie, she thought in anger and frustration, was not worthy of Lucy's love and affection. He was a profoundly stupid and cowardly horse.

She wanted to scream at the fate that had brought her so close to Charlie and Billy, then closed the door on her with a slam. It wasn't fair!

She felt a tug on her foot and looked down to see Adam standing under her, arms raised.

"Let go!" he ordered.

Now that the very real fear of being torn apart by a mountain lion had subsided, she became very much aware of the threat her husband presented. She'd done precisely what he'd told her not to do less than twenty-four hours after he'd told her not to do it.

She clung to the branch now biting into the palm of her hand. "I can explain," she said. Suddenly tired of the deception that seemed to grow and grow and require more and more quick thinking on her already strained brain and nerves, she considered telling him the truth.

Judging by the expression on his face, illuminated by a wedge of moonlight, she thought she might have better luck reasoning with the mountain lion.

The muscle in her right arm spasmed from the strain of holding her, and, with a startled cry, she fell into Adam's waiting arms.

His eyes blazed in the darkness. The tension in his arms was just as frightening.

"Adam, I want to tell you..." she began, but found it difficult to continue when she made a sudden revolution in the air like a windmill, skirts and petticoats flying.

He propped a boot on the rock through which the tree grew and balanced her over his knee.

He'd intended to deliver half a dozen swift, stinging blows to the seat of her drawers. But even through his temper he was sharply aware of the fragility of the rib cage his arm encircled, the narrow white-clad hips wriggling in the darkness and found himself unable to follow through.

Anger still in his hands, he yanked her to her feet again. His hands bit into her shoulders as he gave her a small shake.

"You will not ignore me," he said. "I don't want an explanation, I want cooperation! Do you understand me?"

She wanted desperately not to cry. She gave him the nod she knew he wanted, her eyes burning, her throat aching with the effort to hold the tears back.

He rose into the saddle, reached down for her and hauled her up behind him. She wasn't sure which hurt more, the strained arm with which he pulled her up or the ribs he had bruised when he'd taken hold of her.

She held his muscled waist loosely as they began the long ride home. Amos waited at the mouth of the canyon, gave her one swift, scolding glance, then led the way across the creek.

At the house, Amos came around to help her down and held the reins while Adam leapt down. Then Amos led the horses to the stable.

Adam caught her arm as she would have moved toward the house. Her composure dangled by a thread, and she swallowed hard to maintain it.

"Are you aware how much you've frightened everyone?" he demanded.

She thought it best not to consider the question, to simply avert her eyes and give him the answer she knew he wanted.

"Yes."

"When I came home, Lucy was crying for you."

That was difficult to deal with. She heaved a ragged sigh. "I'm sorry."

"I want you to tuck the girls in and assure them that you hadn't run away, that you were simply lost and that you're happy to be back home."

"Of course."

The front door was thrust open and Bertie burst out, running up to Josie, arms extended. "Mrs. Scofield, you've given us such a scare. Are you all right? Are—"

Then she saw Josie's pinched face and Adam's glower and quickly subsided.

"Well, there'll be a bath ready for you in a minute," she said more calmly. "I've been heating water since Amos and Mr. Scofield took out after you."

Josie tried to swallow the lump in her throat, but it remained. She forced a stiff smile for Bertie. "Thank you, Bertie. I'll say good-night to the girls and be right there."

Jane and Lucy leapt at her the moment she walked into their room and clung to her like little leeches as she walked them to their beds.

Guilt swamped her and sharpened the lump in her throat as they asked eager questions and hugged her as though she were every bit as precious to them as they'd become to her.

She told them everything they wanted to know but altered the truth suddenly when it came to how she'd become lost again. She told them about the mountain lion, minimizing the danger and accentuating the drama, then told them about their father's rescue.

Their eyes grew wider and wider.

She finally coaxed them into their beds with the promise that they could discuss it all over again tomorrow. All the while she smiled and drew blankets up, her pain over the absence of her own children grew, and her frustration over this night's fiasco swelled to make her head pound and her fragile hold on hope fray to fringe.

"Your bath is ready," Adam said from the doorway.

"Papa!" Lucy sat up in bed, her arms stretched toward him. "You saved Mama like a prince in a storybook!"

Josie sidled past him, avoiding his eyes as he entered the room. Then she escaped to the hallway as she heard Jane ask him to repeat everything she'd already told them.

She went to the bedroom, desperately trying to pull herself together. As she entered, Bertie added water to a bathtub that steamed like a hot springs, and Ivy added salts to the mound of bubbles that already threatened to run over the sides. Behind it a fire crackled merrily, in direct opposition to every feeling in Josie's body.

Bertie put the empty bucket down and came to her, leading her into the room and unfastening the buttons at the back of her dress.

"Now, Mrs. Scofield, there's no reason to look as though the world has fallen out from under you," she said with motherly encouragement. "I imagine Mr. Scofield shouted at you and you're feeling small and misunderstood. But it's only because we were all so worried about you."

Josie's clothes fell into a pile at her feet as Bertie's voice droned on with sage, womanly advice. The housekeeper had no way of knowing that none of it applied to her, that she'd taken a husband only to find her children and, in so doing, seemed to have upset everyone's life.

"Let me help you." Ivy lent Josie a supporting hand as she stepped into the steamy fragrant water.

"I'll wash these things for you first thing in the morning," Bertie said cheerfully, gathering up the ruffly pile of clothing. "Shall I bring you a cup of tea?"

Josie opened her mouth to offer a polite "No, thank you," and was as surprised as Bertie and Ivy when what came from her lips was a loud, pathetic sob.

It was the hot water, Josie thought as she placed both soapy hands over her mouth in an attempt to block the sound. She'd built an icy reserve around herself to hold in her despair since Adam pulled her out of the tree and she was forced to accept that her trip to find her children had been aborted once again. But she could retain it no longer. Adam's barely restrained fury, the long, silent ride home, Amos's scolding glance, the girls' obvious relief at having her back and Bertie and Ivy's solicitude chipped away at it.

And as the hot water closed around her, stung her ribs and lapped against the sore muscles of her arms and legs, the wall of control dissolved and loosed a flood of tears she seemed powerless to control.

"Now, Mrs. Scofield." Bertie dropped the pile of clothes and knelt by the tub, stroking her hair as though she were one of the children. "You're safe now. I know that old mountain lion must have been very frightening, but it's all over. Everything's going to be all right. Here, let's take your hair down. That'll help you relax."

Josie sat meekly, still sobbing, hopelessness surrounded with the bubbles as Bertie pulled the pins out of her hair.

Chapter Eleven

Adam paced the length of his office and back again, a glass of bourbon in hand. After half an hour of staring at notes he failed to comprehend, he gave up the attempt to distract himself with work.

He had no reason to feel guilty. Had he been a moment later in pursuit of Josie she'd be with her first husband now, at play with the angels.

He took another swig from his glass as he thought about that large paw with its razorlike claws swiping within reach of her ankles.

The image of large blue eyes came to him, tears of sadness standing in them but prevented from falling by pride and stubbornness. Self-loathing filled him along with the last gulp of bourbon.

He hated the knowledge that he'd caused that look of despair on her face, that he'd probably left bruises on her wrists and her ribs. But he couldn't let her take off on her own across a wilderness she couldn't possibly navigate or survive.

And why in the hell did she insist on trying? He'd done everything within his power to make her comfortable. Much of the time she didn't behave at all like a woman anxious to escape her surroundings. Now that they'd all adjusted to one another, she seemed to enjoy the girls and the Donovans as much as they loved her. And he would swear that there were moments when they made love that she clung to him and kissed him as though her world turned on his presence in it.

He simply didn't understand her.

There was a quick, nervous knock on his office door.

He put his glass down on the desk with a bang and fell into his chair. "Come in!" he called.

Bertie pushed the door open and stepped inside. She frowned in concern.

"Mr. Scofield," she said urgently, "I wonder if I might have a glass of your apple brandy?"

He raised an eyebrow at the unusual request. "Of course, Bertie." He directed her across the room to the table that held bottles and glasses. "Are you feeling ill?"

"No, it's for Mrs. Scofield." She gave him a swift glance over her shoulder as she searched for the brandy in the cluster of bottles. "She's been crying her heart out since we put her in the bathtub and I'm afraid *she's* going to be ill if she doesn't stop. I tried tea and that didn't work. I thought maybe the brandy..."

Her hand finally settled on the squatty bottle.

Adam rose, took the bottle from her, snatched a glass and led the way up the stairs. He didn't want to comfort Josie. In fact, when he thought back to the moment when the cat had leapt at her, he was certain he should have followed his initial reaction.

"It isn't dramatics, Mr. Scofield." Bertie pleaded Josie's case as she hurried to keep up with him. "I've used a woman's wiles myself, and I'm sure her tears are genuine. They just keep pouring out of her as though she's held them back for a long time."

The sincerity of Josie's emotional outburst was obvious to him the moment he opened their bedroom door.

He saw the tips of her knees emerging from the thin layer of bubbles that covered the water. Her head rested on her arms folded over her knees as she cried her heart out.

Ivy held a towel at the ready and knelt beside her, cajoling her. "Mrs. Scofield, you have to come out. The water's cold now and you'll catch your death."

Adam saw the fragile curve of Josie's ivory back, the tremor in her shoulders as she wept, the wet bottom six inches of her dark hair, which one of the women had woven into a braid. She looked small and helpless and abjectly defeated. Guilt scraped at his insides.

He strode into the room and placed the bottle and the glass on the mantel. Then he helped Ivy to her feet and took the towel from her. "I'll take care of Mrs. Scofield," he said, sending Ivy toward her mother, who waited uncertainly just inside the room.

Bertie held her ground for a moment. "She's very upset," she said. "Please don't—"

"Thank you, Bertie," Adam interrupted, then added firmly, "Good night."

When the door closed behind the Donovans, Adam knelt beside the tub and had the impression Josie didn't even know he was there.

"Josie." He tossed the towel over his shoulder and reached out to lift her head off her knees and frame her face in his hands. Her face was red and swollen, her eyes redrimmed and puffy, her mouth contorted in a sob she didn't seem able to stop. Her helplessness unsettled him. This was not the woman who was never at a loss for a clever fib or a glib remark. What had happened to her in the canyon?

"Come on out of there," he said firmly, straightening and bracing his hands under her arms to bring her to her feet. Water rained off her small, firm breasts, her round bottom, her thighs. Flat, leftover suds clung to every curved surface. He ignored that and wrapped the bath sheet around her, then lifted her out of the tub.

He carried her to the braided rug before the fireplace and stood her on it. Methodically, he wiped her dry—shoulders, back, bottom, legs. After several careful swipes down the front of her, he took the nightgown one of the women had laid out on the bed and slipped it over her head.

He poured brandy into the glass and placed the glass on the little table near the wing chair turned at an angle to the fireplace. Then he sat in it and pulled her into his lap.

She continued to sob with a misery so profound he felt as though he would drown in remorse. He doubted seriously that his rough handling of her had been the cause of this, but he was still responsible for her well-being, and she was very far from that state at this moment.

He put the brandy to her lips and, when she tried to resist, insisted that she drink it. Her meek cooperation hurt him almost as much as her sobs.

Josie knew she was creating a spectacle. The Donovans were probably discussing her right now in the kitchen, and Adam looked as miserable as she felt. But she could not explain what had happened to her when she slipped into the hot water and opened the floodgates of emotion.

It was as though every hope she'd clutched to her during the long months since Benjamin's death had swept out of her with the tears. She was now overwhelmed with the sure knowledge that Jones was not Gripper, and that whoever he was, the two children with him were not her own.

The Siskiyou Mountains stretched north into Oregon. Her boys could be anywhere. Red flannel caps could be purchased by anyone with a Montgomery Ward & Company catalogue. She'd been deluding herself all these months with dreams of finding them. The truth was that it would be no easier than finding the proverbial needle in the haystack. It was time to face the truth. Charlie and Billy were lost to her forever.

"Josie, please," Adam said, desperate to end her sobs. He rubbed the blue imprint of his thumb and forefinger on her fragile wrist. "I'm sorry I hurt you. But you came within seconds of being killed. You must listen to me in this."

Josie shook her head as she handed him back the brandy glass. She'd known the chance she took when she set out for the canyon, both in the natural dangers there and in regard to the threat he'd made the night before. She'd known yesterday that concern for her governed his actions, but she'd seen tonight, when she'd fallen into his arms, that it had been more than concern. He'd been truly frightened for her. He loved her.

And that, added to the anguish over her children, upset her world so that she clung to him as the only secure element in it.

"Oh, Adam!" she wept, and fell against his shoulder, sobbing anew.

He held her until she finally fell asleep, exhausted. He placed her in the middle of the bed, shed his clothes and lay beside her. She curled against him in her sleep, an arm hooked around his neck.

He held her close and closed his eyes, feeling as though he'd just fought a war single-handedly.

Josie awoke with a pounding headache. The events of the night before flooded her awareness and she closed her eyes against it. But the memory of Adam's comforting arms holding her through the night would not dissolve.

She stumbled out of bed to the window, parted the curtains and opened it, drawing in a deep draft of fresh air. She felt it fill her lungs and revive the hope and determination that had collapsed the night before.

She knelt on the cold hardwood floor, rested her arms on the windowsill and looked out at the beauty of the land that surrounded the Scofield home.

Beyond the pasture, she could see the lacy white tops of the apple trees. In the far distance was the canyon, though she couldn't see it, and beyond that, against the bright blue sky, was the white mountain that had dominated the landscape for aeons. The air was balmy and suggested that spring had turned to summer in the mountains.

She drew in another deep breath and felt her old spirit renew itself. She'd known the search for her children would be difficult when she'd set out. She wasn't defeated yet. This could very well be just the beginning of her quest.

She frowned at the beautiful mountain, thinking that she just hadn't realized she would become so entangled with Adam and his family that their love would hold her back from what she must do.

The sounds of activity downstairs drifted upward and she pushed herself to her feet and closed the window. She looked at her reflection in the cheval glass and groaned.

She chose a dress sprigged with pink flowers in an attempt to lend color to her pale cheeks, then discovered it accentuated the red rims around her eyes and the black circles under them.

She changed quickly into a blue one, brushed her hair into a high chignon and added a bow to call attention away from her face. Adam would be on his way to the office already, but she didn't want to give Bertie cause for concern or speculation. She had to hide all evidence of this morning's renewed determination for fear the alert Amos or the watchful Bertie would mention it to Adam. Because at the first opportunity, she intended to try again.

She went with a light step down the stairs, turned into the dining room and stopped abruptly just inside at the sight of Adam, still at the breakfast table with Lucy. Jane had left for school.

"Papa's staying home today to take us on a picnic," the child said excitedly.

Josie's and Adam's eyes met across the room, hers darkening with confusion as opposing memories of his anger and his comfort assailed her. Then there was the obstruction he presented to any possibility of her heading for the canyon today. The fatalism with which she accepted this showed in her eyes.

Adam's gaze was confidently calm. He stood with a smile to seat her, apparently prepared to forget yesterday's events. She tried to smile back with equal aplomb.

"Good morning," he said. "We seem to have a genuine summer day, and it would be a shame to waste it at the office."

"A picnic sounds lovely," she lied. She guessed this was an effort on his part to try to reestablish the easy camaraderie into which they'd settled before she'd made her first trip to the canyon. He probably presumed that since he'd imposed his will on her, he thought that would be the end of the matter, and he wanted her to see that he was generous enough to forgive and forget.

As she saw it, her best course of action was to let him believe that was true.

He passed a bright yellow telegraph envelope to her.

"This arrived for you yesterday and was delivered to my office," he said. "In the ... confusion, I forgot to give it to you."

Josie opened it and found a message from Jonathan.

Josie. Congratulations on your nuptials. Stop. Don't worry about things here. Stop. Will solve your mystery. Stop. Delighted all is going well for you. Stop. Love, Jonathan.

The mystery, of course, was a carefully couched reference to Benjamin's death, probably on the chance that Adam read the telegram.

She looked up to give him a faint, wry smile, absorbing the irony of the message.

"It's from Jonathan, congratulating us on our happy marriage."

He nodded, meeting her eyes. "You mean Charlie."

She cursed herself for her stupidity. She had to find her children quickly, before she lost her mind completely.

She replied with a blandly innocent stare. "Of course. Charlie."

Adam, Josie and Lucy spent most of the day in a lush green meadow that edged the southern border of the orchard.

Adam spread a blanket under a sheltering ash tree. They walked hand in hand with Lucy between them pointing out bird's nests that she and Amos had found while he was teaching her to ride Blackie. They lay on their backs in a field of poppies, picking shapes out of the tufty white clouds overhead. Lucy, restless, ran around them gathering flowers, then presented Josie with a cheerful bouquet.

Josie sat up to hug her fiercely, warmed by her sunny personality and touched by her loving gesture.

Adam, leaning back on an elbow, watched their exchange and let himself enjoy it without trying to determine what it meant in regard to Josie. Reasoning through her love of his children and her apparent determination to escape them proved far too convoluted for his basic directness.

Shoes dangling in their fingers, they walked slowly back to the ash tree, stopping to admire a butterfly on a gangly orange flower.

They ate the cold beef and potato salad Bertie had prepared and drank apple juice from a tall, fat jar.

Adam and Josie sat under the tree while Lucy turned cartwheels in the grass.

Adam watched Josie twist nervously at the jade ring he'd bought her several days before. There was an edge of nervousness under the cheerful face she'd put on today. That didn't surprise him entirely, considering the night before, but he suspected that this tension had less to do with fear of him than with whatever it was that seemed to govern her every move lately—whatever it was that had brought her here in the first place.

She was going to try for the canyon again. He knew that as well as he knew her name. He was past being angry over her defiance of his rules, and he was trying to look beyond his concern for her safety. What he wanted to know above all else was what in the hell was driving her. What motivated her to risk her safety and his wrath again?

Was it another man? The Charlie she'd mentioned in a dream on the train? But if so, where was he? Would a lady from Boston be searching for a man at one of the diggings? Somehow, he couldn't imagine that.

Then who or what was she after? He puzzled over the question as she went to keep a close eye on Lucy as his daughter started after a butterfly. She caught up with her and swept her up in her arms, the meadow filling with the sound of their giggles. His heart constricted at the picture they made, at the womanly generosity and tenderness of her every gesture with the child, and the hotly erotic thoughts she made him feel with the most innocent of moves.

He couldn't imagine what motivated Josie. He knew only that fate and a preacher had made her his and she'd come to mean so much more to him than he'd ever expected she would when he'd sent for her. No power on this earth would take her from him.

They ate cake and drank lemonade in the middle of the afternoon, then climbed into the wagon at dinnertime and headed for home.

Lucy, sitting between them on the seat, leaned lazily against her father's arm. "Can't you stay home all the time?" she asked. "It would be nice if every day was like today."

Adam laughed lightly. "I'm afraid not, Lucy. I have to go to work so we have money for the things we need."

Lucy frowned up at him. "Do we need anything else but picnics?"

Did they, indeed. Adam turned to Josie to share the joke with her over Lucy's head, but Josie was lost in thoughts of her own, her eyes unfocused, a tight little frown between her eyebrows.

He accepted once again, as he often did, that though she was with them in body, she was absent in spirit. He guessed this time she was probably plotting her next attempt to ride through the canyon.

He turned the wagon off the road and into the yard, his mind beginning to concoct a plan.

Bertie, wooden spoon in hand, looked up to smile at them as they peered into the kitchen. Ivy, in an apron, stood beside her stirring the contents of a bowl she held in the crook of her arm. Jane sat at the small table, poring over a book. She didn't even notice their presence and only smiled at the page when her father leaned over her to kiss the top of her head. Lucy lay fast asleep in his arms.

"Chicken and dumplings!" Josie exclaimed, the first sign of life she'd shown since they'd climbed into the wagon for the trip home.

Bertie beamed at Josie's obvious pleasure. The last time Bertie had prepared it, Josie had raved. Adam had no doubt she'd prepared it again as an effort to cheer Josie. So she, too, had seen beyond the forced smile to the edgy, pained woman underneath. Josie had become more important than she realized to all of them.

Josie was surprised the following Monday to find herself completely alone in the house just before noon. Jane was at school, Adam had given Amos the day off to repair his sister's roof, and Bertie and Ivy had gone into town to help Prudence Knox on a regular rotation of church cleaning and had taken Lucy with them.

It took her a moment to realize her good fortune. She didn't even change out of the new yellow-flowered dress she wore. She took an old Eton jacket and ran to the stable to saddle Blackie.

From the shelter of the copse of trees behind the barn, Adam watched her clumsy movements with concern. He hoped she remembered to cinch the saddle. She did, getting on her knees under the horse's belly to accomplish the task.

She ran back to the house in a flurry of skirts, apparently having forgotten something. Adam's frown deepened when she returned at a run with his Winchester under one arm. He presumed the box in her other hand to be ammunition. She slipped the rifle into the scabbard, the box into a deep skirt pocket, pulled up a stool to Blackie's side and mounted.

He watched her disappear in a cloud of dust, her seat a little awkward but the set of her jaw and shoulders so determined he felt a sinking feeling in his gut.

He'd known when he hatched this plan that it might reveal something to him he didn't want to know. He was beginning to suspect it would do just that. He'd seen that set to her features twice before, when Betsy Fulton had been unkind to Jane, and when Clayton Brown had tried to force himself on Ivy. Concern for those she loved gave her that consummate stubbornness.

He held Dancer still and let Blackie and Josie get a considerable distance ahead of him. There was little doubt where she was heading. He watched their combined figures grow smaller against the horizon and forced himself to face the fact that in all probability she was riding toward another man.

She was not beset by quail this time or by a mountain lion. It was late afternoon when she cleared the far end of the canyon. She reined in for a moment, stopping to lean over Blackie's neck as though the task of finally reaching the other side after so many false tries had exhausted her.

Then she straightened and kicked lightly at Blackie's flanks to move him forward. Adam followed.

Occasionally she would stop, stand up in the stirrups and look out over the countryside as though searching for a particular landmark or possibly even a structure.

Adam shook his head as he watched her, knowing there was nothing out here besides the diggings. Except the old Porter place, which had been deserted two years ago when Selena Porter had tired of country life and gone back to San Francisco. Will Porter had been right behind her.

But, as the dusk began to gather around them, that seemed to be precisely where Josie was headed. She stopped to do another visual sweep of the countryside after clearing a large outcropping of rock, then stiffened in the stirrups when she spotted what Adam couldn't see from his viewpoint but knew to be there a short distance off the road—the decrepit structure the Porters had abandoned with its broken-down fences.

Adam reined in, pulling himself and his horse into the scrub on the other side of the trail as Josie slid to the ground and stood in the shelter of the rock to survey the homestead.

Adam heard a horse whinny in the direction of the farm. So, someone had moved in there. He remembered vaguely a conversation he'd had with Josie about Reverend Knox bringing food and blankets out here to someone. He remembered that Josie had wanted to make the delivery herself. Did she have a lover in this house? One who'd left her behind in Boston and whom she couldn't live without and had chosen to follow? He frowned, waiting for everything to come together in his mind and make sense. It didn't. A woman didn't usually marry one man as a means of finding another. Of course, in his experience, usual women weren't at all like Josie.

He watched her take Blackie's reins and make her way forward, taking shelter behind a windbreak of pines that surrounded the property.

Adam tethered Dancer to a bush and climbed the gentle slope of a knoll that rose behind the position Josie had taken.

She flattened herself against a tree about fifteen yards from the shabby little house and rubbed Blackie's muzzle to keep him quiet. Lamplight brightened one window, and Adam could see wood smoke curl out of the chimney against the bright moonlight.

And if her lover were in that house, Adam argued with himself, wouldn't she simply run up to it shouting his name rather than skulk toward it, concealed by the trees?

Completely confused, he simply settled down, stretched out just below the brow of the little hillock with a good view of Josie and waited for something to happen.

Sometime later the front door opened and a stripe of lamplight fell onto the warped front porch.

"And don't dawdle!" a gruff man's voice shouted from inside. "It shouldn't take until morning to bring in an armload of wood.

Adam saw two figures step out into the light. One was shorter than Lucy, a small, barefoot boy in pants that were too big and a shirt with the sleeves rolled up so many times the cuffs were a thick mass at his wrists.

He held the hand of a boy close to Jane's age, who was similarly dressed and also barefoot.

Together, the boys walked out of the illuminating light and down the porch steps.

Josie felt her heart stall and every breath in her body leave her. She slapped both hands over her mouth to prevent the shriek that rose to her lips. Charlie! Billy!

She kept her eyes on them as they walked across the dusty yard toward a leaning shed half-filled with split wood. Her eyes devoured them. Their platinum hair shone in the moonlight, and they walked with straight, even strides. She stared at them, mouth agape, almost unable to believe that she'd found them. She'd been in anxious misery for so long, abandoned hope and then found it again, and...

Her heart in her throat, her eyes on the gaping door of the cabin, Josie crept along behind the trees until she was even with the shed. She inched her way around a tree and opened her mouth to call softly to Charlie.

"Well? What are you doin' out there?" the gruff voice demanded, then the man to whom it belonged filled the doorway. Josie shrank back. His bald head almost reached the lintel, and his meaty body filled the opening from side to side. She saw a straggly beard and a big belly and felt a hatred so strong she had to force her brain to engage to prevent her from ruining everything now that she was so close.

Charlie straightened, his puny arms stacked with wood.

"And don't drop it!" Gripper shouted, walking slowly down the steps and toward them. "Or I'll take you to the woodshed myself!"

Every defensive instinct in Josie's body rose, telling her to intercept the man and beat him until he whimpered, then carry her children to safety.

But common sense reminded her that the likely outcome of such a course of action would be quite different from what she imagined. Then she remembered that she'd brought a rifle, but that she'd left it in the scabbard still secured to Blackie's saddle.

She crept back to the horse as Gripper continued to shout. Her fingers shaking, she forced bullets into the rifle as she glanced up to see Billy reach up to steady a log that tottered. Gripper shouted again. Billy started and fell against Charlie, who lost his footing and dropped the wood.

Gripper quickened his stride toward her children, his voice roaring in anger. "I told you to be careful!"

"Henry, my Lord," a woman's high voice shouted from the porch. "Will you leave those boys alone and stop shouting?"

"We took 'em to do chores," he shouted back. "And all hey done is double mine!"

"Well, they can hear you in town!"

"They're gonna hear these two in town for strainin' my >atience."

"Oh, Henry," she returned lightly. "Even sunshine strains your patience. Come inside and leave them be."

Josie ran out into the moonlight just as Gripper grabbed a big fistful of the front of each child's shirt.

"Take your hands off them," she said, her voice quaking with the fear and fury that filled her being, "or I'll shoot you where you stand, I swear to God."

Gripper dropped his hold on the children and turned more n surprise than fear. "Who...?" he began to demand.

Then Charlie's voice said in a small, frail tone of disbelief, "Mama?" Then more loudly, a jubilant note replacing the disbelief, "Mama!" He ran to fling his arms around her waist. "I knew you'd come. I *knew* you'd come!"

"You know what you're doin' with that thing?" Gripper asked, angling his chin toward the rifle.

"Very well," she said, aiming the heavy rifle, intending o shoot at his feet to prove it to him. Then she remembered that she had to work the lever. She bent it forward hen back with shaking fingers and knew immediately she'd done something wrong. The lever wouldn't *go* back.

She'd watched Amos load and fire the rifle twice and tried o memorize every move, but apparently she'd missed something. Cold panic tried to take control of her.

"Henry, what's happening out there?" The woman came o stand on the very edge of the porch, peering out into the yard. "Who's that?"

Gripper ignored her. He reached back to snatch Billy up with one arm around his waist.

But the click of a hammer being pulled back stopped him. Josie turned, as surprised as he was, to see Adam come up beside her, his revolver aimed steadily at Gripper's head.

"Put him down," Adam said, his voice lethally quiet. "Believe me when I tell you that I *do* know what I'm doing. I can part your hair, drill your tooth or pierce your ear."

Gripper put the child on his feet. He ran to his brother.

"Josie," Adam said without taking his eyes from Gripper, "what in the hell is going on here?"

Josie was torn between disbelief that he'd appeared beside her just when she'd been certain her entire plan was about to collapse and the desperate need to get her children away from Gripper. She wouldn't feel safe until she had them home behind the solid door of the Scofield house.

A million details tried to invade her mind. Adam had followed her. He was going to be furious with her when she explained. He would very probably send her away. Though she'd known all along that would be the ultimate result of her plan, it had seemed far less bleak in concept than it was in reality. It occurred to her to wonder just when her plan had altered from finding her children and escaping back to Boston, to fitting her children—and herself—into the life she'd come to know with Adam and his girls.

She pushed all those thoughts aside and concentrated her attention on the needs of the moment.

"These are my children," she said. "I...we..." She drew a breath and began again. "It's difficult to explain, but my mother-in-law gave them to this couple. He says his name is Jones, but it's really Gripper, and our Pinkerton man says he was a petty thief in Boston." She added firmly, "I'm taking them home."

A score of questions rose to Adam's mind, but he decided this was neither the time nor the place to insist on answers.

"We're going to do this peacefully, Mr. Gripper-Jones," he said, leveling the gun at Gripper as the man made an arms-out move indicating frustration.

"They was given to me!"

"He got money to take us!" Charlie said, still clutching his mother. "I saw Grandmother pay him."

Adam had difficulty believing such a thing could have happened in Boston society, but he put that away with all the other elements that didn't make sense. There would be time later to deal with them. At the moment, he was very unclear on just what had happened and knew he hadn't sufficient proof to take him to the sheriff.

"It's illegal to buy and sell children," he said. "If I see your face again, or you give me or this woman or these children the very suggestion of trouble, I'll turn you over to the Siskiyou County Court and let them deal with you. It might be interesting to find out why you've come west under an assumed name."

"Now, you look here . . ." Gripper began to protest, but his wife took hold of his arm and held him back.

"I think he means it, Henry. I told you it wasn't right in the first place."

"Listen to the missus, Mr. Gripper-Jones," Adam said. Without looking away from him he spoke to Josie. "My horse is tethered to a bush at the bottom of the knoll. Bring him and Blackie here."

Josie ran to comply.

"Put one of the boys on each," he directed when she returned.

With a boost from Josie, Charlie leapt to Blackie's stirrup, then hauled himself onto the horse.

"Hold this," Adam said, handing her his revolver and facing her in Gripper's direction. "And shoot if he even flinches."

He took the rifle from her, worked the lever loose, eased the hammer down, then handed it back to her and reclaimed his revolver. "Get the little one," he said.

Josie holstered the rifle, then turned to reach for Billy to find that he had backed away. She held her hand out to him. "Come here to Mama, Billy."

But he took another step back.

She looked into his uncertain, confused blue eyes and faced the fear that had haunted her for the past four months—that her children would forget who she was.

"Billy," she said softly, pain ripping at her as he studied her warily. "Come on, sweetheart. You remember me."

Adam caught her arm and pushed her firmly toward Blackie. "Mount up. I'll get him."

"But..."

"Josie."

She did as he asked, reaching around Charlie to gather the reins.

The gun still leveled on Gripper, Adam reached down to gather Billy effortlessly into one arm, then set him atop the big bay. He climbed up behind him, then sent Josie on her way with a sharp slap to Blackie's rump.

"Remember," he cautioned Gripper, "I don't want to see you ever." Then he holstered his gun and set off after Josie.

At the canyon he took the lead and set a quick pace all the way home.

Chapter Twelve

The Donovans ran out of the house when Adam and Josie rode into the yard. Miles appeared also, and everyone stopped in an uncertain semicircle at the sight of the boys.

Then Bertie came forward to take the now sleeping little one from Adam's arms, and Miles reached up to swing Charlie to the ground. Josie leapt down, hugged Charlie fiercely, then swept her youngest out of the housekeeper's arms and took both children inside.

"I presume it's a long story," Adam said into the surprised expressions of Miles and the Donovans. "Unfortunately, at the moment, I'm not privileged to it. Bertie, I imagine that the boys need food, baths and bed. Once you and Mrs. Scofield have put them down, I'd like to see her in the office."

Bertie and Ivy hurried inside, and Amos took both horses toward the stable.

Miles followed Adam to his office.

Adam was doing his best to contain his temper, but it was bubbling up out of the depths of him now that he'd put Gripper behind them.

"What are you doing here?" he asked Miles with a distinct lack of hospitality.

"I came over after closing the office today to see if you were ill. Two days out of the office is unusual for you. And

I learn from the Donovans that you'd baited a trap for Josie, and they were waiting for you to come home." Insensitive to Adam's dark mood, Miles sat in the chair that faced his desk. "While I helped Ivy shell peas for supper, we went over all the possibilities. Josie is a trained geologist studying the strata in the canyon. Josie is the leader of an outlaw band sheltered there." Miles grinned. "I particularly liked that one. But Ivy thought she might have come all this way from Boston in search of an old love she couldn't forget." He sobered, watching Adam as he tossed his jacket and hat at the small settee and sank into his desk chair. "Funny that I'd put less credence in that possibility, and it turned out to be true. I presume those are her children?"

Adam leaned back moodily. "So it appears. We just stole them away from a couple who'd taken over the old Porter place."

Miles nodded. "So that was the fascination with the canyon."

Adam gave him a grim glance. "Nice of you to conspire with her against me."

"There was no conspiracy," Miles denied calmly. "I didn't lie to you, but it didn't seem gentlemanly to make her out a liar. I thought whatever the mystery was, you'd uncover it. She's bright and charming, but you're not stupid. At least not all the time."

Adam gave him another murderous glance and went to pour himself a brandy. "Why don't you take your amusing self home?"

Miles smiled. "Relax, Adam. The larger your family, the more the voting public will love you should you one day consider running for public office."

"Miles…" Adam warned, walking back to his desk with his brandy.

Miles stood and flexed his shoulders. "I suppose I don't have to remind you that you should hear her out before you start shouting. As I recall, you sometimes forgot that with Maggie."

Adam opened his office door to prompt Miles's departure, then caught a glimpse of the genuine concern in his eyes. He knew he'd waited with the Donovans until this late hour because he'd thought he, Adam, might need a friend when he came home.

He clapped him on the shoulder and walked him to the door. Ivy hurried over with his hat and coat.

"Thank you, Miles," he said, "but I'm certain I can handle my wife."

Miles turned as Ivy held his jacket open. "Some things don't require handling," he said quietly. "Just understanding."

Adam accepted the mild censure with a raised eyebrow. "If you're such an expert on women, perhaps it's time you acquired one of your own."

His jacket on, Miles turned to smile at Ivy, who studied him with frank interest.

"What do you think, Ivy?" he asked, his voice quiet but significant. "Do you think it's time I settled down?"

She smiled and shook her head. "You're a wild thing, Mr. Carver. I think you need to be free."

Miles looked back at her in honest confusion. Adam turned him toward the door. "I'll see you at the office in the morning," he told him.

"That'll be a nice change." Miles bowed to Ivy. "Thank you for your sparkling company this evening, Ivy. I was rather hoping you were right about the outlaw band."

Ivy clasped her hands together at her breast, her eyes bright. "This is almost as exciting. Children are far more precious than stolen fortunes."

With a lift of his eyebrow at Adam, Miles placed his hat at a rakish angle and left.

Adam went back to his office to pour another brandy.

Josie felt as though she rode the very shoulders of God. Nothing else could describe her absolute exhilaration. Seated at the small table in the kitchen, she watched Charlie devour a second plate of Bertie's roast and potatoes while Billy held a tall glass of milk in both hands and swallowed without pausing to breathe.

"Mrs. Gripper was all right," Charlie said as he eagerly accepted another slice of buttered bread from Bertie. "But *he* shouted all the time." He turned to Josie, gray eyes somehow wide with the night's excitement and heavy with the need to sleep. "Grandmother Jerusha said you didn't want us anymore, and that's why she was giving us to Mr. and Mrs. Gripper. But I knew it wasn't true. I knew you'd find us."

Josie held his free hand, still pink from the bathtub, while he forked food into his mouth with the other. "I wanted to get you back more than anything," she said, her heart tearing at what it must have been like for her children to be bundled off with strangers in the middle of the night. "I came to live here so I could look for you."

Charlie accepted that with a complacent nod, the gesture assuring her that he'd never lost faith in his mother.

Billy put his glass down and studied her still with mild uncertainty, a milk mustache surrounding his cupid's-bow mouth. She lifted him out of his chair and into her lap and cuddled him against her breast. She stroked his hair and kissed the baby-fine strands, still damp from his bath.

"He'll be asleep in a minute," Bertie said, smiling fondly at the child. "Are you sure you wouldn't like something besides that coffee? You and Mr. Scofield both missed supper."

Josie shook her head, the very sound of Adam's name invading her euphoria to remind her that she had to explain her actions to the man responsible for getting her children to safety, the man she'd lied to and married under false pretenses. The impending confrontation gnawed at her, but, for the moment at least, it couldn't eclipse the ecstasy of having her children in her arms at last.

"Who's the man?" Charlie asked, running the last bite of bread around his plate, collecting tiny pieces of meat. Table manners, Josie decided, could wait until tomorrow. "The one who scared Mr. Gripper." That notion seemed to please him as he opened his mouth wide as a big fish and popped the bread inside.

"That's my husband," Josie said, wondering just how long that would be a reality. "This is his house."

Without warning, Charlie's eyes filled with tears and a suddenly stricken look drained his face of color. "Papa's dead, isn't he? I heard Grandmother tell Mr. Gripper. That Papa was dead and you didn't want us anymore."

For a moment Josie's euphoria over finding her children was eclipsed by the memory of her arrest in the early hours of the morning after Benjamin's murder. She'd been mired in grief and confusion, and wondering how to tell her sleeping children their father had been murdered.

Then she'd been shocked to find herself arrested, handcuffed, and locked away with no opportunity to even kiss the boys goodbye, much less try to explain to them what had happened.

Hatred for Jerusha rolled up in her afresh, but she forced it aside to deal with her weeping child.

Josie extended her arm and Charlie walked into it, tears falling. "I wish I could tell you that part wasn't true, either, sweetheart, but it is. Papa's gone. But you and I and Billy are together now and everything will be fine."

"Are we going back to Boston?"

Quite possibly. She squeezed him and smiled into his face. "I'm not sure, Charlie. I have to think about the best thing for all of us. For now, Bertie and Ivy made up a room for you upstairs, and we'll have many fun things to do."

He squeezed her tightly. "I'm glad you found us, Mama. I missed you."

Tears welled up within Josie, but knowing Charlie would misunderstand them, she swallowed them back. She stood with Billy, now asleep against her shoulder, and took Charlie's hand. "Come on. I'll tuck you in bed, and tomorrow I'll show you the stables and the barn and the orchard and the creek where we have picnics."

Charlie rubbed a hand over his stomach. "Right now I'm pretty full."

She laughed and led him upstairs.

Ten minutes later Josie closed the bedroom door quietly behind her, both boys fast asleep. She turned to keep her appointment with Adam and found Jane and Lucy standing in their doorway, their eyes wide with surprise.

"Who were *they?*" Jane asked as Josie turned them both back into their room.

It was time to start telling the truth, Josie knew. These two girls had come to mean as much to her as Charlie and Billy did. She had no idea what fate she faced at the moment, she knew only that whatever pain she caused these children, even though it had been inflicted to save her own children, would haunt her always.

"They're my little boys," she said, putting Lucy back in bed and pulling her covers up. "Tomorrow morning I'll introduce you."

Jane sat on the edge of her bed with a frown. "Papa said you didn't have children."

"Your papa didn't know," she said carefully. "A very mean lady had stolen them from me, and I came here to find them."

Lucy turned onto her side, her head propped on her hand. "And you and Papa just found them tonight?"

Josie nodded.

Jane sat propped against her pillows as Josie pulled the blankets up over her. Then she cut incisively to the heart of the matter. "You mean you didn't come here to be with us?"

"Yes, I did." Josie prayed God would understand and forgive the fib. "Your papa told me how wonderful you were, and I thought this would be a very nice place to live while I was trying to find my little boys."

Jane looked mildly suspicious but reached her arms around Josie's neck to hug her good-night. "How old is the big one?" she asked.

"Eight," Josie replied.

Jane looked satisfied. "Ha! I'm older."

"Yes, you are. Good night, darling." Josie moved to Lucy's bed and adjusted her covers again. "Sleep tight, pumpkin."

"Can we still call you Mama?" Lucy asked in concern.

Josie hugged her again for good measure, misery beginning to overtake her earlier euphoria. "Of course. Now I have two little boys and two little girls."

Lucy smiled brightly. "Good night, Mama."

I just don't know how long your father will allow that situation to be, she thought as she closed their door and took a moment to square her shoulders and brace herself to meet with Adam in his office.

Adam had poured a third brandy then poured it back into the bottle, deciding he was going to have to have his wits about him for this encounter. He had to be controlled by logic, not alcohol, and not the fury he'd tried to use the alcohol to dilute.

He understood her desperation to find her children. He loved his own enough that nothing save death would take them from him. But though he still knew none of the details, he knew she'd used him and his family in a big way, and he wouldn't forgive her for that.

It also troubled him that she'd made him feel like a monster for having stopped her search for her children the night he'd found her trapped by the cat. God! What little the two brandies had done to settle his anger was undone as he considered that. It frothed in him when she rapped lightly on the office door.

Josie was surprised by his coolly polite, "Come in." But she knew the moment she stepped into the room that there was nothing cool about his anger. It stood between them like a heat mirage she'd read about in a dime novel about the plains. It kept her at a distance and promised pain if she ventured too close.

"Would you like a brandy?" he asked, still with that chilling civility.

She was about to refuse, then decided she might need it.

"Yes, thank you," she said.

She moved toward the settee, where they sometimes talked when she had something to discuss with him while he worked. But he pointed her to the chair that faced his desk, then went to pour her brandy.

She understood the snub. This was not a family discussion. This was the conducting of business—probably that of her return to Boston as quickly as possible. After he told her what he thought of her.

She sat in the chair, prepared to accept whatever he had to say. She took the brandy with another thank-you and swallowed a deep sip while he walked around the desk to his chair.

He sat and leaned back in it. He had shed his vest and collar and his white shirt was open at the throat. His dark features against the snowy white seemed hotter, darker, more threatening. But she found the cool dispassion with which he studied her the most alarming of all.

"I presume you have an explanation," he said. "I'd like to hear it."

She took another quick sip and wished it were that simple, that she could open her mouth and a logical, chronological explanation would come forth that would help him understand a mother's anguish, which had made her set out to lie to him.

But it was all so entangled, all so hurtful to rethink and relive. Yet she had to. She tried to sort through her mind for a beginning, because, even now, there were some things she would tell him and some things she would not. Because she realized with a sudden sharpness that was a pain unto itself that she loved him and she didn't want to leave him.

Deliberately passing over her humble beginnings, wharf-rat childhood and her father's deathbed request that his employer care for her, she began.

"I ... explained that Benjamin was a wealthy man," she said. She waited for his confirming nod but he didn't seem willing to help her with even that simple courtesy. So she went on. "He was murdered in his office at the wharf, just after Christmas."

She saw a flare of surprise in Adam's eyes, but he reacted in no other way except to continue to watch her with that penetrating gaze.

She took the last sip of brandy, placed the glass on the edge of his desk and joined her hands together.

"My mother-in-law, Jerusha, a cruel and bitter old woman who'd resented my presence in her household since the day Benjamin brought me home, told the police she'd gone to the wharf to deliver a message to him that night and that she'd seen me run out of his office in the darkness."

The only expression on his face was a small furrow between his eyebrows. "Did you?" he asked.

"No," she replied, beyond affront that he'd asked the question. "But Jonathan, my attorney, wasn't able to prove that until several months later. The intervening time I spent in prison."

Surely that would bring a reaction. It didn't. She resisted the temptation to reach across the desk and shake him. She suspected that could prove fatal.

"Go on."

"While I was in prison," she said with quiet clarity, her heart ripping as she relived those days in her mind, "Jerusha gave the boys to Gripper and his wife and paid them to take them away.''

This time he did nod, probably because that was something he'd heard for himself from Charlie. She was encouraged by even that meager response.

"I was delirious with joy when Jonathan secured my release from prison, then, in the carriage on the way home, he had to tell me that my children were gone. Jerusha had disappeared, and I had no way of knowing even which direction they'd taken." Panic closed her throat for a moment as the horror of that afternoon and the grim torture of every day that followed was reenacted in her mind. She drew a deep breath to steady herself.

"The only clue we had was a conversation one of the maids had overheard in which Jerusha had referred to the man as Gripper. Jonathan has several unsavory connections who sometimes help him in investigations, and he discovered from them that Gripper was a petty thief who was heading west to evade the law. Apparently Jerusha found him through the butcher's delivery boy, who's been to jail several times. She paid him well. Someone at the railroad office recalled selling four tickets that night to California to a very anxious man and woman with two children. One child was asleep, and the other, he thought, was trying to get away from the couple."

His expression grew neutral again. "And you came out to search all of California on your own in typical illogical fashion."

She felt so battered at the moment she couldn't even muster resentment for the accusation. "Jonathan hired a Pinkerton man," she said patiently, then explained about his accident and long recuperation, and that he'd learned only that the Grippers were heading for the Siskiyou Mountains. She met his eyes. "Then I intended to search the Siskiyou Mountains in typical illogical fashion. But Jonathan wouldn't help me."

He raised an eyebrow at that. Before he could suggest that Jonathan was a man of great wisdom, she went on. "Because of the murder, all of my husband's money was legally entangled, and I had very little of my own. And Jonathan refused to lend me the money because he was certain without masculine protection I would fall victim to some form of predator." She sighed. "I was about to set out on foot when your letter arrived in Jonathan's office. It was the first glimmer of light in that darkest time of my life."

Adam could only imagine how horrible that time must have been for her. But he could *feel* how horrible this time was for him. While he could empathize with her, he couldn't quite sympathize.

"And it never once occurred to you to tell me the truth?" he asked. "That a man with children might understand your desperation to find your own?"

"No," she replied candidly. "First, if you'll recall, I didn't know at the time that you had children. Jonathan somehow passed over that part of your letter while trying to find the parts that answered my questions. And secondly, your letter sounded so..." She searched for a diplomatic word, certain this was not the time to use *pompous*. "So...concerned with finding a lady of good breeding and fine manners. You were obviously in search of a woman to round out your life, so to speak, not one who would bring problems into it. And even if the inconvenience of trying to find my children didn't upset you, you'd probably have wanted to know *how* I'd managed to lose them. And I felt very certain that if I explained that they'd been taken from me while I was in prison, you'd have quickly decided to search elsewhere for a wife." She looked him in the eye again. "And I needed so much to get here. Marrying you was my only chance."

He held her gaze evenly. "And what were you planning to do when you found the boys?"

Again, she made herself reply honestly. "Go back to Boston, try to untangle Benjamin's affairs by helping Jonathan and the police find his killer, and obtain my sons' inheritance for them."

That set a match to Adam's temper. He wanted to stand, to storm across the office, but he made himself remain in his chair. He was afraid movement on his part would lead him to her, and he simply didn't trust himself. But his voice did raise several decibels.

"And what about *my* children?" he demanded. "The woman they've come to think of as their new mother simply disappears?"

Tears burned her eyes and her throat, but she held them back. "If you'll recall," she said calmly, "I tried to withdraw when you told me you had children. You were the one who wouldn't hear of it. You're partially responsible for this..."

He shot out of his chair, no longer concerned with whether or not he hurt her. But he paced in the opposite direction anyway. Then he spun on her, his eyes dark with fury.

"Don't try to put responsibility for this tragic little opera at *my* feet. You lied from the beginning, and you lied every moment you spent with my daughters and with me."

She sat quietly as he marched past the back of her chair. That must seem a very true statement to him, though in her heart she knew it to be false. Everything she felt for the girls was deeply sincere, and even now, as he raged around her, she loved him with all her heart. Life could be vicious, she thought with sad acceptance. It had restored one love to her and robbed her of another.

"There is a solution," she said reasonably. "If you could arrange transport for the boys and me back to Sacramento, I'll see that Jonathan returns all the expenses you've incurred on my behalf when Benjamin's estate is finally settled. Also..."

He came around her to sit on the edge of his desk. "You will remain here," he said implacably, folding his arms. A small silence followed his pronouncement.

Josie blinked. His expression made it obvious this had not been a decision reached out of a desire to forgive and forget. "Surely you don't want me to stay after..."

"No, I don't," he replied brutally, "but Jane and Lucy have been hurt sufficiently for their little lifetimes, and since I've fulfilled your purposes in this marriage, it seems only fair that you now fulfill mine."

She didn't want to leave, but neither did she want to stay simply on sufferance.

"But I've been in prison," she reminded him. "If anyone finds out, your position in the community..."

"Yes, well, I'll be quiet about it if you will."

He was quite serious. He intended to make her stay. She couldn't deny the little bubble of joy that rose in the turmoil within her.

"My children will stay with me," she said firmly on the chance he was entertaining an alternative solution to their sudden presence in his life.

His level gaze condemned her for thinking he would do otherwise. "Of course," he said quietly.

She felt herself relax. "How," she asked practically, "will you explain them to everyone?"

"You left them behind with friends in Boston until you were settled here. Everyone should understand that."

"They won't question why we haven't mentioned them?"

"You've missed them so much, it was difficult to talk about them—or whatever seems logical to you."

She nodded, the little bubble of joy creating another. She had her children, and she was staying. In the dark heart of all the problems that surrounded her at the moment, that was enough to create the hope that one day she might find a way to make Adam understand and forgive what she'd done.

"They're very nice little boys," she said quietly.

He dashed her hope instantly. "I'm sure they are. Take after their father, no doubt." He stood to go back behind his desk and pull a sheaf of papers toward him. "Go to bed, Josie. I'll be sleeping down here from now on. We'll have to continue to share the wardrobe, but the room is yours."

"Adam." She stood to lean across the desk and place her hand over one of his. "That isn't what I want," she said softly. "You know how I..."

He drew his hand away, the look in his dark eyes pushing her back several paces. "You've already gotten what you want, Josie. This is what *I* want. Good night."

Josie checked all four of the children before climbing into her cold and lonely bed. She lay huddled in the middle, burrowing her nose in a spot on Adam's pillow that smelled of his bay rum cologne. She felt as though her body might tear itself apart with conflicting emotions. Elation and despair could not coexist. But for now at least, they had to.

She had found her children and lost Adam in the process. She closed her eyes and said a prayer of gratitude and one of supplication. "Please," she pleaded, "help me find the strength and the patience to win him back."

Sleep claimed her while she prayed.

Chapter Thirteen

Adam forked a thick piece of bacon into his mouth and reviewed his notes for a civil dispute case for which he must appear in court this afternoon. The material was so foreign to his beleaguered brain that it seemed as though an eternity had passed since he'd taken these notes—or that some-one else had taken them.

Someone else had, he thought dryly—the man he'd been before he'd learned his marriage was a sham and his wife a deceitful liar. He'd known all along that she was keeping secrets. He'd just never suspected they involved a murder, prison and two children. Not that any of that mattered as much as her dishonest wifely "performance."

He sipped his steaming coffee and listened to the quiet sounds of Bertie at work in the kitchen. He'd dressed early, smuggling clothes from the bedroom, where he resolutely kept his eyes from the graceful figure at sleep in the bed, one slender, naked leg hanging over the side. He'd intended to leave before anyone else was up and take his breakfast in town. But Bertie, preparing to feed two extra mouths, was already slicing bacon and bread. She'd insisted on fixing his usual morning fare.

He took another sip of coffee and tried to turn his mind back to the case. But a new disturbance prevented him from doing so—a feeling that he was being watched. He glanced up at the window, beyond which a hawthorn tree was in full bloom, but not even a bird looked in at him. He turned to his right, saw nothing, then looked down and found himself the object of the frank study of a pair of dark gray eyes. They belonged to Josie's youngest. Adam recognized one of his patched shirts, which had apparently served as a nightshirt and hung to the boy's toes.

"Good morning," he said. "Are you hungry?"

The gray eyes continued to stare with an intensity he began to find unsettling. Then the boy raised his arms to him.

Adam had been a father too long to misunderstand the gesture. He lifted the grave little child onto his lap.

"Are you Charlie?" he asked.

The blond head shook. Adam noted in amazement that it seemed to be covered in very fine corn silk.

"Billy, then."

Adam was rewarded with a quiet "Yes." Then, apparently deciding he'd studied Adam sufficiently, he turned his attention to his plate.

Adam handed him a slice of crisp bacon. The child studied it, took a bite, then leaned back in the crook of Adam's arm and proceeded to eat it.

"You have the same charming skills your mother has," Adam said, moving his notes to the other side of the table.

Since Billy seemed to want nothing more of him than a comfortable place to sit and food to share, Adam tried again to peruse his notes.

Josie wasn't certain what had awakened her, but she sat up to a brilliant early morning and for the first time in almost five months felt a burst of joy rather than the grim reality of loss with which she had started every day since learning her boys were gone.

They were home now. She was home. She just had to make Adam understand that.

She dressed hurriedly, checked the bedroom next to hers and found the girls still asleep. She felt a moment's concern that Jane wasn't up, then remembered that it was Saturday.

She peered into the next bedroom. Charlie lay half in and half out of the blankets, his hair tousled, his arm, clad in one of Adam's shirts, hanging over the side of the bed. Josie went to resettle his blankets and to simply admire for a moment the contentment with which he slept. Happiness made her want to shout.

She turned to check on Billy and straightened with a start. His bed was empty. Panic took her in a stranglehold for a moment until she could assure herself that he hadn't been stolen from her again. He'd simply awakened early and gotten up to explore.

She closed the bedroom door softly and hurried downstairs, afraid he might wander out of the house if no one was up.

The smell of bacon frying told her that Bertie, at least, was up. Josie looked in the parlor, checked behind and under things because Billy used to love to hide. When that search proved fruitless, she rounded the corner into the dining room and stopped still in the doorway.

Billy, still in the oversize nightshirt, sat in Adam's lap at the head of the table, munching on half of a biscuit. Adam spooned a dollop of jam on the other half, his free hand holding the child in place, long fingers splayed against and almost covering Billy's little torso. Before Adam could put the biscuit to his mouth, Billy held out his piece, a ragged bite missing.

Adam put his biscuit down and reached for the jam pot. "Of course you want some," he said conversationally as he carefully spooned a small amount while Billy watched in anticipation. "Bertie makes the best peach jam in the county. There. What do you think?"

Billy took an enormous bite, smiled up at Adam, then let his head loll back against the man's arm as he chewed.

Whatever notion she might have entertained that Adam would let the anger and resentment he felt toward her affect his treatment of her children was immediately banished. Josie found herself not only surprised but a little jealous of their intimacy. She wondered how long they'd been up that this easy camaraderie could have formed already.

Then she remembered that Adam had held Billy all the way back from Gripper's place. He had provided the paternal touch even a child that age realized was missing from his life. And, in the way of children, he was not shy about staking his claim on what he wanted.

Bertie bustled into the room from the kitchen side and put more bacon and biscuits on the table.

"Oh, Mrs. Scofield," she said. "Good morning!"

Adam and Billy both looked up, Adam's relaxed countenance stiffening, Billy's gaze only mildly interested. She felt suddenly like an intruder.

"Come and sit down," Bertie called cheerfully. "Before Billy eats all the bacon. I'll go put your eggs on."

"Thank you, Bertie." Josie went to her place at Adam's right, bravely facing down both their stares.

She saw her husband watch her warily as she placed a hand on his shoulder and skimmed her lips within inches of his as she leaned down to kiss Billy on the cheek. Had she been braver, she'd have kissed him, too, but self-preservation prevailed.

She sat down and smiled amiably at Adam. "Would you like me to take him before he gets jam on your shirt?"

"Actually, you're just in time," he said. "I have to be off to the office." He stood with Billy riding his arm and leaned down to place him in Josie's lap.

Billy protested, holding both arms out to Adam and crying, "No! No! No!"

Adam, in the act of leaving the room, came back, a frown between his eyes. He looked to Josie for an explanation.

She shrugged helplessly, holding the squirming, scream-ing child to her. "I can't explain it," she said. "He seems to have taken to you."

Bertie, bearing a plate with two eggs, sunny-side up, placed it before Josie and wiped her hands on her apron. "Forgive me, but what's so difficult about this? The girls took to Mrs. Scofield because they needed a mother. It only stands to reason that the boys will take to you, Mr. Sco-field, because they need a father. It's one of life's very ba-sic family recipes."

Adam took one of Billy's grasping little hands in his and kissed it. Josie went weak with emotion.

Then another level of chaos was added to the room as the girls ran in, still in their nightgowns, pink-cheeked from sleep.

Billy's attention was suddenly diverted by their squeals. Jane insisted on holding him and Lucy, twice his size though less than two years older, stroked his hair.

Josie smiled up at Adam. "You should take the oppor-tunity to escape while you can."

He returned a look that was far different from the loving one he'd given the child. "I'm too securely caught in the trap for that," he said, and it was clear he wasn't referring to Billy's instant attachment to him. Then he reached for his jacket, kissed each child on the head and left the house.

By noon, Josie was convinced that no punishment Adam could inflict on her for her deception could rival that brought about by the very achievement of her goal.

In King's store she was forced to raise her voice to main-tain order, something she'd never done before, either with her boys at home in Boston or with the girls since she'd ar-rived in Yreka. But it seemed that was all she'd done all morning.

From the moment Charlie had wandered downstairs and found girls at the breakfast table exclaiming over his little brother, he'd been insufferable. At first Josie thought she'd somehow brought the wrong child home—that some impostor had come west with Billy and that sweet-natured, kind-hearted Charlie was still somewhere in Boston.

"Who are *they*?" he'd demanded, pointing to Jane and Lucy as though they were leprous.

"They're my husband's children. This is their home." She'd made polite, cheerful introductions all around, certain her own hopeful attitude would inspire the same reaction in the children. She'd been sorely mistaken.

Charlie immediately took the defensive. "How old are you?" he demanded of Jane.

"Nine," she'd replied with obvious relish. "Older than you."

They'd stared at each other in what Josie understood to be the face-off in a struggle for leadership of the pack.

"But I'm a man," Charlie said.

Jane had been unimpressed. "You're a boy, and I'm still older."

Charlie had turned to Josie and said unequivocally, "I'm not living with girls. I want to go home."

Josie had pulled a chair out for him and said kindly but firmly, "This *is* home, Charlie, and the girls are both very nice, as I'm sure you'll discover when you stop being rude to them. Now, eggs and bacon?"

He had glowered across the table as though to tell the girls that he would see about that. "Yes, please."

Josie was grateful Ivy had insisted on accompanying her on the shopping trip for clothes for the boys, because it was she who sat with the children in the back of the wagon and maintained order.

But now she was on an errand for her mother and Josie was alone in the mercantile with four children doing all within their power to humiliate her in front of the other patrons.

While Josie had been occupied with finding garments for Billy, Jane had apparently placed a saucy straw hat on her head. Charlie had told her she looked like the ice cream vendor's donkey in Boston. She'd shoved him angrily, he'd grabbed her, and together they'd fallen into a carefully stacked mountain of canned and boxed goods.

Josie turned in mortification. Lucy, clutching Winifred, had pointed at Charlie. "It wasn't Jane's fault," she said loyally. "Charlie said she looked like a donkey."

"You will both restack those just as you found them," Josie said firmly, "and I don't want to hear a word out of either of you until the job is finished."

"Really!" a disdainful, vaguely familiar female voice said. "It seems you've brought a tribe of wild Indians to town with you, Josie."

Josie turned again to look into Betsy Fulton's beautiful but coldly smiling face. It occurred to her that the sunny morning was simply too full of unpleasant surprises. But the children had already created a scene. She wouldn't be baited into another.

"Hello, Betsy," she said. She couldn't bring herself to say that it was nice to see her again, so she settled for, "You're looking lovely."

Betsy gave an unconscious nod, apparently well aware of the fact. "And you're looking embarrassed," she said in a tone that pretended to be discreet but was loud enough to be heard in every corner of the store. She pointed with a frown to Charlie, face like a thundercloud as he restacked the store display, and Billy, looking like a little ragamuffin as the clerk pinned up pants that were far too long. "Who are the little orphans?"

Temper made Josie clasp her shopping bag in both hands so that she wasn't tempted to use them to commit murder.

"They're not orphans," she replied with cool courtesy. "They're my children. Now that I'm settled, I've brought them out from Boston."

Betsy frowned in genuine surprise. "But I thought you didn't—"

"Betsy, please!" an older woman called from across the store. "I'll be late for my fitting if you don't come this instant!"

"Coming, Aunt Priss," Betsy promised, then turned to Josie with a quick, pained perusal of her yellow dress. "We're on our way to Madame Elise's. I see you haven't had the opportunity to visit her. Would you like to join us?"

Josie forced a smile she was sure failed to be gracious. "Thank you, but I'll be busy here for some time."

"Pity," Betsy said, then, with another disapproving look at the children, hurried to catch up with her aunt as the woman left the store.

Josie sighed and turned at the sound of a squeal. Lucy, who'd reached into a pickle barrel, intent on a little shopping of her own, was now invisible except for white stockings and black button-up shoes protruding over the edge. With a groan, Josie went to extract her.

"Lucy Scofield, you smell like a pickle," Adam said with a laugh that was half amusement, half confusion as she climbed into his lap in the parlor, unmindful of the fact that Billy was already there.

Josie, sitting on the settee with Jane beside her as they worked on their embroidery, looked up to explain. By unspoken mutual agreement, Adam and Josie had decided for the sake of the children and at least the appearance of family harmony to continue the little habits of their everyday lives, despite the gulf that had opened between them.

She related Lucy's tumble into the barrel, leaving out Charlie and Jane's animosity toward each other, and the embarrassing mess that had followed. She was a little surprised word hadn't gotten to him from Betsy or one of the other patrons present at the time.

"Ivy and I washed her in vanilla water, but it doesn't seem to have helped a great deal."

Adam frowned at his youngest daughter. "You fell *into* the pickles?"

Afraid a scolding might be imminent, Lucy quickly diverted attention from herself. "Jane and Charlie knocked over all the cans in King's window."

Adam's eyebrow went up and his frowning gaze turned to his older daughter.

"Charlie started it!" she said in defense of her behavior. "He said I looked like a donkey, so I pushed him." When her father's expression didn't seem to lighten with her explanation, she added lamely, "I forgot the cans were there."

"Well, it was a stupid hat!" Charlie stood in the doorway, covered in dirt from head to toe.

Josie closed her eyes and wondered what precisely she had done to offend the fates.

Adam, applying all the tenacity of which his legal mind was capable, found himself struggling to keep up with what was beginning to sound like a reign of terror perpetrated by his family at King's.

"What hat?" he asked.

"I tried on a hat," Jane said, sending Charlie a look of utter dislike. "He said it made me look like an ice cream vendor's donkey."

Adam's gaze turned to Charlie, who shifted slightly in the doorway but didn't flinch.

"Yes," the boy admitted. "That's what I said."

In the less than twenty-four hours that Josie's boys had been in his home, he and Charlie had barely had the opportunity to exchange names, but he could see defiance written clearly in the boy's face. He guessed that they would gradually adjust to each other, but he couldn't be sure. The boy appeared to have more of his mother in him, and several months in the hands of a bully under what had to have been frightening conditions didn't seem to have diluted it.

It was more likely, he thought, that their acceptance of one another would be the result of a confrontation rather than any easy adjustment. But until that day came, he could afford to be understanding about what was probably the result of a squabble for position in the family hierarchy.

Adam smiled at him. "Let me tell you, Charlie, that women respond more pleasantly to compliments than insults."

"She's a baby," Charlie said scornfully.

"I'm still older than you!" Jane said with a fulsome glower.

"That's enough," Adam said mildly. "I think it would be good of both of you to remember that you're not savages. Disputes shouldn't be settled by pushing and shoving, particularly in public. Charlie, ask Amos to run a bath for you."

Charlie remained where he was, looked from his mother to Adam and declared simply, "I don't want to take a bath."

Josie fought every maternal instinct that demanded she place herself between the child and the man and explain them to each other before whisking Charlie off to handle the matter of his defiance herself. But that would never do. She was going to have to take him aside at the first opportunity and let him know a few of the things she'd learned about Adam Scofield.

Adam saw that he was being measured. He was accustomed to that. Opposing attorneys did it to him all the time.

"I'm afraid that doesn't matter in this instance," he said without raising his voice. "What does matter is that you're very dirty and I want you to take a bath."

Charlie turned to Josie in supplication. "Do I have to?"

Josie didn't hesitate. "Yes, you do. And right now."

Charlie stalked off, looking as though he'd been betrayed by his last friend.

That issue settled, also by the unspoken but mutually accepted knowledge that parents must function in tandem,

Adam excused himself to go to his office, and Josie took Billy upstairs to bed.

Later, when the girls were tucked in, Josie looked in on Charlie, who'd gone to bed voluntarily after his bath.

"I don't like him," Charlie said, arms folded atop the covers, eyes staring straight ahead as she sat on the edge of the bed beside him.

"I would guess after your behavior today, it would be difficult to find anyone in this house, or anyone who was near King's store today, who likes *you*."

"I want to go home."

"Charlie, this is home. I've explained that."

"It's not home to me."

"The home you remember no longer exists for us, Charlie. Papa's gone, and the house no longer belongs to us. I know how much that hurts, but that's the way things are. You have to learn to be happy here."

"I won't."

Yes Josie thought. *That's what I once thought. But you'll learn differently, just as I did.*

"We'll start again tomorrow," she said, leaning over him despite his belligerent posture to kiss his cheek. "Since school is almost finished for the summer, we've decided not to send you until next fall. So, you've a whole summer ahead of you to learn to ride, to fish in the creek, to meet other children and to have a good time."

His side-glance told her that was a slim possibility, indeed. Then he turned onto his side and said good-night.

Josie went to her room, restless and depressed. She had faith that the children would adjust to one another eventually, but she wondered what good that would do when, underneath their civility, their parents were at odds.

Josie pushed her window open and leaned out to draw in the smell of roses in Bertie's garden, the clean fragrance of grass and the distant sweetness of the orchard.

And as she knelt down to let the breeze sweep her face, she saw Adam walk across the yard toward the fields, hands in his pockets, shoulders square under his white shirt.

She watched him longingly, wishing that she had the right to reach for her shawl and run out to join him, hand tucked into his arm. But she knew that to be simple wishful thinking. His reaction would be to give her that cold gaze that held her at a distance more surely than a pitchfork would have. And today had felt as though it were a year long. She simply hadn't the resilience.

After church on Sunday, Josie and Adam had to explain why there'd been four children between them in the pew rather than two.

Adam made introductions, and Josie calmly gave everyone the explanation she'd given Betsy. If they were surprised, they were gracious enough to accept her explanation without question.

She held her breath as Nan, the older woman from the sewing group, pinched each little chin in welcome and seemed not to be aware that she'd seen the boys once before.

The Scofields stayed for a cake social on the church lawn. Adults gathered in groups to exchange gossip while the children played, mothers shouting cautions about their Sunday clothes. The pastor's eldest daughter and several of her friends gathered the little ones into a circle for singing and playing games.

Julia had a new collection of magazines and novels for Josie and asked excitedly if she'd be going to the party to be held in two weeks' time at the Journal Residence.

Josie shook her head. She'd learned that the famous home of Robert Nixon, Jr., the publisher of the Yreka *Journal,* was often the setting for wonderful parties. But Adam had mentioned nothing to her about attending and, she guessed, given the present state of their relationship, probably would not.

Josie shook her head. "I've nothing to wear to such an occasion. I'm afraid most of my Boston clothes are—" she ran a disparaging hand down the elegant but sedate brown suit she wore "—frumpy. Suitable for church and travelling and shopping, but not for parties."

Julia rolled her eyes. "Well, my dear, that's easily remedied if you can get your husband to plump your allowance for a week or two. My couturier could have you outfitted like Princess Eugenie herself in time for the party."

"Madame Elise?" Josie guessed.

"Yes," Julia replied. "You know her?"

"No." Josie laughed. "But Betsy has suggested on more than one occasion that I've desperate need of her services."

Julia's eyes rolled again. "That little trollop. Did you know that my husband found her in the hay with Drake Morgan, her father's business competition?"

Josie couldn't help the interest the news generated within her. "No!"

"Skirts up, drawers down," Julia smirked. "Fulton hired George after he fired Adam and Miles, and George had gone out to look over the property and buildings to update his will, and he walked into the barn and, well . . . George looks like he hasn't a frivolous thought in his head, but he never misses an important detail."

"Julia!" Josie said, looking around to make certain no one had overheard.

"In any case, I'll be paying Madame Elise a visit tomorrow. Why don't you come with me?"

Josie shook her head. "I don't believe we've been invited. Adam hasn't said anything."

Julia dismissed that possibility with a wave of her hand. "Of course you've been invited. Adam is always invited to everything. In any case, I'll pass your house on my way into town. If you want to come with me, be ready. I'll be going first thing in the morning."

Josie heard Julia's instructions, but what caught her attention was the scene taking place several yards away over her friend's shoulder.

A group of six or seven children were gathered around two boys who danced around each other, fists raised like little boxers. One of them was a burly boy whom Josie had seen arrive with Betsy's aunt. The other was Charlie.

Even before she could react, she saw Charlie run at the bigger boy, driving his head into his stomach and knocking him to the ground.

With a little cry, she ran in their direction. It wasn't long before she realized that separating two young boys determined on fisticuffs was a dangerous business. She'd been kicked in the shins, the shoulder, and barely dodged a flying fist.

Strong hands suddenly lifted her bodily out of the way, and Adam reached down to yank one boy up by the back of his shirt and then the other.

"Roger!" Betsy's Aunt Priss exclaimed, arriving on the scene in high dudgeon. She pulled the child to her and wrapped her arms around him protectively. Over the boy's bright red hair she stared fiercely at Charlie. "*You're* the boy who almost destroyed King's store last week. Apparently no one's taught you manners since then! Someone ought to give you a good whipping!"

Josie moved to interfere, but Adam put a hand out to hold her back. He shifted the hand that clutched Charlie's shirt to his shoulder and asked quietly, "What happened, Charlie?"

Charlie opened his mouth as though to speak, then firmed his lips and shook his head.

"You *see* what happened!" Aunt Priss said indignantly. "Roger's eye is already swollen like a frog's!"

"Charlie?" Adam asked patiently.

Charlie looked back at him, gray eyes wide and moist with tears he refused to shed. Josie's stomach tensed with the effort to let Adam handle the situation. She could see in the boy's eyes that he'd had a reason he refused to reveal.

"See? He had no reason. Except that he's a bad-mannered bully!"

Josie saw Adam's temper slip when he turned to the woman and said coolly, "I don't think you can call him a bully, Mrs. Fulton, when your boy is twice his size."

"Roger's the bully." Jane stepped forward out of the group of children who'd surrounded the boys. "We were playing ball. When Charlie's team beat Roger's team, Roger called Charlie a stupid orphan and threw the ball at his stomach. It wasn't Charlie's fault, Papa. Roger started it."

The other children confirmed her story with nods of agreement.

"Nobody would say so because Roger beats you up if you don't do what he says." She fixed Roger with a superior glance. "But I'm not afraid of him."

After a moment of grumbling, the crowd dispersed. Aunt Priss dragged Roger off to their wagon, and Adam straightened Charlie's shirt.

"Do you feel all right?" he asked, bending over him. "Where did the ball hit you?"

"I'm all right," Charlie said, looking from Jane to Adam in faint confusion. "It hit my belt buckle."

Josie leaned down beside them to wipe Charlie's dirty face with her hankie and smooth his hair. Her heart bled for him and all he'd had to bear since his father died.

He pushed her away, putting a hand to his mouth in sudden urgency. "I think I have to..."

Adam towed him swiftly to the backside of a tree. He looked pale and big-eyed when they reappeared.

Josie put her arms around him and looked at Adam in concern. "Do you think the ball might have injured him? Should we take him to Dr. Reed?"

Adam shook his head. "My guess is this has more to do with the four pieces of chocolate cake he ate and the tension of the moment than the blow to his stomach. But I think it's time we got everyone home."

Adam lifted the children into the carriage, then offered Josie a hand up, his expression once again carefully neutral.

Jane and Charlie, side by side in the second seat, looked at each other in suspicion.

"I still don't like you," Charlie said.

"I told the truth because it was the truth. I still don't like you, either."

Well, Josie thought, resisting the impulse to turn to Adam to share the grimly funny moment. *One phase of my life is very much back to normal.*

Chapter Fourteen

Josie sat propped against her pillows atop the covers, dressed for bed but too wide-awake to sleep. The children had been in bed for an hour, and the Donovans had retired. She imagined Adam was still at work in his downstairs office. The house was unnaturally quiet.

She'd tried to begin one of the new novels Julia had given her, but she was too restless for an endeavor that required concentration. She leafed through the *Police Gazette*, but that didn't suit her mood, either. She wasn't certain if it was Charlie's pugilistic performance that had brought on the mood, but she felt defensive and edgy herself—and very lonely.

She finally crept quietly down to the kitchen in search of leftover brown Betty and a glass of cider. She was surprised to find the lamp still lit and stared at it for a moment, wondering if Bertie had somehow forgotten it.

"Raiding the icebox?" a male voice asked from the far shadows of the kitchen. Josie spun around with a little cry to find Adam in the portable bathtub, naked shoulders and upper chest visible above the water, a lean, angular leg hitched over the side. In his hand was a small glass of something golden that caught the lamplight.

For a moment, Josie was paralyzed. Lust rose in her like a sudden storm, hot and sparking lightning. Its power emanated everywhere—from the tips of her fingers to her toes and all places in between.

Adam saw her eyes ignite. Against the lamplight, he also saw the small, elegant curves of her breasts and hips under the thin cotton gown. He could remember the feel of her roundness against the palm of his hand as though he held her now—as though there was no shadowy kitchen between them, no gulf of suspicion and hurt feelings. He was grateful that the bathwater was high enough to conceal his body's immediate and powerful reaction to her.

Josie felt drawn toward the tub as though she were being pulled by a rope. She stopped within a foot of it, realizing that the clear water hid little. She moved her gaze to his face, noted that he'd washed his hair and that it lay slicked back, the natural part already forming, a fallen curl already drying on his forehead. She had to clutch the side of her nightgown to avoid reaching for it.

His chin and jaw were beginning to darken with beard, and his eyes—his eyes studied her with a lust that equalled her own.

"Adam..." she whispered.

"I'm here," he replied softly. "In the flesh, so to speak."

He was. Splendidly. She struggled to keep her eyes on his face and resist the irresistible seduction of the moment. If she reached for him and he rebuffed her, she would be crushed. But if she didn't try...

She reached intrepidly for the cloth and soap on a stool beside the tub and walked around behind him. If he repulsed her effort to help him bathe, it wouldn't be quite the same as rejecting her.

"Why are you bathing in here?" she asked, tossing the cloth over his shoulder into the water and rubbing the soap, which was already damp, between her hands. Her breathing was shallow and she concentrated on remaining calm.

He drew his leg into the water and, raising both knees, leaned slightly forward over them to allow her access to his back. Triumph swelled in her.

"I didn't think you'd want me bathing in your room," he said, reaching out to put his glass on the stool.

Bracing herself for the impact on her senses, Josie ran her soapy hands across his hard, square shoulders, down his well-muscled back, along his arms to his elbows, then repeated the process again with slow deliberation.

Adam thought he probably deserved this torture, the insistent prodding of her small, mobile fingers, the sensation of them moving over him, tracing the lines of his shoulders and back. He remembered that she'd once touched him in that same way while she learned about his body with flattering fascination the first time they'd made love. That memory had plagued his sleepless nights.

Her hands dipped a little lower along his spinal column, lower than they'd ventured on their first pass.

She grew serious for a moment.

"Julia told me that Mr. Fulton has fired you and Miles and hired George."

Adam had difficulty thinking about business. "Yes," he said simply.

She sighed, and he felt her breath against his wet shoulder. "I'm sorry. I feel . . . responsible."

"Don't," he said. "The Donovans are like family to me. I wouldn't let anyone hurt Ivy and get away with it. And I wouldn't expect you to. Miles and I have more cases than we can handle, even without Fulton's business."

Relieved that he didn't blame her, Josie began to soap his back and shoulders with fresh enthusiasm.

"Julia," she said chattily, "also told me there's a party at the Journal Residence and that we've been invited."

He had to repeat her words in his mind to distract himself from her attentions. He'd put the invitation aside, reluctant to have to pretend to be lovesick newlyweds in a situation considerably more intimate than the church social. Although he had to admit that he did feel seriously lovesick at the moment.

"I didn't think you'd want to attend," he said. "You'll have to pretend that we're happy newlyweds, that you married me because you love me."

Josie ignored the taunting words, choosing to follow instead what seemed to be a promising path. "Would you hand me the cloth, please?" she asked, reaching her hand over his shoulder to receive it.

Adam reached for the cloth, wrung it out and placed it in her palm.

She ran its nubby softness over his back. "Julia said your presence would be expected."

"I imagine it would."

"Then I would be willing to give a creditable performance," she said airily, "if you think you are capable of doing the same."

Adam hesitated for a moment. He still held his anger over her deception closely. And the notion that all the warm, comfortable moments they'd shared and all the nights they'd loved each other with unrestrained passion had been calculated to keep him satisfied with her so that she could remain with him to do her searching still cut him deeply. His pride and his willingness to share had been assaulted.

"I'm not sure I can," he admitted honestly.

Josie dropped the cloth over his shoulder again, satisfied that it landed in the water with a plop, splashing his face. Frustration made her want to rake her nails over his back, but she forced herself to think rationally, to behave fairly. After all, this was all her fault in the first place.

"Of course you can," she said, dabbing at his back with the towel she took from the stool. "You pretend to care for my children as though they were your own. Certainly you can pretend that you love their mother?"

He shrugged a muscled shoulder. "I can hardly fault your children for what you've done."

She sat back on her heels with a gusty little sigh. Why was she surprised that he refused to forgive her? He'd told her that night that he wouldn't. Still, she had to applaud the fairness with which he dealt with her children.

"I want you to know," she said, "how grateful I am that you haven't transferred your anger with me to them."

"That would be petty and small."

Yes. Rather like refusing to forgive a woman who is very, very sorry.

Josie pushed herself to her feet. "I will need a gown for the party," she said, walking around the tub as he reclined again. "I brought no evening dresses with me from Boston. Julia is going to see Madame Elise tomorrow."

He nodded. "She's a client. I'm sure she'll open an account for you."

She turned to face him. "Then you think you *can* give a persuasive imitation of a loving husband?"

He inclined his head gravely. "I will make my best effort."

Josie, prodded by a touch of devilry, looked doubtful. "It's been some time since you've behaved like one."

She saw the challenge leap to his eyes. Her heart thumped against her breast.

Adam's gaze ran over her body, beautifully delineated once again by the lamplight through her gown, and decided that she might be right.

"Come here, then," he said, "and remind me how it's done."

He held a hand out in clear invitation. Josie hadn't the will to resist, though she could see in his eyes that this was more game than real emotion. But her entire life's creed had been to take what she could get and build on it.

She went toward him and put her hand in his. She leaned over the tub as his eyes drew her to him. His hand slipped up her leg under the nightdress as she leaned even farther to place her hands on his shoulders, her eyes ensnared by his.

His hand rose up her thigh to shape her bottom. She lowered her lips to his.

The old familiar quiver began deep in her being, and she knew just an instant of the powerful chemistry they shared as his tongue dipped into her mouth—then a high-pitched shriek filled the air.

Startled and dangerously overbalanced, Josie fell into the water and Adam's lap.

"Oh my God! I'm so sorry!" Bertie stood in the middle of the kitchen, a horrified expression in the wide eyes visible above the hands crossed over her mouth. Behind her, Amos looked both mortified and amused.

Bertie's gaze ran over Adam's bare chest and Josie in her wet nightgown pressed to it, her legs now bare to her thighs kicking futilely at the air.

"I saw the light," Bertie chattered in explanation, "and thought I'd forgotten to turn it down, or worse, that there was an intruder, so I woke Amos and brought him with me. It never occurred to me that you...that the two of you..."

"It's all right, Bertie," Adam said, laughter in his voice. "I appreciate your vigilance."

"But I'm so sorry I...I didn't mean to..."

Amos turned his flustered wife to the door and smiled over his shoulder at Adam. "Good night, Mrs. Scofield, Mr. Scofield."

"Good night, Amos."

As the door closed behind the Donovans, Josie looked into Adam's eyes and knew the moment was lost. The spell that had made him invite her closer had been broken by Bertie's intrusion. He knew what he was doing. And she could see in the depths of his gaze that he would make love to her if she made the proper move or said the right word. But not because he loved her, because he wanted her.

And, fortunately for her, the broken spell had reeled her back to reality. She didn't want to play games with him. She wanted to love him. And she wanted him to love her.

"This is the last time," she said, pushing against him and the tub to try to get to her feet, "that I come downstairs at night in search of refreshment."

As her efforts to reach land were proving futile, Adam braced an open hand against her bottom and pushed. She landed on the kitchen floor, the wet skirt of her nightgown bunched and wrinkled around her waist.

Josie blushed and straightened it.

"I'm quite refreshed," Adam said with a smile.

With a scolding frown she said good-night and left the kitchen.

Adam watched the delicious sway of her hips under the wet and clinging fabric and groaned. He'd lied. He was not refreshed at all. He was frustrated and in pain.

"You look ravishing!" Julia Burton exclaimed as the Scofields wandered into the group with which she was engaged in conversation. "I *knew* Madame Elise would make you look like a queen, Josie. Adam Scofield, you have on your arm the most beautiful woman in the Journal Residence this evening."

Adam gave Josie a loving, possessive glance that made her tingle...until she remembered that it was all for the sake of appearance.

She smiled back at him, relieved to be able to show the love she truly felt. Since it was wasted at home, she kept it to herself. But here, tonight, she'd determined to let it free. He would simply think she was performing, and there was little danger of his rejection, since he was performing, too. All she need do to perfect the evening was pretend that his performance was real.

The crowded conditions added a wonderful dimension to their charade. They held each other more closely when they danced because there was barely room to move. When they chatted in the parlor, Adam was forced to sit on the arm of the chair Josie occupied because there weren't enough to seat everyone. When they moved to the porch for fresh air, it, too, was so crowded that Adam leaned against a pillar and pulled Josie close to him as they visited with Miles. Josie, cradled against Adam's thigh, had difficulty concentrating on the conversation.

Until Betsy Fulton appeared.

"Why, hello, Josie and Adam. Miles." The last she added with a venomous glance at him. This time the gentleman trailing Betsy was considerably older, Josie noted, and had an air of boredom and dissipation. Was this Drake Morgan? she wondered. She saw Adam and Miles exchange a look.

"I'm still confused about your children," Betsy said. Everyone within earshot, and their number was considerable, turned to listen. "Adam told everyone you just sent for your boys to join you, but it's curious you didn't simply bring them with you."

"I explained—" Josie began politely.

"That you were waiting until you were settled," Betsy interrupted. "Yes, I remember. I suppose since you were purchased or freighted or whatever the proper term is, sight unseen, so to speak, perhaps you were afraid you wouldn't meet with Adam's approval and might be sent back."

The cruel and audacious suggestion left everyone silent. Even Betsy's escort gave her a startled look. Josie wasn't concerned for her own reputation, but since it was inextricably entangled with Adam's, she was embarrassed for him.

He, however, seemed to be suffering no such discomfort. Clearly, and loudly enough to satisfy every ear now straining for a reply from one of the Scofields, Adam said, "Josie was *invited* to join me because she wasn't afraid to do so, and because she was genteel and well mannered, something you might not understand since you seem to have limited experience with either quality. And if it will relieve your curiosity, sending her back has never once crossed my mind. Excuse us."

Adam led Josie back inside with a firm grip on her arm.

"Liar," she whispered for his ear alone.

He gave her a quick, annoyed glance, leftover temper still radiating from him. "I believe that's a case of the pot and the kettle, Josie."

She was flattered by his defense of her but filled with guilt that she'd placed him in a position of having embarrassing questions asked of him in front of his friends.

"I'm sorry," she said softly as he led her toward a buffet table where a line was beginning to form.

"That wasn't your fault," he said, taking his place behind Reverend Knox and pulling Josie in front of him. "It was hers."

"Was that Drake Morgan?"

Adam frowned down at her. "How did you know?"

"Julia told me they were seeing each other." Quietly, she related the scene George had come upon in the barn.

Adam raised an eyebrow. "Morgan owns the logging company in direct competition with Fulton."

Josie nodded knowledgeably. "So Julia told me. Mr. Fulton doesn't mind Betsy seeing Morgan?"

"I'm sure he would if he knew. He seldom socializes, so he isn't here. And Betsy and Drake didn't arrive together, so all anyone could report to him about tonight was that they spoke to each other and probably had a dance."

Their discussion of Betsy's companion was terminated when Reverend Knox turned and smiled warmly at them. "Well, Scofields! I've been looking for someone to bore with my youngest's latest exploits."

Throughout the rest of the evening Josie was aware of Betsy's eyes on them. Despite the fact that Adam kept Josie close beside him, and always had a proprietary hand on

her arm, she felt sure that Betsy suspected that things were
not as they appeared.

"Josie," Adam finally said impatiently when they were
dancing once again, "I feel as though I'm holding a corset
with a stone statue in it. Will you please forget Betsy?"

"I'm sorry," she said, beginning to weary of the strain
this performance was placing on both of them. She felt sure
guilt was readable on her face, and Adam seemed to be
growing more and more tense as the evening progressed.
"But she's always watching us. I *know* she suspects something."

"The way you're behaving, it's little wonder." He spun
her in a wide turn that brought them to the open doors
leading to the porch. The fragrance of roses beckoned from
the garden. "She's on the lawn watching us from behind her
fan while pretending to converse with Morgan and another
couple. Shall we destroy her suspicions once and for all?"

Concerned about precisely what he meant, Josie hesitated over an answer. But that didn't stop Adam from going forward with his plan.

He led Josie out to the porch to a spot behind a pillar that
did not conceal them entirely. And Josie knew her gold dress
shone brilliantly even in the shadows.

Adam turned her toward Betsy and took her in his arms.
Josie's went around his neck without conscious direction
from her, and her heart began to pound as his lips came
down on hers.

He was crushing her, and his mouth on hers prevented her
from drawing a breath, yet his kiss filled her with a sense of
freedom she hadn't felt in several weeks. After all the dis-
mal days when they'd been coolly civil to each other and the
lonely nights they'd spent apart, this was like coming out of
a dark, dank tunnel into the light.

It was all they'd begun to feel for each other recaptured.
It was...

"Adam!" she whispered in a high voice when his left hand began to gather up the side of her skirt and petticoats.

He kissed her into silence. "Hush," he said as he nipped at her ear. "The men have their backs to you, and she can only guess what we're doing."

She gasped against the front of his coat as he held her firmly to him with one hand and ran the other over her lace-and-cotton drawers.

"Adam, I don't think..."

The admonishment went unfinished as his hand dipped into the waistband and molded a trembling curve in his palm. It was warm and firm and she pressed her mouth against his coat again for fear of making a sound that would turn the men's heads in their direction and leave Betsy in no doubt whatsoever about what they were doing.

She found herself erasing the presence of spectators from her mind, studying the small swing in the corner and wondering if it would hold them.

Then there was the sound of an indignant huff and the pattering feet returning to the house.

"Betsy?" a woman's voice said in surprise.

Other footsteps moving more slowly also returned to the house.

The sudden silence reminded Josie that this had all been staged with a definite purpose in mind—to convince Betsy that Adam was pleased with his bride. It was no one's fault that her body seemed unable to recognize that fact though her mind knew it. The heart of her femininity was already pulsing madly, and she had to marshall every particle of self-control she possessed not to move against his hand and encourage him further.

"They've...left," she said in a strangled voice. She pushed against his shoulders, afraid her weakening willpower wouldn't hold out another moment.

Adam felt her reaction to him, felt the unconscious upward movement of her knee that pressed her against him and invited more.

Josie felt his hesitation and began to come to her senses. There were scores of people just a few feet away. There were probably guests wandering in the gardens and, worse, this *had* just been a casually written little drama intended to deceive—just as so much of her life had been lately.

With a sudden little burst of self-pity and a sense of abuse being heaped upon her by life in whichever direction she turned, she pushed against Adam more firmly and, when he didn't free her, punched one small fist against his shoulder.

"Let me go at once!" she ordered in a whisper.

Adam had had enough of trying to guide their lives safely through all the perils and pitfalls she put up in their paths. He was tired of his actions being nothing more than *reac*tions to control the damage caused by hers. He decided that he wasn't yet finished with her.

Closing both arms around her waist, he lifted her off the floor and walked to a shadowy corner where a wicker chair stood against the latticed side of the veranda.

Josie hung in surprise from his arms. "Adam, what are you—"

His purpose was clear the next moment when he propped his foot on the seat of the chair and placed her astride his knee.

"Are you insane? There are people . . ."

He reached into the front of her drawers and gently but confidently right inside her. She emitted a high-pitched and not very quiet little cry.

"I suggest if you don't want an audience," he said quietly, "that you keep your voice down. They're far enough away to notice nothing if you will hush."

"The audience we were concerned about," she said breathlessly, "has left. This is not necessary! Ah!" She closed around him tightly, thinking to prevent him from moving any deeper, but all that did was heighten the sensation of his intimate touch. After the desert of feelings of the last few weeks, she felt her resolution slip.

"I believe it is," he said, molding his other hand around the back of her thigh. "You seem to forget that you do not control every move we make. *I* brought you here, *I* got your children from Gripper, and *I...* " He stroked a fingertip across the silky little bead inside her and heard her whispered cry. She wrapped her arms around his neck. "I," he whispered as he stroked again and again, "am the only one who can make you feel this way."

His hand around her thigh supported her weight as she strained off his leg and against his hand, her breath stopping, her muscles taut, her eyes closed, until her stillness shattered in a bouquet of little cries and shudders.

She finally fell against his shoulder with a broken sigh. He eased her bloomers back into place and smoothed the petticoats and shimmering gold skirt that still rode his knee. Then he bracketed her waist to lift her off him and set her on her feet.

Her blue eyes were filled with fire in the shadows, and he could see heat in her cheeks. "You did that deliberately!" she accused.

He raised an eyebrow. "Of course I did. It's difficult to do that accidentally."

"I mean," she said, adjusting the bodice that had slipped a little in her enthusiastic response to him, "that you were flexing your muscles, demonstrating that you have the power to make a wanton out of me in the shadowy corner of a veranda."

The other eyebrow went up. "I suppose that's unheard-of in Boston."

"What's unheard-of," she said, her voice growing hoarse with anger and hurt feelings, "is to deprive a woman of wifely considerations night after night, then take her out to a party and treat her like a woman who charges for her services!''

He shook his head, apparently unimpressed with her vehemence. ''That's not at all what happened, and you know it, Josephine. I believe you're more upset that you enjoyed it than that it happened. And if you miss your wifely considerations, remember what brought this about.''

''I didn't say I missed them,'' she said. ''I pointed out that...'' The argument stalled on her lips as she felt the little pulse that still beat where he had touched her, a tangible testament to her body's more than eager reaction to him. Denying that she'd missed making love with him would be a lie. And she simply couldn't tell one more.

Instead, she turned, prepared to stalk away from him into the ballroom.

He caught her arm at the door and said with a smile as several dancing couples turned to watch them, ''If you storm away from me, you'll undo the image we've spent the evening creating, and Betsy wins.''

At the moment, she almost didn't care. But he was right and she had to be sensible. So they left the party as they'd arrived, arm in arm and with cheerful smiles.

After a silent ride home, Josie left Adam at the bottom of the stairs with a polite but stiff good-night.

Adam let her go, almost relieved to have her out of his sight. She'd been wreaking havoc on his nerves, his emotions and his frustrated masculinity all evening.

He'd known he was in trouble when she'd drifted down the stairs punctually in that gold dress. It revealed ivory shoulders and the swelling fullness of breasts that rose above the construction of the garment with every sigh. It clung to a small waist, then swept grandly to the floor, concealing all manner of treasures he knew by heart—and had finally had to touch once more.

He poured a brandy and sat at his desk without lighting the lamp. He was beginning to understand why he was having such difficulty letting go of his anger over her deception and admitting to himself and to her that he adored her in spite of it. It was because what he felt for her was so strong that it threatened to overpower him.

He'd loved Maggie like that, with a totality that had claimed him so completely that when he'd lost her he had felt for a long time as though he'd died himself.

That kind of love was frightening. And he was a man who liked to think of himself as fearless. But he remembered how afraid he'd been for her when he'd drawn a bead on that mountain lion, then, later, how worried he'd been when she wouldn't stop weeping.

He downed the last mouthful of brandy and laughed at himself in the darkness, a curious peace settling over him. It was pointless to be afraid of a threat that had already overtaken him. He loved Josie utterly and completely, every bit as much as he'd loved Maggie. All that was left to do was find a way to deal with it.

Chapter Fifteen

"Mama, Charlie is kicking me under the table!"

"I am not! Lucy's just a big baby. I moved my foot and it touched, but I didn't kick her."

"That was *my* piece of chicken!" Jane shouted.

Against the loudly spoken protests, Billy banged his cup on the tabletop again and again.

Josie, who was helping Bertie pare potatoes, exchanged a weary look with the housekeeper, put her knife down on the cupboard and went to the table with her most severe expression. She'd brought the children in for lunch an hour before to put a stop to a quarrel that had begun upstairs where they'd been playing in the girls' room. But everyone still seemed far more interested in arguing than in eating. Even usually amenable Billy was being difficult

"I think everyone needs a spring tonic," Bertie said from the rocker where she sat with a bowl of peelings in her lap and a basket of potatoes at her feet.

Hands on her hips, Josie looked from one pugnacious little face to the next.

"I'm going to give everyone a good spring spanking if this quarreling doesn't stop," she said firmly. "It's a beautiful day outdoors. I want you to go outside and find something to do. If you can't play together, then play separately. And you remember what the boundaries are."

Three heads bobbed up and down. Charlie rolled his eyes. "I want you to stay out of the stream and away from the toolshed."

As they went outside, Josie gathered up their plates and frowned at the housekeeper. "Do you think they're ever going to learn to live together?"

Bertie grinned. "One day, when they realize they'll be a help to each other in life instead of someone to get between themselves and the attention they want from their parents."

Josie lifted the back of her wrist to brush the hair from her eyes. "That sounds like something that won't develop until they're almost grown."

Bertie's grin widened as she nodded. "I believe you're in for a long siege."

"What do you mean you're leaving early?" Miles asked, looking up from his desk as Adam, jacket on, stood in his doorway. He shook his head in a disparaging way. "Honestly, Adam, you're becoming quite pathetic. You've taken more time off in the weeks you've been married to Josie than you have in all of our years in partnership. Why don't we simply build on a room for Josie, and you can bring her in with you every morning and visit her several times a day for the sake of your voracious virility."

Adam leaned a shoulder against the doorway. "You're envious because you've spent so much time playing the rogue bachelor about town that you'll have to work all night tonight to be prepared for court tomorrow. And my going home early has nothing to do with my virility."

Miles dropped his pencil and leaned back in his chair. "I'm willing to believe that. Certainly you've expended it by now."

"Of course not," Adam denied seriously. "It's infinite. But the children were quarreling when I left Josie this morning, and she's had her hands full trying to help our children learn to coexist. I thought I'd bring her into town for dinner.''

Miles looked suddenly grave. "Did Betsy's questions last night upset her?''

"Somewhat." Adam knew that *he* had upset her more than Betsy had. "That's one nasty young woman.''

Miles nodded. "Well, enjoy your evening. If you decide to take pity on me, bring that pretty little Ivy into town with you and leave her here to help me with my work.''

Adam gave him a reproachful look over his shoulder as he headed for the door. "She's a very nice young lady, Miles. And Amos is very protective, and very strong.''

When Adam could find no one in the house, he followed the sounds of angry shouts to the back door. He was concerned for a moment when he saw splashing in the stream and Bertie standing on the bank, shouting anxious directions.

Then he saw as he drew closer that Josie had everything under control. She stood in the stream past her knees, had each of the two smallest children by a hand and was bringing the very reluctant older two to her by the power of her voice and her glare.

She gave each child a sharp smack on his or her backside, then handed them up to Bertie. The girls and Billy marched past Adam, screaming in indignation, followed by Bertie, who bit back a smile. Charlie stalked past, hands in his pockets, lip quivering.

Adam went to the edge of the bank and gave Josie a hand up. She leaned heavily on him, encumbered by her skirts.

Apparently forgetting she was angry at him, she poured out a story of daylong mutiny and mayhem. "We couldn't stand them in the house a moment longer," she said, pulling at her sopping skirts, pushing at her hair, wispy wet curls hanging in attractive disarray, "so I sent them outside to play, telling them specifically to stay out of the water. When

I looked out to check on them, of course they were all in the creek. Charlie with Billy on his shoulders! I'm sorry. I promise not to make a habit of striking the girls. I've never disciplined that way. But today there was simply no other way to get their attention!"

He nodded with grave sympathy. "I understand completely. I once had a similar dilemma involving a young lady, a canyon and a mountain lion."

Josie, struggling to make progress toward the house in her wet skirts, stopped to give him a scolding glance. Then she grinned. "Well, at least neither of us can question where our children's bullheadedness comes from."

"Come here," he said. "It'll take us until morning to get to the house at this rate." He swung her up into his arms.

Surprised by his good humor, and surprised by the instant evaporation of her own bad temper, she raised a curious eyebrow. "Why are you home in the middle of the afternoon?"

"I came home to take you to town for supper."

She blinked. "Why?"

"Because I thought you might like a change of scenery after the day you've had. I could see it developing when I left this morning."

"But you took me to a party last night."

He walked effortlessly toward the house into which Bertie and the children had disappeared. He hesitated over a reply. Last night Betsy had appeared, and then there'd been the veranda incident. Although he'd found it delightful, Josie had taken a very different attitude about it.

"It was *your* fault!" Jane's accusatory voice drifted out to them as they approached the back of the house. "You dared me!"

"If you hadn't been squealing like a pig," Charlie retorted, "we wouldn't have gotten caught!"

"Upstairs with the lot of you, and get out of those clothes," Bertie ordered, "before I finish what your mother started with a wooden spoon!"

Josie sighed wearily. "I believe I would very much like to go to town for supper."

Josie felt slightly off balance, not quite sure what Adam expected of her tonight. She sat across from him in a dark green dress, her hair swept up in a simple knot. Serviceable crockery and cutlery was spread between them on a checkered tablecloth.

Though the Siskiyou Hotel's dining room hadn't the sophistication of the Sacramento Palace, where she and Adam had shared their first dinner, it reminded her sharply of that night. And he was watching her consideringly as he had then, as though understanding her was not a simple matter. So many of her problems had been resolved since then—and several new ones created.

"You look melancholy," Adam observed over the unpretentious pot roast before him. "Are you worried about the children?"

She was, of course. Their hostility toward one another was always on her mind. And it was easier to nod than to admit she'd been thinking about him.

"I'm at my wit's end," she said with a grim smile and a shake of her head. "Your girls were darlings until my boys arrived. And my boys have always been sweethearts. But together they're like some wild Mongol horde bent on war and destruction!"

He grinned and she shook her head, now spilling out all her concerns. "I know Charlie is often the instigator. He's always been stubborn, but never so deliberately difficult." Her eyes filled and she put a hand to a suddenly dangerous quiver in her bottom lip. "I hope the time with Gripper hasn't affected him so that he will never be the child I knew again."

"Josie." Adam put his fork down and reached across the table to cover her hand with his. "Are you the same mother he knew before your husband was murdered, before you were imprisoned, learned your children were taken from you and were forced to find the surest way to the Siskiyou Mountains to find them?"

She didn't have to consider. "No," she said in a small voice. "Of course not."

"Then you can't expect that all this hasn't changed him, too. But I think your concerns are misplaced."

She looked up at him with hope. "You do?"

"Yes. He hardly seems broken by what he's been through. Instead, I would say that his stubbornness probably served him well. And as soon as he realizes that he's among friends and doesn't have to fight *us,* he'll settle down—and so will our lives."

Josie took comfort in his theory—and felt her love for Adam grow in proportion to the enormous generosity he showed for her children. They'd disrupted his life a great deal in the past two weeks, and while never letting a serious infraction slide, he seemed always to find a just solution to the endless quandaries they created.

"You think that day will ever come?" She allowed her mind to create a vision of the six of them living in familial harmony. The vision was so beautiful it hurt. But could it ever really be?

He smiled and picked up his fork once again. "Yes. But then, we have to consider that this stubbornness of Charlie's was inherited from you and is of a particularly virulent strain."

She gave him a smilingly reproachful glance as she, too, went to work on the succulent roast. "It just so happens Benjamin was very stubborn."

"Ah. Of course." He poured more wine into her glass. "In any case, Charlie isn't responsible for my girls' bad behavior. They've been defensive and jealous, but that should stop, too. You proved this afternoon that all the children will be treated the same whether they began as yours or mine.''

She frowned, disheartened once again. ''Now every one of the children hates me.''

He shrugged that off. ''That's a parent's lot in life. Eat your supper. I'd like to stop and see Miles before we go home.''

The night was cool and fragrant, a light, scented wind coming down from the direction of the white mountain. Adam took Josie's elbow as they stepped off the boardwalk and into the street to cross to the office.

Longing rose in her, made her want to turn into his arms and beg him to take her home and make love to her, to put aside this friendly neutrality that was almost worse than the anger. She yearned desperately for the passion and humor they'd once found together.

But she knew she'd dealt their relationship an almost fatal blow, and this slow rebuilding was necessary and important and probably more than she deserved.

She walked beside him quietly, fighting the terrible loneliness of having him so near yet still not close enough.

''Adam!''

They turned simultaneously to see James Forsythe locking the bank. Josie recognized him as the husband of Milly Forsythe, an outspoken member of the group she'd met at Julia's home. She'd seen him at several after-church socials. He was short of stature and as cheerful as he was round.

He waved as he pocketed his keys and came toward them. He doffed his hat to Josie and smiled apologetically at Adam.

''I hate to bother you on what looks like a social evening, but might I have just five minutes of your time? We have a problem with a depositor, and Mr. Proctor, the bank president, asked if I would discuss it with you before we do anything further."

Adam nodded. "Of course. We're heading toward the office anyway."

"But I have to show you bank records. Will you come back with me? I promise not to keep you beyond five minutes."

Adam pointed Josie to his office. "Go ahead and sit with Miles. I promise I won't be long."

It was only moments later that Adam and Forsythe stood in front of the bank again as the bank manager locked the door. The night was quiet, except for the muted sound of a hurdy-gurdy coming from Duenkel's Saloon down the street.

Suddenly the loud pop of a rifle shot split the stillness, coming from the direction of his office. It was followed instantly by the high, shrill scream of a woman. Josie's scream.

Heart in his throat, Adam ran across the street, followed closely by Forsythe. He burst inside and stopped a moment at the door, relief filling him at the sight of Josie kneeling in the middle of the floor, apparently unharmed. Then alarm filled him anew as he saw that she cradled Miles's head in her lap and that a large dark red stain covered the shoulder of his white shirt.

"I'll get Dr. Reed!" Forsythe said, and disappeared at an awkward run.

Adam went to kneel beside Josie and Miles on the floor. "Are you all right?" he demanded of Josie. "What happened?" He pulled his jacket off as he spoke and placed it over Miles, who was ashen and gritting his teeth.

"We were just standing together talking," she said anxiously, holding a small, blood-drenched hankie to the wound. Her eyes were wide and distressed. "Then I heard this strange sound and he fell. He's losing so much blood, Adam!"

"James went for the doctor." Adam leaned over his friend and held Josie's hankie away to take a closer look. "I suspect it looks worse than it is."

"You...*would* say that," Miles objected in a very thin voice. "It isn't your shoulder."

"Be quiet and save your strength," Adam said.

"Why?" Miles asked, wincing against the pain. "So you can impugn my masculinity by suggesting that it doesn't hurt?"

"I didn't say it didn't hurt," Adam corrected with a grin, encouraged by Miles's perversity. "It's just not likely to bring about your death, so I'd just as soon not listen to you groan. Josie's sensitive about these things."

"Adam, really!" Josie scolded with a dark glance as she stroked Miles's sweat-beaded forehead. "This is no time for levity."

The doctor arrived with Forsythe and the sheriff, and the men lifted Miles and carried him to the settee in Adam's office. Dr. Reed pulled off his jacket, rolled up his sleeves and tore Miles's shirt to study the wound.

"Nice and clean," he said after a moment. "Bullet went right through. All we have to do is clean it out and stitch it up." He grinned into Miles's pale face as he reached into his bag. "Won't be much worse than that time Milo Busby shot you for makin' eyes at his wife at the Fourth of July picnic."

"She made eyes at me first," Miles said with a weak smile. "And she never mentioned being married."

Josie knelt beside Miles and held his hand while the doctor poured laudanum on a cloth, then held it to his patient's nose. Adam and the sheriff wandered out of the room with the bank manager.

When Adam returned half an hour later, Miles was singing softly, his words incoherent under the influence of the drug. The hole in his shoulder was now covered with a thick white dressing and bandage. Josie, face white and pinched, helped the doctor pull his coat on over his bare chest.

"Who would want to shoot Miles?" she asked, carefully buttoning the coat.

Adam shook his head. "I don't know. Possibly someone on a case he's working on. Or someone unhappy with us for having defended Mr. Fong. Whoever it was was standing outside the back window. Miles made a perfect target in the lamplight."

The doctor rolled down his sleeves and pulled his own jacket on. "There's no one at home to take care of him, is there? He won't be able to use that arm for a few days."

"We'll take him home with us," Adam said.

Adam and the sheriff placed Miles gently on a blanket in the back of the wagon, then covered him again with Adam's jacket.

The doctor shook Adam's hand. "I took good small stitches, but don't jostle him too much."

"Thanks, Doc."

When they arrived home, Adam went in search of Amos to help him carry Miles into the house. With him came Bertie and Ivy, but it was obviously Ivy who considered herself in charge of the invalid's welfare.

Once Adam insisted Miles should be lodged in the master bedroom, Ivy directed his transfer there, was very specific about his placement on the bed, then helped Adam undress him with a clinical detachment that was almost professional.

She sat in the chair by the bed and calmly insisted that everyone else retire.

Amos and Bertie went back to their place, and Josie looked in on the children. She was grateful to see that they'd all slept through the commotion.

Adam went down to his office, puzzling over why and by whom Miles had been shot. Everyone liked Miles, so reason suggested one of their clients, but even that possibility seemed remote. Except for the Fong case. And he and Miles had worked on it together. Why would someone have attacked Miles and not him? It didn't make sense.

He was suddenly very tired of things in his life that didn't make sense. Unfortunately, Miles's shooting was a tangle he could not unwind at the moment, and his friend was safe upstairs. But there was another knot in his life that he intended to undo tonight.

It wasn't until that decision crystallized in his mind that he became aware of the absolute stillness of the house. Where *was* Josie? She'd been in the bedroom when they'd all fussed over Miles, then the Donovans had gone home to bed and she had disappeared.

With Miles in the bed she'd occupied, she had nowhere to sleep. At least, she probably thought she hadn't.

Shirt unbuttoned, he prowled through the house in search of her. When he could not find her in the parlor, the dining room or the kitchen, he went back upstairs.

He peered into the girls' room and found them both fast asleep and no one in the rocking chair. He pushed open the door to the boys' room and found them, too, asleep. But he saw a figure sitting up in the window seat that looked out through sheer curtains onto bright moonlight.

She unfolded herself gracefully from the cushioned seat and hurried toward him on tiptoe, gauzy white floating about her, dark hair tumbled around her shoulders. "Is something wrong with Miles?" she asked in an anxious whisper.

He caught her wrist and pulled her out into the hallway, closing the bedroom door.

"No, he's sound asleep with Ivy stationed in the chair beside his bed like a militant angel." He frowned down on her, hands on her hips. "But there must be something wrong with you. Did you intend to sit up all night on the window seat?"

Josie's heart began to tick erratically. He'd obviously come upstairs specifically in search of her. She was afraid to consider what that meant on the chance she was mistaken. She tried to appear unperturbed.

"Unless you've lost count," she said mildly, "you'll notice that with Miles in the master bedroom, there is no bed for me."

"Yes, there is," he corrected, his eyes dark in the shadowy hallway. "Come with me." He took her arm and drew her with him to the top of the stairs.

She pulled against him on the brink of the first stair. Since he was already down one, they looked each other in the eye. The lamp on the landing cast a frail light on them.

"Why?" she asked.

He was momentarily surprised by her question. Then he thought himself a fool for letting anything about her surprise him. "Why?" he repeated. "So you don't have to sleep on the window seat."

"I'd prefer that," she said honestly, "than to sleep in the comfort of the office folding bed if that truly was the only reason you came looking for me."

He folded his arms. "I came looking for you because I thought you might prefer to sleep in my arms."

The very suggestion made her heart race, but she had to clarify an important distinction.

"I would, but not if it's just because our estrangement has grown tiresome for you."

"Hasn't it for you?"

She knew the answer was in her eyes and she let him see it. "This would be a new start for us, Adam. Me being honest with you, and you forgiving me. This would be like the wedding night of a real marriage. I won't come with you on any other terms."

"Very well," he said. "If you want to set terms, I have a few of my own." He placed one hand on the railing and the other loosely on his hip. "There will be no more dishonesty between us. And you will accept my judgment on where you can and cannot go unescorted.''

No more dishonesty between us. A jolt went through Josie. She'd never told him that the story about her blue-blood Boston beginnings had been a lie. And somehow now, with the future of their fragile and mending relationship and the happiness of all four of their children dependent on this night, it didn't seem the moment to bring it up. Yet not to would be a breach of his terms. For one extended moment, she didn't know what to do.

Adam saw her hesitate, chafing as usual over any restriction placed upon her. Even if he had to put a full-time guard on her to save her from herself, he was putting this marriage on an even keel once and for all.

His jaw firmed with purpose, Adam bent his knees, positioned a shoulder at Josie's waist and slung her over it.

''Adam!'' she cried, then, remembering the invalid and the sleeping children, shouted in a whisper, ''Adam! What are you doing?''

He carried her down the stairs and around the corner into the office. ''I'm taking you to bed,'' he said, leaning down to deposit her in the chair that matched the settee. He'd placed a hand on each side of the chair, blocking her in. ''I'm going to presume you're in cooperation with my terms, and I assure you that I'm in compliance with yours.''

''But...''

''I've said all I'm going to say, and I trust you have, too.''

She opened her mouth to deny that, but he put an index finger over it.

''While I open out the bed, I want you to go to the linen closet for a sheet and blankets. I'm afraid we'll have to share a pillow.''

Josie accepted that she simply hadn't the character to fight him further. She'd tried to tell him, and the chance of that part of her past being revealed was remote at best. Her fears on that score were probably unfounded.

Adam folded down the walnut-framed mirror against the wall that became a sturdy, if slightly narrow, double bed. He and Josie put the linens on together, Josie finding it easy to accept this bountiful gift of his love and forgiveness and put aside all other concerns. Their marriage had been born out of her desperation, wounded by her deceit, and was now being restored to her whole because of her persistence and Adam's generosity. They deserved to be together.

Josie turned the blankets back, and Adam tossed their single pillow into the middle of the head of the bed. Then they faced each other across the relatively narrow expanse of mattress with new wonder—as though it truly were their first time.

Josie came around the foot of the bed to Adam, a playful smile in place. She pinched the skirt of her nightie between thumb and forefinger and held it out.

"I seem to be prepared, and you aren't," she observed. "Shall I help you?"

My God. It had been too long. The prospect alone robbed him of his voice. "Please," he said finally.

She took one of his hands, turned it and held it against her breast. She removed the gold cuff link there. Then she took the other and did the same.

Adam let himself enjoy the warm softness of her against the back of his hand without trying to touch her. He would have all night to savor her. At this moment, the taunting promise of her was building inside him.

She slipped the shirt off his shoulders, folded it by the sleeves and placed it over the back of the chair. Then she came back to him, kissed her way across his shoulders, then placed her hands on them and pushed gently until he sat on the edge of the sofa bed. She knelt to pull his boots and socks off. Then she lifted his bare feet and swung them up onto the bed.

Adam lay docilely as she unbuckled his belt, then worked with concentration on the buttons of his pants. The rasp of her knuckles low on his stomach, then over his wide-awake manhood, elicited a series of small groans from him. When she unbuttoned his underdrawers, he expelled a strangled breath.

"Am I hurting you?" she asked with a teasing smile. "Shall I stop?"

He caught the skirt of her gown in one hand and swung himself to his feet. "That offer comes too late," he said, his eyes dark with passion. He pulled the nightgown up to her waist, then crushed her to him, his hand stroking over her bottom with possessive tenderness. He kissed her lips, delving deep with his tongue, taking charge of the encounter she'd led so deliciously thus far.

He lifted the gown up and off her. Then he pulled her to him, her crushed breasts against his ribs a sensation that drew another broken sigh from him.

"Josie. My God. It feels as though it's been so long."

She rubbed gently against him, her eyes closed against the indescribable wonder of vulnerable softness against solid muscle. "It's been an eternity for me," she admitted in a whisper.

"Then let's not wait another moment."

It was an almost physical effort to step back from him and tug at his pants. He sat to help her remove them, then said with a little laugh, "If you pause to fold them, I'll swat you."

She tossed them aside with a laugh, then uttered a little squeal of surprise as he caught her wrist and yanked her into his arms. He caught her and turned her so that she landed on her back in the middle of the mattress.

Josie's heart was rocketing, and everything else within her body seemed to be in a state of strained waiting—sensitized and pulsing like a telegraph line waiting for a message.

She stared into his eyes, only inches from hers, and combed her fingers into his thick hair, thinking how desperately she loved him, how critical he'd become to her sanity, to her security, to her very life.

"I love you," she said, wrapping her arms around his neck and pulling him to her. "Adam, I love you so much."

He laughed a little at her vehemence and turned onto his back, bringing her with him to avoid strangulation. But the seriousness on her face stopped his laughter and humbled him.

"I love you, Josie." He kissed her temple and her cheek and stroked a hand up the thigh hitched around his waist. "You've become the very heart of my life in such a short time. I love you. I do."

She braced herself on her hands and looked down at him, her brow still pleated. "Tell me you forgive me."

He made a self-deprecating sound. "I forgave you the moment you explained to me how the children had been taken from you. Pride insisted that I make you suffer for having deceived me so completely." He grinned. "Usually I'm very difficult to trick."

"Say it," she insisted.

"Very well. I forgive you." He slid both hands up her thighs then down to her knees and up again, feeling the stillness that overtook her and meant she was waiting for him. "Now can we put conversation aside and do what we came to do?"

Feeling lighter than air now that the words she'd dreamed of hearing had been spoken, Josie smiled devilishly into his face as she levered herself several inches backward.

"I thought we came to save me from the window seat?"

He feigned ferocity. "Nothing is going to save you if you don't...ah! You little witch!"

Small hands closed around him and every coherent thought in his head fled. All that existed in this suddenly red-hot world was need—need for her—need to be inside her.

She withheld herself until the last moment, gauging the precise instant to take him into her. He was on the brink of madness when she finally enclosed him. He heard his own gasp as he plunged inside her and erupted on the instant—a long, shuddering release making him mad with pleasure for long, blissful moments.

When he could finally focus again, he noted her smug expression. She well deserved it, but he tapped the thigh under his hand and scolded, "It isn't nice to gloat."

She smiled gleefully at him, still containing him, wriggling to let him know she could create a reason to gloat all over again if she chose.

"Of course it is. You gloat all the time when I obey you without argument."

He raised an eyebrow. "And when has that happened?"

She leaned down to kiss the jut of his ribs. "I'm often amenable. You just don't notice because you've come to expect it of me."

"All right," he said, pulling her down to him and holding her to him while he turned and placed her under him. "Let's see how obedient you can be." He placed her arms out at her sides at a right angle to her body. Then he leaned over her with a wicked smile, his eyes gleaming and dark. "I don't want you to move your hands," he directed softly. "I want you to keep them at your sides. Do you understand?"

Flushed with pleasure and excitement and the very smallest suggestion of danger, Josie nodded against the pillow.

"And I want you to close your eyes."

Josie hesitated only a moment, then complied, a frisson of anticipation running along her spine.

Against the dark backdrop of closed eyelids, lighter shapes shifted and changed as Josie anticipated his touch. It took so long that she fidgeted a little, then finally felt it— a gentle kiss against the underside of one breast. Another kiss fell right beside it, then another, until he had wreathed her breast in kisses and she felt the sensitive nipple, already beaded, await his attention. She breathed a sigh of satisfaction when his mouth closed over it, stroking the tense little mound with his tongue.

Then he began on the other in precisely the same way. Her fingertips stirred restlessly against the folded-back bedspread as he took that breast into his mouth. Energy was beginning to roil within her like the gathering of a storm.

She uttered a little gasp of surprise when he lifted her leg and kissed the back of her thigh. A little string of gasps continued as his lips and hands stroked over her leg from her ankle to the juncture of her thigh and torso—front and back, outside and inside. The gasps rose in tone and increased in speed as he attended to the other leg and kissed and stroked his way up the inside of her thigh.

She had now locked her fingers on the bedspread. She was beginning to move restlessly.

"I asked you to be still," he reminded gently, contemplating his next move. Although her hips were tilted up toward him, he concentrated a series of nibbles and kisses across her waist and over her stomach instead.

Her brow furrowed and she gasped again.

Small, taunting little strokes of fingertips and tongue touched her everywhere, generating a tingle under her flesh that made her mad with the need to feel Adam against her, to break her promise of obedience and reach up to drag him down to her. And she wanted him desperately, precisely where he chose not to touch her.

"Adam . . ." she said on a long broken whisper.

"Yes, my love?"

His voice sounded smug. Without being able to look at him she gave him a moue of disapproval. "Revenge is no more admirable than gloating," she pointed out in a strangled voice.

"Each of us has such bad habits," he agreed with no suggestion of remorse in his tone.

Then she felt his index finger against her femininity, and that mad little pulse that was already ticking began to work even faster.

Then his finger was inside her, gently probing, exploring, retreating. She brought two handfuls of bedspread several inches off the bed in her fists.

"Adam . . ." she said in a breathy whisper.

"Yes, Josephine." His fingers dipped into her again and she groaned as he found the little pearl that would enslave her to his will.

"I want to touch you," she pleaded.

"I asked you to lie still."

"Ah!" she gasped, her hips rising to his touch. Her voice was desperate. "Adam, what do I forfeit if I disobey?"

But it was too late to consider it. Pleasure swept over her like a wind, around and around her in a tightening circle until he caught her to him and her shudders racked both of them.

He finally settled her on his shoulder and pulled the bedspread over them. She snuggled against him, her mouth reaching up to his, her eyes languid but shiny.

"One more night without you," she said with complete sincerity, "and I might have gone into a decline."

He kissed her soundly.

Chapter Sixteen

"I will be late again tonight," Adam said as he shrugged into his coat. "With Miles malingering, I may never enjoy a family life again."

Josie looped her arms around Adam's neck and smiled into his eyes. "I'll wait up for you."

Adam pulled her to him and kissed her with slow deliberation. Then he kissed the tip of her nose. "You're keeping me so busy during the night that I'll be a broken man by fall."

She nipped his bottom lip. "I've seen no evidence of that yet." Then she adjusted his tie and smoothed his lapels. "And Miles is *not* malingering. He was shot a mere four days ago. You can't expect him to be prepared to wrestle."

Adam grinned. "Don't be so sure of that. I went into his room this morning to ask him a question, and I believe he was going a round with Ivy."

Josie appeared delighted. "I've been hoping that would happen!" She followed Adam out onto the porch. "I believe Ivy's had her eye on him for some time."

Adam opened his mouth to add a comment to her statement but was halted by the startling sight of Charlie and Jane side by side on their knees around a mud puddle at the far end of the yard.

Adam turned to Josie with an inclination of his head in the children's direction. "Am I feverish, or do you also see Charlie and Jane working in harmony?"

Josie nodded. "They're digging worms to go fishing. I'm giving them one more chance to sit on the stream bank and fish without jumping in."

"They're actually learning to coexist?"

"In small ways. I think we're making progress. The little ones are still dawdling over breakfast. As soon as they're finished, we're going to help Bertie with the laundry since Ivy is so gainfully occupied."

He kissed her cheek. "I'll spend all day thinking about tonight."

She hugged him fiercely. "So will I."

Josie watched Adam ride away, then went into the dining room to check on Lucy and Billy, who had abandoned the rest of their breakfast in favor of singing the few lines Lucy knew of "My Darling Clementine." Josie cleared away their plates and brought the children outside with her to help Bertie.

By midmorning Charlie and Jane were down at the stream and the younger children were napping on a blanket under an ash tree. Josie hung the wash on the line while Bertie continued to scrub.

Josie folded a bed sheet over the line and tugged tightly to make it smooth.

The sudden pop of a gunshot startled everyone into stillness. Bertie looked up with a frown, and Josie turned, a knot tightening in her stomach. Amos came running from the barn with a rifle, and the upstairs window in the room Miles occupied flew open.

The sound came again, and Josie heard a curious whine in her ear, then a sudden burning there.

"Get down!" Amos shouted as he turned in the direction from which the sound had come—the copse of trees behind the house.

Josie looked up to see Charlie and Jane wandering back toward the house as though wondering what the noise was.

"Get down!" she cried, using her hands in a pushing motion to emphasize the command.

Charlie fell to his knees, pulling Jane with him.

Lucy sat up on the blanket, shouting in a frightened voice, "Mama?"

Josie rose to run toward her but Miles's voice stopped her. "Stay there!" he called, then ran from the back door of the house to the children's blanket, wearing cotton underdrawers and a shirt he'd thrown on. In his hand was one of Adam's rifles. Ivy appeared in the kitchen doorway, a hand to her mouth in alarm.

Absolute stillness fell over everything. Then there was the sound of a horse's hooves galloping away. Amos ran into the barn and emerged in a moment on Blackie, hurrying off in pursuit.

Miles stood cautiously, ordering everyone to stay put. Then he ran at a crouch to the trees. He was back in a few moments.

"There must have been only one," he said. "But I want everyone inside anyway."

Josie ran to Lucy and Billy while Bertie met the older children halfway across the lawn, waving them to hurry.

"Miles, what is happening?" Josie demanded anxiously, the still-sleeping Billy on her shoulder, Lucy clutching her skirts and beginning to cry. Ivy ran out to pick up Lucy and frown in concern at the fresh stain on Miles's shirt.

But Miles was more concerned with the blood on Josie's ear.

"What? Oh." Josie put a hand to her stinging earlobe and drew away blood. "Yes, I heard something funny," she said. She noted the blood on the sheet behind which she'd been standing. Then, with a sharp thud of her heart, she saw the perfect bullet hole through the fabric she'd been holding tautly with her hands. She could look right through it to the front of the house. A fraction of an inch to the left and the bullet would have penetrated her brain instead of the sheet.

She turned to Miles, who was also staring at it.

"All right," he said briskly. "In the house. Everyone inside. Josie, come on."

"It was meant for me," she said in grim amazement, turning back to stare at the hole. "The other night when you were shot, you had stepped in front of me to offer me the box of candies." She turned to him again, her eyes wide with the realization. "Someone is trying to kill *me.*"

He took her arm and pulled her toward the house.

When Amos returned more than an hour later to report that he'd lost the rider in the canyon, Miles sent him to town to notify Adam and the sheriff.

Amos returned with the two men shortly after noon. Ivy kept the children occupied upstairs while everyone else sat around the dining room table to relive the morning's events.

Josie repeated everything clearly and calmly to the sheriff. It occurred to Adam that anyone who didn't know her might think she truly felt calm. Her voice was quiet, her hands still, but he'd seen this tension in her before, the night they'd found her children.

The moment the sheriff had finished with Josie, Bertie and Ivy set about preparing lunch. Adam took Josie into his office and pulled her into his arms. The tears he knew she was barely holding back erupted.

"No one will hurt you as long as I draw breath," he said, kissing her temple. "You know that." He stroked comforting circles up and down her back, rocking her gently from side to side as though she were Lucy.

"Oh, Adam," she said after a moment, drawing back from him. He laced his fingers together and held her loosely in the circle of his arms, looking down at her with a frown of concern. Her words had such a fatalistic sound. "You can't save me from him."

"From whom? You know who shot at you?"

She shook her head. "No, I mean you can't stop him. He's probably some emissary from God."

Adam put the back of his hand to her cheek to check for fever. Her eyes were wide and soupy and had a vaguely unfocused look, as though she were not quite here with him. It gave him an uncomfortable feeling.

He gave her a little shake until she looked up at him, but still her eyes had that strangely resigned look. On a woman who never resigned herself to anything, the expression made him even more uncomfortable.

"Josie, what are you talking about?" he demanded, forcing a stern tone into his voice in an attempt to bring her out of that trance.

She sighed wearily and tried to push out of his arms, but he refused to free her. She finally rested her arms on his and closed her eyes. When she opened them again they were sad.

"I'm not supposed to have this," she said with a shake of her head.

"Have what?"

She stroked gently up his arms just once. "This," she said. "You, the children, the house, the . . . peace of the last few days. Josie Denehy is not supposed to be happy."

"That's absurd."

"No," she said with complete conviction, "it's not. Jerusha hated me, Benjamin was killed, my children were stolen from me. I lied to you and cheated you. Miles was shot. I'm responsible for everything that's happened."

"Josie..."

She had to tell him. He had to know that he could never be happy with her. She was somehow marked.

"I'm responsible," she said, looking directly into his eyes, "because I'm still lying to you."

She waited for surprise, anger, condemnation. Instead, his gaze ran over her face with a look still so possessive and indulgent that *she* was the one surprised.

"Adam," she tried to clarify, "I haven't told you everything."

He nodded, his gaze more accepting than condemning. "I know." He pulled her to the settee, sat her down, then sat beside her at an angle and delved into the breast pocket of his jacket.

He removed a yellowed newspaper clipping and handed it to her. She unfolded it with trepidation, suspecting what it contained. It was a news story about herself that Jonathan must have kept from her at the time of Benjamin's murder. It referred to her as a woman "who rose from slum child to society matron," divulged every detail of her marriage to Benjamin from the arrangement he made with Will Denehy to care for his daughter after his death, to statements from Jerusha of mistrust and dislike.

"She liked to think of herself as a highborn lady," Jerusha was quoted as saying. "But one could see through her when one knew the truth."

Then there was open speculation that Josie had played on Benjamin's sympathies before her father's death, then endeared herself to him after it so that he would "succumb to her charms," offer marriage, beget heirs, then sit innocently by while she plotted his demise so that she and her children could inherit.

Angry tears clogged her throat as she slowly refolded the clipping. "And I imagine you wonder if this is true," she asked in a husky voice.

"No," he replied quietly. "I never considered it true for a moment."

She looked up at him, surprised anew by his generosity. How could he not wonder? She passed over the subject for a moment to a question that could be answered.

"How did you come by this?" she asked.

"Betsy did a little research to discredit you for getting the better of her and sent it to me at the office about a week ago."

"A week?" she asked in surprise. That would have been before Adam had brought the wounded Miles home and taken Josie down to his bed in the office. There'd certainly been no evidence that night that he'd been angry with her.

He read her mind. "Yes, I knew that night," he said.

"But why don't you believe it?" she challenged. "I used you for my purposes, just as they say I used Benjamin."

He smiled and reached a hand along the back of the settee to cup her head in his hand. "Never in the way the article suggests. You used me to have a sort of base of operations. You never used my money or my possessions for your personal gain. And I remain in perfect health."

"I lied to you about being from an important Boston family. My mother was a housemaid who died when I was very young, and my father was a laborer for Cross Shipping. Benjamin respected my father, so when my father knew he was dying, he approached him with brash Irish nerve and told him I would have no one and asked if he'd be responsible for my care. He agreed. Everything I learned about behaving like a highborn lady, I learned from Benjamin."

Adam ran a thumb across her cheek to wipe away a tear. "I imagine you learned so well because it's instinctive with you. You were born with the natural grace that sets a woman apart. And now I understand your fearlessness and why you're so quick to fight your own battles. You were forced to be courageous very young.''

''I loved my father very much,'' she said in a ragged whisper.

''As far as I'm concerned, a man whose dying thought is for his daughter's future is as highborn as they come. I can't think why you felt you had to hide that from me.''

Josie lowered her eyes guiltily. ''Jerusha hated my past as much as she hated me. I lived with that feeling of being less than quality for so long that when your letter came and you listed all those specifications Jerusha always insisted I'd simply painted on myself, I thought you'd feel the same way she did.''

For the first time in their interview, his look became judicious. ''And now?'' he asked ominously.

''Now,'' she whispered, another tear spilling over, ''I wish I'd trusted all you seemed to be that night on the hotel balcony in Sacramento and told you everything!''

That was precisely what he wanted to hear. ''Come here,'' he said.

She flew into his arms in a torrent of tears. He leaned back in the corner of the settee and cradled her in his lap, holding her close.

''Oh, Adam,'' she wept. ''If I had any strength of character, I'd leave my children with you and ride away. I'm not supposed to be happy. Everything in my life is taken from me eventually. It's only a matter of time.''

He pulled her away from him so he could look into her eyes. ''That's idiocy, and you know it. It's simply leftover hysteria from this morning. We all work for what we deserve, and if anyone deserves to be happy, you do. Now, I don't want to hear that again.''

She sniffed, and he could see residual fear in her eyes from the morning's episode. ''This morning everyone, even the children, was in danger because of me.''

"Everyone was in danger," he corrected, "because of the man with the rifle. Is there any reason to believe that it's the same person who killed Benjamin?"

Josie thought a moment and shook her head. "I truly don't know. Jonathan promised to send me a telegram if there was any progress in the case, and so far we haven't heard from him."

"Well, who stood to benefit from Benjamin's death?"

"The children and I inherited the house and half of everything else, including the business. Jerusha and Daniel shared the other half."

"Daniel?"

"Benjamin's brother," Josie explained. "But he wouldn't want to hurt me, he was always kind to the boys and me. And he's been in Europe since before Benjamin was killed. We couldn't even locate him to bring him home for the funeral. And Jerusha is in her eighties. I can't imagine she would travel this far to try to kill me."

Adam inclined his head in agreement. "But she might hire someone."

Josie laid her cheek against his shoulder and sighed. "I suppose Betsy has told everyone?"

"No," Adam said. "I don't believe she has."

"Why not?"

"Because I told her if she mentioned it to anyone, I would see that her father learned she was intimate on a very regular basis with Drake Morgan. Thank Providence for Julia's fondness for gossip."

Josie raised her head to look into his eyes. "Would that stop Betsy? She *is* a grown woman."

Adam nodded. "Her father would disinherit her in an instant, and she couldn't live without trips to San Francisco and access to the finest fashions."

She sat up a little farther, her hands on his shoulders. He leaned his head back to look into her eyes. They widened dramatically.

"Maybe it's Betsy!" she said. "Maybe she's angry that you haven't sent me away as she obviously hoped you would."

"Then wouldn't she be shooting at *me?*"

"Not if she wants to get rid of *me.*" Her eyes narrowed as she considered. He bit back a smile because Betsy's inclusion in the mystery brought it down to a less lethal and more feminine level that made it suddenly filled with drama. He was pleased to see that the fear had left her eyes, and they were now filled with earnest speculation. "Perhaps she took up with Miles only to get to you—the handsome, wealthy bachelor she's probably always admired from afar. What?" She frowned at his sudden laughter. "You don't think that could be possible?"

"That she has desired me since she was fifteen?" he asked with an arrogant inspection of his fingernails. "Certainly. I do cut a handsome figure and she's been after every man in town at one time or another. But when Amos gave chase this morning, he said he caught only a glimpse of his quarry, but that it was a large man."

Josie frowned at him, suddenly serious. "Gripper?" she asked.

"Possibly." He stroked her cheekbone with his thumb, wanting to erase that look of fear. "It seems a logical conclusion. And we'll know very shortly. Miles and the sheriff and I have been discussing a plan," Adam said, suddenly serious once again. "I'll tell you about it when we've worked out all the details. In the meantime, no one will leave the house for any reason. Is that clear?"

She sat up again to ask with interest, "What kind of a plan?"

He pinched her chin between his thumb and forefinger. "An answer to my question first, please."

"Yes, it's clear," she said dutifully. "I will keep the children inside."

"And yourself."

"And myself. What kind of a plan?"

"I'm not certain. Some pretense of moving you to safety in the hope that we'll draw the man out. Meanwhile, Amos and Miles and I will take turns keeping watch. I promise you nothing will happen that we aren't prepared to handle."

Josie smiled and hugged him, secretly hoping that he was right and she was wrong about what fate had in store for her. So far, everything wonderful had been taken from her—her parents, Benjamin, her children, though Adam had helped her retrieve them. Had that simply been a temporary reprieve or a serious turn in a new direction? Time would tell.

It was 2:00 a.m. Adam, the rifle across his knees, sat in a chair on the front porch in the darkness, his feet propped on the railing. Miles had watched from noon to four the previous afternoon, Amos from four to eight, then Miles had insisted on taking the eight to midnight watch so that Adam could go to bed with Josie and lie with her until she slept.

"Your arm must be paining you by now," Adam had said to Miles in concern. "I'll take the watch. Josie understands. She'll be fine."

"She was frightened this afternoon," Miles insisted. "She needs you, at least until she falls asleep." Then he had grinned. "Ivy promised to sit with me for a while."

"Aha! And will you be watching or sparking?"

"I'm quite competent to do both at the same time."

Adam knew that to be true. There was very little Miles couldn't do with a woman in his arms. Of course, this time, one arm was injured.

Adam had gently pried himself from Josie's sleeping grasp at midnight and come down to relieve Miles. Ivy had just gone to bed and left a full pot of coffee beside Miles's chair and an empty cup for Adam.

The coffee had long since grown cold and the night was as still and quiet as it had been two hours before. Adam had little difficulty staying awake. What troubled him most was a painful longing to be back in bed with Josie curled against him, clutching him as though he comprised her whole world. That feeling would never grow old for him.

A small sound behind him had him on his feet and spinning around, rifle levelled as he cocked it. Then he expelled the breath trapped in his throat and every muscle relaxed as he saw light eyes and lighter hair in the shadows of the porch. Flattened against the front door in a white nightshirt that fell to his knees was Charlie.

"It's me," the child said in a small, startled voice.

Adam nodded and lowered the rifle. "I see that," he replied quietly. "Is something wrong?"

Charlie took several hesitant steps toward him. "I'm not sleepy," he said.

Adam resumed his chair and propped his feet up again. "Do you want to watch with me?" he asked.

Charlie came to stand by his chair. Adam was pleased to see that the boy's gaze had lost its earlier hostility and suspicion. But it remained uncertain. He wasn't sure what Charlie wanted from him and decided that all he could do was wait until he asked for it—whatever it was.

"What are you watching for?" Charlie asked, leaning an elbow on the back of Adam's chair.

"Movement," Adam replied. "The moonlight is bright, so it would be easy for us to see anyone trying to come across the meadow or the yard." He reached down for the flannel jacket he'd brought out with him and placed it around Charlie's shoulders.

Adam and Charlie stared out in the same direction.

"Mama's asleep," Charlie said conversationally. "I checked on her."

"Thank you."

"I had a papa, you know."

"Yes, I do. Your mama told me that he was a good man." There was a minute's silence.

"Somebody shot him," Charlie said in a very composed voice.

Adam glanced at him and saw lips pursed tightly together. "Yes, I know. I'm sorry. Your mama misses him, too."

Charlie turned to him, frank eyes just inches from his. "Will you be able to stop that man from hurting Mama?"

"Yes," Adam said without hesitation. "I promise you that."

"I wouldn't know what to do if she was gone," he said, his voice tight with emotion. "When Grandma sent us away, I just kept dreaming Mama would find us. But I was scared she wouldn't—that Billy and me would never see her again. And then—there she was."

"Yes," Adam said, feeling an echo of painful guilt at the memory of all he'd put her through because of her trips to the canyon. "She worked very hard to find out where you were."

"But she wouldn't have been able to get us away from Mr. Gripper—'cept that you were there." Charlie came around the chair and turned so that his back was to the railing as he looked Adam full in the face. Again Adam got the impression the boy wanted something he was reluctant to ask for.

Adam, operating on instinct, took a chance and grasped the boy's arms through the jacket and lifted him into his lap. Charlie sat stiffly for one surprised moment, then melted sideways against his chest and leaned his head against him.

Charlie raised a hand and pointed south, past the barn and the stables. "I'll watch that way," he said, indicating the direction that would not require him having to move.

Adam nodded and wrapped his arms loosely around him. "Good. I'll watch the meadow."

After a moment, Charlie observed sleepily, "Jane wouldn't like it if she saw me sitting here."

Adam smiled into the darkness, hearing the satisfaction in the boy's voice. "No, but then you probably don't like it when she sits with your mama, so it's only fair."

Charlie curled comfortably against him, apparently considering that an equation he could live with. Then he went to sleep.

Chapter Seventeen

Adam shouldered his way into the kitchen at just after 6:00 a.m. and stopped right inside the door, surprised to find Miles already at the small table, a coffee cup in hand. Miles had not noticed him but stared off into space, his gaze unfocused, a frown line between his brows.

"You look like a troubled man!" Adam observed, snagging a cup and going to the coffeepot on the stove to fill it. "Been reviewing your sins, have you?"

Miles focused on him, also failing to notice his taunting. "I've been thinking about life," he said. "My life."

Adam nodded, sitting across from him. "Cause for concern, for certain. What, specifically, about your life?"

"The lack of a woman in it," Miles replied.

Adam raised an eyebrow. "Ah," he said, grinning. "So a brush with mortality has turned your thoughts to settling down and begetting heirs?"

Miles gave him a censorious look and shook his head. "No. It turned my thoughts to how alone I am. No parents, no blood relatives..." He gave Adam a fractional smile. "No caring friends."

"Miles," Adam said in quick denial, "had you died, Josie would have mourned you, I'm sure."

Miles finally drew a deep breath and looked at his friend steadily. "Do you wish to hear this or not?"

"Is it going to be tedious?" Adam laughed at Miles's expression of affronted dignity and became serious. "I apologize. Of course I want to hear that you're giving serious thought to courting Ivy with the ultimate intent of asking Amos for her hand. I presume you want my opinion on whether or not marriage is worth the trouble."

Miles made a small sound of surprise, then shook his head and asked, "Well, is it?"

"Yes. Definitely."

Miles narrowed his gaze. "Now, think. Remember what Josie has put you through. Remember that you now have four children instead of two, and a woman whose obedience you'll never be completely sure of."

"Obedience isn't everything. And one child causes such upheaval in one's life that whether the number is one or four makes little difference—except in the positive aspect of having them. More hugs, more laughter..."

Miles blinked at him. "Adam, you've hardly had more laughter with that pugnacious little Charlie."

Adam remembered this morning and smiled as he put his cup to his lips. "I know," he said. "But I see it coming."

"So you're pleased that you sent for your Boston bride."

Adam let himself think about Josie for a moment, about all they'd shared in the time he'd had her, and a flood of love washed over him.

"She's so much more than I'd hoped to find. I sent for a companion, a woman who would be my friend. And she came instead with love and passion. Fire has warmed man and kept him alive since the very first Adam. Sometimes we get comfortable and forget that we need it."

Miles frowned. "Ivy thinks I should remain free."

Adam laughed and shook his head. "You poor innocent. She says that only to ease your fears. Once you marry her she'll shackle you with all the charm and sweetness at her disposal."

"Josie has you shackled?"

"Hands and feet," Adam answered without hesitation. Then he grinned. "But that means she can have her delicious way with me."

Miles winced in sympathy. "You're besotted."

Adam sipped his coffee and swallowed. "Guilty," he said.

"Of what?" Josie demanded cheerfully, tying on an apron over a pink-flowered dress as she walked into the room. She leaned over Adam to kiss him soundly.

He caught her around the waist before she could move away and pulled her into his lap. "Of being besotted with you as Miles has accused me."

Josie looked into his eyes, her own wide with pleasure. "Are you really?"

"Yes. Very."

She hooked an arm around his neck, and kissed his forehead. "I'm happy to hear that, my love. But doesn't it strike you as strange that Miles should accuse *you* of such a thing? Have you seen *him* watching Ivy?"

Miles opened his mouth to defend himself, then found that he couldn't.

"Oh, no," he said with feigned grimness, looking from one face to the other. "I see what this new alliance means. Instead of Josie having a positive effect on you, you've had a negative effect on her. She's going to begin making my life difficult, too."

Josie stood and went across the small table to kiss his cheek. "And I'm going to begin right now by preparing your breakfast. I presume Bertie and Ivy are seeing to the animals since Amos is still on watch?"

Miles nodded and got to his feet. "I'll bring in more wood for the stove. Bacon crisp and eggs over lightly, please."

"My pleasure," she said, then went to give him a quick hug. "Thank you for taking Adam's watch last night. That meant a lot to me."

Miles grinned at her, then he went out to the woodshed.

Josie gathered what she needed for breakfast while Adam watched her with a deep satisfaction in the simple pleasure.

"Why was Charlie asleep in our bedroom chair this morning?" she asked, placing an iron skillet on the stove with a clang.

"He stood part of my watch with me," Adam replied. "When I came up to bed, he was sound asleep in my arms so we slept in the chair so as not to wake you."

Josie turned away from the stove, her eyes wide with pleased surprise. "He watched with you?"

"He came out to express a few man-to-man concerns about whether or not I could keep you safe. Once I assured him I would, I think he decided I could be trusted."

"Oh, Adam." She came to wrap her arms around him and press his cheek to her breast. "Thank you."

"I did nothing significant," he denied. "I told you harmony would come about eventually."

For the first time since she'd arrived downstairs, she let him see the fear in her eyes as she glanced toward the meadow beyond the window. "Harmony is a curious word to use for the position we're in."

He pulled her back into his lap. "We're going to solve that problem as soon as the sheriff arrives to escort you into town to take the stagecoach."

"The stagecoach?"

"We're certain whoever shot at you is watching us, waiting for another chance. So I'm going to put you on the stage, as though you're being sent to Redding to keep you out of harm's way until we can locate whoever's after you."

She set her mouth in a stubborn line. "I will not go to Redding."

"I said *as though* you're being sent to Redding," he reminded her, then his look altered subtly. "And in any case, didn't we just have a discussion about obedience?"

She grinned and leaned an elbow on his shoulder. "I heard you tell Miles that obedience isn't everything."

"You were eavesdropping?" he asked in a threatening tone.

"No, I was coming to fix your breakfast. I just happened to hear my name mentioned, and you were saying such lovely things about me, I didn't want you to stop." She kissed his eyes, the straight line of his nose, his cheekbone, then grazed her lips across his before dipping inside with her tongue and kissing him deeply, erotically, promisingly. "And as soon as the danger is behind us, I'm going to show you how much I appreciate all the lovely things you said."

Miles burst back into the room, dropping an armload of wood by the back door. "Sheriff's here, Adam. Are we ready?"

"Almost." Adam stood, easing Josie to her feet then catching her hand and bringing her upstairs with him. As they hurried, he explained.

"I want you to get your travelling bag and stuff some things into it so it will look full. Put on your cape and a hat. The Donovans will stay behind to watch over the children while Miles and I and the sheriff surround you like an army to take you into town. This should convince the man after you that I'm sending you away."

In the bedroom, where the still-sleeping Charlie had moved from the chair to the middle of the bed, Adam helped her gather what she needed to look convincing.

"Actually," he said quietly, "all three of us will be with you, waiting for him to make his move. All the way to Redding if necessary." He watched her in the mirror as she pinned on her chip-straw hat with shaking fingers. "There's no need to be afraid. I'll be with you all the time. And so will Miles."

"I'm not afraid," she lied. She knew he was confident he could handle this situation, but he'd been a part of her life such a short time. He didn't know what life was really like for Josie Denehy Cross Scofield. Despite her faith in him, she couldn't help feeling a strong sense of foreboding, a feeling that even Adam Scofield couldn't fight fate—and fate had decided that Josie Scofield could be teased by happiness but never really possess it. Everything she'd had in this house at the foot of that majestic white mountain had just been a trick to make it all hurt that much more when it was taken away.

Adam watched her eyes and knew what she was thinking. He turned her around and framed her pale face in his hands. "I promise you," he said with the complete confidence that so defined him, "that when this is over, you will have lost nothing. We will all be together, all six Scofields, and we will dance at Ivy and Miles's wedding."

There was a rap on the bedroom door. "Are you ready?" It was Miles's voice.

Adam kissed Josie lightly, his eyes filled with love. "Are we ready?"

"My future obedience," she said to Adam in a small shaky voice, "depends on the perfect execution of this plan. Remember that. If you are even scratched, I will never listen to you again."

"Oh, Josie," he said, grinning as he picked up her bag and turned her toward the door. "Be prepared to mend your ways."

The stagecoach was stuffy and smelled of a previous passenger who either had not been in the habit of bathing or had bought a second passage for a pig. Josie's stomach roiled violently, and her heart pounded against her breast like something trapped and terrified.

She was desperately afraid Adam's plan was not going to work. In fact, she was sure something had already gone wrong. At the station, Adam had held her close and kissed her goodbye in front of everyone and presumably whoever was after her, then, while the driver checked the harness, he rode away. She resisted an urge to lean out the window and demand to know where he was going, to call him back, but he had promised her all would be well, and, the dubious events of her past aside, she was doing her best to trust him.

She saw the driver and the man riding shotgun climb up into the driver's box. One was tall with a full beard and mustache, the other portly and dirty. Then an obviously heavy trunk was loaded atop the coach by two other men while they complained loudly that the railroad building its way from Redding to Yreka should have to ship its payroll by stagecoach.

As the coach pulled away with the driver's profane call to the horses, Josie looked around worriedly for some sign of Miles and the sheriff. "We'll be with you all the way!" Adam had promised. Josie closed her eyes and prayed. *Please, Lord, let them truly be here. Let that be Miles and the sheriff in the driver's box and Adam in the trunk. Please, Lord.*

Josie leaned back and employed herself with yet more prayer while she watched the quiet countryside. The morning remained sunny and bright, and they were almost to Kilkenny's when she began to wonder if Adam had misjudged her pursuer.

Then, as they rode through a narrow lane thick with trees on both sides, she heard a gunshot, then a man's loud voice shouted, "Stop the coach!"

Josie's heart lurched and the breath seemed to stop in her lungs. She would have sworn that her blood stopped flowing.

The driver required some distance to rein in. When he finally did, Josie peered out the window to see two men on horseback, bandannas covering the lower halves of their faces. One was tall and slender, the brim of his hat low over his eyes. The other was also tall, but thick and meaty with a belly that made Josie feel sympathy for his horse. Despite the bandanna, Josie recognized Gripper.

"Come down!" The more slender of the two men, and the one who seemed to be in charge, called up to the driver. "And throw down the trunk."

This was not going at all the way Josie had hoped. She should have known. Adam had been mistaken. Perhaps he wasn't in the box, and he'd been left behind after all.

She watched the driver leap down, then reach up for the trunk. Josie studied him carefully and was certain he was Miles under a beard and mustache more appropriate to a costume party than to try to fool a villain.

And he was taking such care in receiving the trunk that there was little doubt it contained something that would not be well served by a fall from the top of the coach.

He supported it against the side of the coach while the man riding shotgun leapt down and helped him lower it to the ground. The second man, though dressed in dirty clothes and chewing crudely on a plug of tobacco, was very obviously Yreka's sheriff in disguise.

Josie's heart sank to her toes. This plan was not going to work. It was obvious that theatrics were not her protectors' strong suit.

"Throw your guns away," the man demanded.

Miles and the sheriff complied.

The bigger man got down from his horse and hurried awkwardly to collect them. The corpulent form of the man who'd taken her children had been emblazoned on her brain since she'd first seen him standing in the doorway of his cabin.

"Josie, you may come out now," the other man called.

Josie searched her mind desperately for a plan of her own, but fear overrode all else. She was vaguely surprised to find that it was not fear for herself—it was fear for Adam, whom she was now convinced had been smuggled aboard the coach in the payroll trunk, and for Miles, whom she'd come to love like a brother, and for the sheriff, who'd endangered himself to help her.

"Josie!" The voice was louder, deeper.

She pushed open the door of the coach. The driver, Miles, moved to help her down.

"No!" the man shouted, then swung a long, slender leg over his horse's rump and leapt down. "Allow me," he said in cultured tones that belied the common roadside attack.

A gloved hand reached up to help her down. Josie studied it, then his masked and shadowed face, the bedeviling need to know his identity almost overriding her fear.

Impatient, he bracketed her waist with his hands and swung her down. She looked up into his face again, trying to focus on the eyes in the shadow of his hat.

He laughed suddenly, as though this were an after-church social rather than a prelude to murder.

"You still don't know me, sister-in-law?" he asked, then yanked the bandanna down and swept his hat off in a mockery of a bow.

Josie went cold with disbelief. He bore a strong resemblance to Benjamin, but his features were more finely cast, giving him a handsomeness his brother hadn't had.

"Daniel?" she breathed.

He shook his head over her continued surprise. "Well, did you seriously think I would allow you and your little upstarts to take half of my money?"

Josie stared at him, speechless, remembering all the evenings she and Benjamin and Daniel had lingered over dinner and made plans for the company, or sat on the balcony on summer nights and told stories on one another. He'd always brought gifts for the boys when he travelled.

"But," she said finally, "you were always so kind."

He shrugged a shoulder. "What better way to convince you that I posed no threat, so that when I was finally able to make my move, you would be as stunned as you are now and would say in that shocked voice, 'No. It can't be Daniel. He was always so kind.'"

Everything inside her went cold and hard. "*You* killed Benjamin?"

"Yes," he said, a small smile of satisfaction on his handsome face. "I should never have been born a second son. I could never simply love him and wish him well and be happy with what he left. I've always wanted it all. For a while, I took comfort in the fact that at least I had the looks and the charm and the ladies. Then he married you."

Josie, a block of ice in her chest, found she still needed to understand. "You mean under all that pretense of kindness, you hated me like your mother did?"

"No," he denied quickly. "I loved you. Or, rather, I lusted after you. You were my ideal—young, beautiful, warm, intelligent. I considered trying to take you away from Benjamin, but you were so pitifully loyal. You mistook all my overtures for brotherly affection and concern and responded in kind." He shook his head and sighed. "You're a most frustrating woman."

"So you murdered Benjamin and sent your mother to tell the police that she'd seen me at his office."

"No," he denied again. "As far as she knew, I was still in Europe, missing all Jonathan Dunlop's urgent messages to bring me back. Actually, I'd come home several days before to settle the money issue once and for all. If Mother thought *I'd* shot her favorite son, she'd have killed me without a second thought. Her decision to tell the police she saw you at Ben's office was her own. She saw a chance to hurt you and took it. Served me well for a while—got rid of you *and* the children, but now the money's tied up and I still can't get to it."

She bunched her fist and struck him hard in the chest. She heard Miles gasp and take a step toward her. Gripper drew a bead on him but Daniel stopped everyone with a raised hand as he drew a labored breath.

"You bastard!" she accused. "I spent two months in prison, then was released to discover that your mother had used that time to give my children to a petty thief who took them three thousand miles away from me!"

Daniel shook his head and did not even pretend regret. "But you found them, didn't you, and acquired several more and another husband. Poor Mother. She was so sure she'd destroyed you, she took the *Oceanic* to Europe. I hid on the docks for several weeks, preparing to pretend to arrive home, grief-stricken and solemn after finally receiving the news that had chased me across the continent—that of my brother's murder and his family's tragic separation.

"I planned to take over the running of the company, enjoy my brother's home and assets, and wait for the boys to be declared dead after seven years." He sighed as though weary of the inconvenience she and her children presented. "Then I began to hear the gossip circulating around Boston. You were safe. You'd found your children. And your husband and Dunlop were in contact about the boys' inheritance. I broke into Jonathan's office and saw it for myself on Scofield and Carver letterhead."

That Adam had been in touch with Jonathan was news to Josie. "You did?"

Daniel nodded. "I'm afraid your husband's actions brought you to this sorry pass. You see, Josie, I can't give up the money now. I need so much to live the life to which I've grown accustomed, but I carouse and gamble at too earnest a rate. I'm beginning to outrun my money. So I'm afraid I'll have to have yours."

"You can have it," Josie said. "Anything set aside for me or the children is yours, including the house."

He raised an eyebrow. "You'd give up the brats' inheritance?"

"My children have a new home and a new father," she said. "I'll go with you if you'll leave these men alone."

Daniel shook his head apologetically and placed a hand on her shoulder. "My dear Josie, you've nothing with which to bargain. I don't intend to take you anywhere, I simply intend to be rid of you. I tried twice, but apparently I'm not as good as I thought. Once I hit Carver, and yesterday I missed entirely." He shook his head wearily. "So I went in search of Henry Gripper, whose whereabouts I discovered among some things Mother left behind. He was more than willing to help me waylay you."

Of course. Fate had decreed it. "Very well, then send the coach and the payroll money on to Redding and do what you have to do."

Daniel laughed. "Ah, Josie. So heroic. But, you see, you and your husband underestimated me."

She didn't like the sound of that, or the sudden light that ignited in his eyes and vanquished the mad good humor.

He reached out to Miles and yanked the beard off. "Did you really think I was that stupid? That I wouldn't recognize the sheriff and your husband's partner through the ridiculous disguises? It's almost an insult."

Then, without warning, Daniel turned his gun in the direction of the trunk and fired rapidly four times.

Josie screamed and ran to it, falling to her knees and fumbling with the locks, crying, "Adam!" in one long, loud wail. No! her mind denied as her blood ran cold with horror. No, no, no!

"Right here, Josie," Adam said, coming out of the trees on Dancer, his revolver aimed at Daniel. Daniel turned to him as though to fire, and a shot exploded. Josie screamed again.

The rifle flew out of Daniel's hand and a red stain began to spread on the forearm of his suit coat. Miles grabbed Daniel and stuffed him into the coach, while the sheriff chased down Gripper, who'd chosen to run. Adam followed on his horse, heading him off. The sheriff leapt at Gripper and brought him down.

The sheriff was saying something about putting him away for a long, long time and seeing that Daniel went back to Boston, but Josie couldn't quite hear the details. Her heart had lurched at the sight of Adam, safe and sound, and at the realization that things had turned out as he'd predicted after all. Now her heart didn't seem to want to settle down.

It was beating rapidly, and there was a buzzing in her ears and a curious warmth inching upward from her feet, catching her in sticky fingers.

She had a blurred image of Adam galloping back to her, smiling that confident smile. Then, as he watched her, something changed in his eyes and he was off Dancer before he'd even managed to stop him. His arms were reaching for her, but that warm, sticky something already had a hold on her and was pulling her down.

It was happening all over again at triple speed. She was sitting in a stagecoach and watching Adam climb into a box, which was then closed and lifted onto the top of the coach. Curiously, her mind could foresee what would happen, and she knew it was critical to get Adam out of the box.

But the driver roared a command and the horses tore away from the station at high speed. And somehow time and distance had compressed, and when they rounded the corner out of town, they were suddenly in a narrow road flanked by trees.

There was an order to halt, the box was thrown down from the top of the coach, and Josie watched it take an eternity to fall, as though each second of time had been elongated to a minute. Then it hit the ground with a crash and broke apart. Adam lay there, still and silent.

"No!" Josie shouted, leaping out of the coach. "No, Adam!" But Daniel Cross suddenly appeared and fired four times into Adam's body.

"Adam!" Josie screamed.

"Josie! Josie? It's Adam. Open your eyes, I'm right here, Josie."

Josie heard her name from a great distance, but she had to…had to…what? She pulled against a force trying to hold her down, hold her back.

Then she felt herself being shaken and opened her eyes to protest—and saw two familiar faces looking at her. The second she didn't even take time to identify because the first was Adam's.

"Josie?" he asked, as though not entirely certain she was out of the dream. "Are you with us?"

"Adam," she said, pushing against his restraining hands to touch his face. It was warm and smooth and banished completely the dream of a moment ago. He was very much alive.

"Are you with me?" she asked in an exhausted whisper.

"Forever," he said, pulling her into his arms with relief. "My God! You scared the life out of me."

She crushed him to her, enjoying the deliciously familiar solidity of his muscle against her own vulnerable softness, the firm splay of his hands against her back, moving gently up and down, comforting and supporting her.

Then her brain registered what he'd said and she pushed away from him, temper flaring in her relief.

"*I* frightened *you?*" she demanded. "You told me you would be with me all the way!"

He kept a grip on her arms and replied calmly, "I was."

"I thought you were in the trunk!" she said angrily. "The men who loaded it made such a point of being careful with it, then when Miles and the sheriff eased it down, they treated it so..."

"That was part of the plan," Adam explained patiently. "We knew Daniel was watching us. He had to believe I was in the trunk, too, so he wouldn't realize I followed him all the way out of town to the lane where he stopped you."

"But you didn't tell me that! I saw him shoot four times into the trunk and thought—"

"Josie, we were in a hurry, if you'll recall. There wasn't time to explain every little detail. I expected you to trust me."

Her sudden temper deflated as she recalled how easily she'd been convinced that it had all gone wrong.

"In fact, you promised to trust me," he reminded.

She subsided, nodding guiltily. "I did. But I was sure deep down that..." She winced as she added the words she was certain he wouldn't be pleased to hear. "I was sure that you were wrong."

He nodded as though he'd suspected that all along. "And now that it's over, is there something you'd like to tell me?"

She looked into his eyes, delighted to have been mistaken. "I apologize for not trusting you. You were right and *I* was wrong."

"Very good. And what are you going to do in the future?"

She smiled, unwilling to let him believe she'd be too amenable. "Become a hurdy-gurdy dancer? Write stories for the *Police Gazette?* Join Mrs. Brady in a march on Sacramento for..."

Adam shook his head and turned to the older man who sat on the opposite edge of the bed, grinning. "You see what I am up against?" He turned back to Josie, trying valiantly to suppress his smile at her apparently thorough return to good health. "Would you like to give me an answer that will *not* earn you retribution?"

She laughed impenitently and looped her arms around his neck. "I will believe in you and trust you implicitly. Always."

He finally nodded his approval. "Much better." He indicated the older man still watching them with a smile. "You remember Dr. Reed."

"Yes, of course," Josie said. "I'm afraid we've been claiming more than our fair share of your attention."

He snapped his bag closed and stood. "You don't seem to require me anymore today. I'll have a quick look at Miles's shoulder and be on my way."

The moment the door opened as the doctor left, the children rushed in, Charlie in the forefront, Jane following, the two little ones behind them.

Adam let them sit with Josie for several moments as she reassured them that she was fine and that normal life would resume as of this moment. But she was still pale and he knew how important it was for her to rest.

"You mean we can go fishing in the stream?" Charlie asked.

She nodded. "But no one is to go in it," she insisted. "Is that clear?"

Josie received four hugs and kisses, then each of the children kissed and hugged Adam, including Charlie, who held on to him an extra moment. Then he looked up into Adam's face, eyes shining. "You want to come fishing?" he asked.

Josie saw pleasure flash in Adam's eyes even as he shook his head. "Thanks. This afternoon I'd better look after your mama."

"Tomorrow?" Charlie persisted.

Adam nodded. "Tomorrow."

Smile wide, Charlie ran from the room to follow the other children.

Josie fell back against her pillows with a smile for the little miracle that had just transpired. Then she shook her head with sudden grimness as she remembered how this had all come about.

"Can you believe," she asked Adam, "that a woman could do what Jerusha did to my children and calmly book a transatlantic passage?"

"I'll wire Jonathan," he said. "We'll find her."

Josie shook her head and reached for him. He'd sat at the foot of the bed while the children visited and now moved up to sit beside her.

"She's an old woman," Josie said, looping her arms around Adam's neck. "I don't want our children to see us seeking revenge."

"Even so," he said firmly, "my job is justice. I'm going to have Jonathan look for her."

Josie stroked his dark hair and smiled into his eyes, all her old burdens lifted as he held her. "I want only love and kindness in our lives, Adam." She pulled him close and kissed his neck. "I can't wait for the six of us to take up our lives again like a normal family."

She waited for his agreement, and when it didn't come, she leaned back in his arms to look into his face. Did something remain unsettled? Was there still some threat of which she was unaware?

"You don't agree?" she asked a trifle nervously.

"Well," he said with a smiling glance down at the blankets then up into her eyes. "It seems you've made a small miscalculation there."

What? Still not entirely attuned to being completely loved and totally cared for, she entertained the thought for just a moment that she'd somehow misunderstood. That the miscalculation involved her concept of their relationship. Then she looked into his loving dark eyes and shook off all the old fears.

"What miscalculation?" she asked.

"Well, it seems that by next year, there will be seven of us," he said, watching her face carefully, a smile about to burst from his.

Her eyes widened and she put a hand to her mouth.

He nodded. "That's why you fainted. The doctor suspects you're with child."

She gasped behind her hand, then sobered and asked Adam uncertainly, "Are you pleased?"

"No," he replied, letting her believe for one moment that he wasn't as punishment for having asked the question. Then he, too, laughed. "I'm ecstatic." He held her close again and they laughed together.

"But five children under ten years old," Josie said in mock horror. "And Ivy soon to be married. There are days when I don't know what I'd do without her."

Adam pulled her away to look earnestly in her eyes. "Every moment that passes," he said, "I thank God for the impulse that led me to listen to George Burton and write that letter. And I thank God that you needed me enough to write back."

She blinked in surprise. "Even for the reason I did?"

He shook his head. "That no longer matters. All I care about is that the girls and I have you and the boys. It doesn't matter how we came together. Only that we stay this way."

Josie held him fiercely, her heart full. "Yes, Adam. Oh, yes."

* * * * *

MORE ROMANCE, MORE PASSION,
MORE ADVENTURE...MORE PAGES!

Bigger books from Harlequin Historicals. Pick one up today and see the difference a Harlequin Historical can make.

White Gold by Curtiss Ann Matlock—January 1995—A young widow partners up with a sheep rancher in this exciting Western.

Sweet Surrender by Julie Tetel—February 1995—An unlikely couple discover hidden treasure in the next *Northpoint* book.

All That Matters by Elizabeth Mayne—March 1995—A medieval about the magic between a young woman and her Highland rescuer.

The Heart's Wager by Gayle Wilson—April 1995—An ex-soldier and a member of the demi-monde unite to rescue an abducted duke.

Longer stories by some of your favorite authors. Watch for them in 1995 wherever Harlequin Historicals are sold.

HHBB95-1

Where do you find hot Texas nights, smooth Texas charm and dangerously sexy cowboys?

Crystal Creek reverberates with the exciting rhythm of Texas. Each story features the rugged individuals who live and love in the Lone Star state.

"...Crystal Creek wonderfully evokes the hot days and steamy nights of a small Texas community...impossible to put down until the last page is turned."
—*Romantic Times*

Praise for Bethany Campbell's *Rhinestone Cowboy*

"...this is a poignant, heart-warming story of love and redemption. One that Crystal Creek followers will wish to grab and hold on to."
—*Affaire de Coeur*

"Bethany Campbell is surely one of the brightest stars of this series."
—*Affaire de Coeur*

Don't miss the final book in this exciting series. Look for **LONESTAR STATE OF MIND** by BETHANY CAMPBELL

Available in February wherever Harlequin books are sold.

CC-24

Harlequin® Historical

Why is March the best time to try Harlequin Historicals for the first time? We've got four reasons:

All That Matters by Elizabeth Mayne—A medieval woman is freed from her ivory tower by a Highlander's impetuous proposal.

Embrace the Dawn by Jackie Summers—Striking a scandalous bargain, a highwayman joins forces with a meddlesome young woman.

Fearless Hearts by Linda Castle—A grouchy deputy puts up a fight when his Eastern-bred tutor tries to teach him a lesson.

Love's Wild Wager by Taylor Ryan—A young woman becomes the talk of London when she wagers her hand on the outcome of a horse race.

It's that time of year again—that March Madness time of year—when Harlequin Historicals picks the best and brightest new stars in historical romance and brings them to you in one exciting month!

Four exciting books by four promising new authors that are certain to become your favorites. Look for them wherever Harlequin Historicals are sold.

MM95

On the most romantic day of the year, capture the thrill of falling in love all over again—with

Harlequin's

Bachelors

They're three sexy and *very single* men who run very special personal ads to find the women of their fantasies by Valentine's Day. These exciting, passion-filled stories are written by bestselling Harlequin authors.

Your Heart's Desire by Elise Title
Mr. Romance by Pamela Bauer
Sleepless in St. Louis by Tiffany White

Be sure not to miss Harlequin's Valentine Bachelors, available in February wherever Harlequin books are sold.

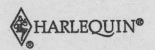

HARLEQUIN®

Deceit, betrayal, murder

Join Harlequin's intrepid heroines, India Leigh and Mary Hadfield, as they ferret out the truth behind the mysterious goings-on in their neighborhood. These two women are no milk-and-water misses. In fact, they thrive on

MISCHIEF & MAYHEM

Watch for their incredible adventures in this special two-book collection. Available in March, wherever Harlequin books are sold.

REG4

Fifty red-blooded, white-hot, true-blue hunks
from every State in the Union!

Look for MEN MADE IN AMERICA! Written by some
of our most popular authors, these stories feature some
of the strongest, sexiest men, each from a different state
in the union!

Two titles available every month at your favorite
retail outlet.

In January, look for:

WITHIN REACH by Marilyn Pappano (New Mexico)
IN GOOD FAITH by Judith McWilliams (New York)

In February, look for:

THE SECURITY MAN by Dixie Browning
(North Carolina)
A CLASS ACT by Kathleen Eagle
(North Dakota)

You won't be able to resist MEN MADE IN AMERICA!

If you missed your state or would like to order any other states that have already been
published, send your name, address and zip or postal code, along with a check or
money order (please do not send cash) in the U.S. for $3.59 plus 75¢ postage and
handling for each book, and in Canada for $3.99 plus $1.00 postage and handling for
each book, payable to Harlequin Reader Service, to:

In the U.S.	In Canada
3010 Walden Avenue	P.O. Box 609
P.O. Box 1369	Fort Erie, Ontario
Buffalo, NY 14269-1369	L2A 5X3

Please specify book title(s) with your order.
Canadian residents add applicable federal and provincial taxes.

MEN195

This February, Harlequin and Silhouette
bring you seduction and danger with

Three elusive professionals who thrive on danger—and
do their best work at night!

Three complete novels by your favorite authors—in
one special collection!

CATSPAW by Anne Stuart
CODE NAME CASANOVA by Dawn Carroll
IN FROM THE COLD by Lynn Erickson

Whose heart will they get caught stealing next?

Available wherever
Harlequin and Silhouette books are sold.

HARLEQUIN®

Don't miss these Harlequin favorites by some of our most
distinguished authors!
And now, you can receive a discount by ordering two or more titles!

HT#25577	WILD LIKE THE WIND by Janice Kaiser	$2.99	☐
HT#25589	THE RETURN OF CAINE O'HALLORAN by JoAnn Ross	$2.99	☐
HP#11626	THE SEDUCTION STAKES by Lindsay Armstrong	$2.99	☐
HP#11647	GIVE A MAN A BAD NAME by Roberta Leigh	$2.99	☐
HR#03293	THE MAN WHO CAME FOR CHRISTMAS by Bethany Campbell	$2.89	☐
HR#03308	RELATIVE VALUES by Jessica Steele	$2.89	☐
SR#70589	CANDY KISSES by Muriel Jensen	$3.50	☐
SR#70598	WEDDING INVITATION by Marisa Carroll	$3.50 U.S. $3.99 CAN.	☐ ☐
HI#22230	CACHE POOR by Margaret St. George	$2.99	☐
HAR#16515	NO ROOM AT THE INN by Linda Randall Wisdom	$3.50	☐
HAR#16520	THE ADVENTURESS by M.J. Rodgers	$3.50	☐
HS#28795	PIECES OF SKY by Marianne Willman	$3.99	☐
HS#28824	A WARRIOR'S WAY by Margaret Moore	$3.99 U.S. $4.50 CAN.	☐ ☐

(limited quantities available on certain titles)

	AMOUNT	$
DEDUCT:	**10% DISCOUNT FOR 2+ BOOKS**	$
ADD:	**POSTAGE & HANDLING**	$
	($1.00 for one book, 50¢ for each additional)	
	APPLICABLE TAXES*	$_____
	TOTAL PAYABLE	$_____
	(check or money order—please do not send cash)	

To order, complete this form and send it, along with a check or money order for the
total above, payable to Harlequin Books, to: **In the U.S.:** 3010 Walden Avenue,
P.O. Box 9047, Buffalo, NY 14269-9047; **in Canada:** P.O. Box 613, Fort Erie, Ontario,
L2A 5X3.

Name: _____

Address: _____ City: _____

State/Prov.: _____ Zip/Postal Code: _____

*New York residents remit applicable sales taxes.
 Canadian residents remit applicable GST and provincial taxes.

HBACK-JM2